Memory Stands Still

M. Kate Allen

Thea Press

Memory Stands Still
by M. Kate Allen

Thea Press
P.O. Box 24905
Tempe, AZ 85285
www.theapress.org

For more information about M. Kate Allen, see www.lifeloveliturgy.com

2021 Cover design by Andrea Dobbins and Megan Hall.

ISBN-13: 978-1-956604-00-9 (Paperback)

For Dad-
may his memory be a blessing

Then I saw a lamb, looking as if it had been slain, standing at the center of the throne…

-Revelation 5:6

Chapter 1

If Angela Bridges was going to accomplish anything, she needed to clean up her mess. She tied back her long, wavy brown hair in a loose braid and snatched up papers and books from furniture and the floor, delivering them to more appropriate places. Dirty clothes went in the hamper. Shoes were set down by the front door. Wearing a loose t-shirt and red fleece pajama pants over her curvy frame, Angela readied her office, which was really a nook in her upstairs bedroom, so she would be able to concentrate on more important work: drafting her entry for Cleveland's first bi-annual urban development contest.

It was Angela's third of four semesters in her urban planning Master's program at Cleveland State University, and the contest had been announced to all the students in her program a month ago. The prize was fifteen thousand dollars along with up to ten million dollars allotted for carrying out the proposed development. Terry Keating, a well-known architect who lived in one of the grand houses of Fairmount Boulevard in Cleveland Heights, was single-handedly funding the contest. Wealthy people could do things like that, Angela mused.

When she was finished tidying, Angela pressed the back of her golden-brown hand against her forehead and descended to the kitchen to prepare a pot of hot black tea. On her trip to San Francisco the previous summer, Angela had visited a tea shop in Chinatown. The shopkeeper poured her a cup of her finest tea, sweetened with ginseng. Angela bought a pound of it before she walked out the door, ignoring the hole it burned in her wallet.

With the pot of tea and her favorite red, purple, and orange striped mug in hand, Angela climbed the finished wooden stairs and sat down, swiveling her chair to face the desk. As she poured the steaming tea into her mug, she reviewed the application form.

The First Bi-Annual Amateur Urban Development Contest of Cleveland

Requirements:
-Cover Letter
-Proposal, including the address and name of the proposed development site; CAD blueprints, sketches, or a model of the project; and a 1,000-word description of the project
-Applicant must be a non-professional or unpaid professional in the fields of urban development and architecture

Guidelines:
This contest seeks to bring about the renewal of an abandoned site in the city of Cleveland. Contestants should take the history of the site into consideration when forming the proposal. The winning proposal will represent a harmony of old and new.

Angela considered Cleveland's landscape as her sea-green eyes searched her cream-colored walls for ideas. Downtown had a lot going for it between three major sporting venues, the Rock and Roll Hall of Fame, the Theater District, and the Flats. There were a number of houses on both the West Side and the East Side—Angela's being one of them—that had been built in the early twentieth century and were beginning to look worn. A house in a residential neighborhood, perhaps as a safe house, might be a possibility. There were also a number of abandoned factories in mid-town on the East Side that Angela observed on her commute to work.

The deadline for the proposal was December 31, just ten weeks away. A whole world could change in that time, or nothing at all. Angela sipped her tea and closed her eyes. It wasn't just the space that mattered—it was its history. Regarding a building as a mere shell, empty of story and meaning, would result in failure. Every building has a story. Every building began just like this, with a person sitting at a table, imagining a building into life. The tales of the workers who created the building became part of the story. The ways in which the building was put to use were part of the story. The people who frequented (and didn't frequent) the building were part of the story. How a building might be renewed was just one late chapter in the story of a building, and the key was to ensure that that new chapter took the prior chapters into account.

Angela opened her eyes, took another sip, and stared at the corkboard in front of her. There she had pinned sketches of her work, pictures of people she loved, and memorabilia from events she had attended. Her proposal would resemble this corkboard. So which came first: choosing the site, or choosing the story?

A vision of Angela's friend, Bill, came to mind. Bill Kinsman was a connoisseur of art and architecture, even though music was his passion. Perhaps what she needed for this proposal was a tour of the city.

She pulled her cell from her pocket and typed in his name to pull up his number. The phone rang, and she looked out the window.

"Hello, darling," he greeted her.

"Good afternoon, friend! How are you?"

"I've been better and I've been worse, but I'm glad to be talking to you," he said.

"What's wrong?" she asked. She looked back at her wall. She loved watching the shadows of the leaves outside her window when they danced across her room, but there was no dancing today.

"The clouds are getting to me," he replied.

"Well, what do you say you overcome those Cleveland clouds by taking me out? I could use your expertise."

Bill's tone turned sultry and Angela could imagine his smirk. "What sort of expertise would you be looking for?"

Angela grinned and rolled her eyes. "Gross. No, I want you to help me figure out which building to use for my urban development proposal. You know the stories behind our city a whole lot better than I do, and I need some stories if I'm going to find the perfect spot."

"Ah, you've decided to take me seriously, then."

Angela rolled her eyes again and smiled with relief. "So you want to come over around three?"

"How about you come over at four, and we'll end the evening with dinner at Mama Santa's."

"Deal. See you then."

"*Ciao, bella*," he said. She pressed the end button. Her phone read 2:34pm. She looked out the window at the breeze-blown autumn leaves in her front yard, then looked back at the application form for the urban development contest. Summoning the streets of Cleveland to her imagination, she reviewed the neighborhoods and buildings that stood within them. What memories would she discover? Would she trample on the graves of those who would have been better off resting forever?

At 3:45, Angela stood from her desk and stretched her arms above her head with a yawn. Her mind palace of Cleveland was a facade, one that she would have to build up with the beams of stories beyond her imagining. She descended the stairs, grabbed her black knit beret and dark green pea coat from their hook in the front closet, and put them on as she exited her front door. Her spacious porch was one of her favorite parts of her 1920s two-story house, but she didn't notice it as she descended its steps toward her car.

The air was crisp and cool, painting a blush on her cheeks that she observed in her rear-view mirror. Her 1994 Saturn was a handy car, if an old one. She'd been driving it since driver's ed, and her parents had given it to her as a gift when she'd graduated from college. She pulled out of her driveway and headed south on East 82nd Street.

Wind blew red and gold leaves off tall tree branches and across Cedar Avenue as Angela ascended the hill toward the Cedar/Fairmount neighborhood. Bill was waiting for her in front of his apartment building door when she pulled in.

Bill lived in an apartment just outside the city limits in Cleveland Heights. Nighttown, a high-end Irish pub that nearly always required a reservation to get in, was just across the parking lot from him, and he was one of their most popular servers. He greeted all his customers in a faint Irish brogue, which inspired the ladies — and a few of the men — to stare at him with sparkling eyes.

Bill was a bear of a white man who reveled in sartorial splendor. His gray checked silk scarf was wrapped around his neck in a neat loop, and he wore a lavender button-down shirt with black slacks. His hazel eyes met hers as he stooped into the car, and his black hair was gelled flat except for the front, where it was spiked upward. "My dear, are you going to drive this poor beast forever?"

"She is not a beast, and she's holding up quite well, thank you very much! There, there, Felicity, he didn't mean it," Angela said as she petted the dash of the car. Bill shook his head with a sigh and buckled up.

"Before you begin driving, tell me what area interests you most. If there's a neighborhood that intrigues you, that would suggest a story."

Angela thought a moment. "How about if I let Felicity take us where she wants to go?"

Bill chortled and shrugged. "Fine. Felicity," he said in a dramatic voice, "lead us where you will." Angela grinned and backed out of the parking space.

Soon they were coasting back down the steep hill of Cedar Avenue, with thick, tall trees and ivy cascading on either side of them. They exited to Euclid Avenue, which was flat and built-up. "Well, Felicity seems to have some intuition about architecture," Bill said. Angela snorted. "Did you know that Euclid Avenue used to be called Millionaire's Row?"

Angela glanced at her friend, then back at the road. "Euclid Avenue used to be called Millionaire's Row?" As she drove past the Cleveland Clinic, she knew what lay ahead—abandoned factories, open lots, graffiti-covered shops, and dilapidated houses.

"At the turn of the twentieth century, the steel and auto industries were booming here," he said. "Carnegie Avenue is named after the famous steel industrialist, Andrew Carnegie. The Rockefellers lived here as well—portions of Cleveland Heights and Mayfield Heights constituted the Rockefeller estate, which was a country estate at the time."

"It certainly isn't the country now. Wasn't the neighborhood in *Leave it to Beaver* based on homes Mayfield Heights?"

"Yep. The hills that we know as Cleveland suburbs were built up before the Great Depression and then again after World War II. Mayfield Heights represents more of the post-war architecture that *Leave It to Beaver* made famous. Millionaire's Row was where many wealthy industrialists built their city homes. Most of them were abandoned after the Great Depression and eventually torn down. You'd never know that Euclid Avenue used to be the place to live in Cleveland, would you?"

Angela shook her head. "I mean, now they have the dedicated bus lanes here for the Euclid Corridor, but it seems more like an excuse to get people from University Circle to downtown as quickly as possible."

"I think that's the idea," Bill said. "So, have you come across anything interesting yet?"

Angela had been eyeing the buildings as they continued toward downtown. "There was one at 61st that looked interesting—a factory of some kind. I'm not sure what I could do with a factory building in mid-town, though."

"Because you have so much trouble thinking of ways to transform spaces," Bill replied, rolling his eyes.

Angela blushed. "You know me, it's hard to draw an idea out of here," she said, pointing to her head. As Bill well-knew, Angela had an idea about virtually every space she came across. Interior design and architecture had been her hobby since her days of building Lincoln Log homes large enough for her My Little Pony dolls. Every detail of every space was up for evaluation.

"Remember that time we went to the Federal Reserve and you gave the greeter your business card and asked him to call you if they wanted to hire you as an interior design consultant?" Bill asked.

"Yeah. He looked at me like I had three heads."

"You do, Ang, and I wouldn't give up any one of them for anything." Angela swatted his arm and smiled.

They were nearly into downtown and needed to find another route. "What about Superior?" Angela suggested, turning right down East Ninth Street.

"One building in particular stands out for me: the former Church of St. Mary Magdalene."

Angela wrinkled her nose. "A church?"

"Hey, First English Lutheran Church was transformed into some amazing condos right near my apartment building."

Angela thought of the church on Derbyshire Road with its bright red doors. It had been converted into the center of a luxury condominium complex in the early 2000s. "I know, but that seems like a strange way to deal with a church. Sacred spaces are supposed to be sacred spaces, not homes for people with too much money."

"Honey, if I had the money, I'd move there in a quick second. I'd love to live in a place that was a house of God. It would make me feel like a god," he said.

Angela turned right onto Superior Avenue. "You kid," she said flatly.

"Only a little. Anyway, let me tell you about the Church of St. Mary Magdalene. It was built by German settlers in the 1840s, if I remember correctly. It closed a few years ago when the Roman Catholic bishop decided to oust the liberal Catholics from their home—or that's how the rumors in the papers go.

They up and moved to another site and pissed off the bishop like you wouldn't believe. The building shut down because the diocese couldn't afford to keep it open anymore, and they desanctified it. They can't tear it down because it's on the National Register of Historic Places. They've just put it on the market."

Superior was a wide avenue lined with young trees and old buildings. Red brick factories, starting with the converted Tower Press building at East 19th Street, lined the south side of the street. Just across the street from the Tower Press building, a wall of glass with seams of brick formed the front of the contemporary *Plain Dealer* building, where Cleveland's print news journalists could be seen typing away at their flat-screen computers. Smaller businesses lined the north side of the street, and Angela caught occasional glimpses of Lake Erie in between them as she drove. At East 40th Street, Angela slowed to a stop for a red light. The Church of St. Mary Magdalene stood on the southeast corner of the intersection. It was an old stonemasonry structure with a tall bell tower over the central doorway.

"That building looks like it would collapse if a tornado came within five miles of it. Look at the cracks in the masonry!"

Bill turned his head as they drove past. "One of my buddies was a member there. When they were kicked out of their building, they were devastated. Those old stones and everything inside them shaped their community identity, and they had to start over again when they were forced to move out. The amazing thing is that they stuck together at all. Most folks from closed parishes scattered to other churches, but his community still thrives."

Angela watched the belfry disappear in her rearview mirror and looked ahead. "If only more of Cleveland had been like that—strong enough to stay together in the midst of chaos."

"And that's where you come in, Ang. You get to be the woman who brings an old story to new life. You just have to be ready for that story to find you."

Angela stopped at a red light at 55th Avenue. "Which way next?"

After many miles touring the streets of Cleveland's East Side, Angela pulled into a parking spot that opened up on Murray Hill Road. The scents of pasta sauce and pastries complemented the timbre of Italian music wafting through Little Italy. Glasses clinked as couples and groups of friends toasted each other in their al fresco seating. The dusky air was chilly and tinged with sweet. The smells of oregano, tomato sauce, and melted cheese greeted Bill and Angela as they entered the red-brick, white-trimmed, multi-story building.

The foyer of Mama Santa's wasn't crowded that night. Within five minutes a female server escorted the pair down the main hallway and into the dining room on the right, seating them near the front window. Angela shrugged off her coat but left her scarf in place. "It got warm tonight, didn't it?" she said, opening her menu. When she looked up at Bill, he was staring over her shoulder.

"He looks pretty warm, doesn't he?" he replied at

last. Angela turned her head, catching sight of a thirty-something stocky server with slick black hair and bright brown eyes. Bill purred, and Angela nudged his leg with her toe. "Maybe you should say something to him."

The black-haired server approached their table next, and Bill reddened, lowering his eyes to his menu. "Would you like to start off with a glass of wine this evening?" His voice was a silky baritone. Bill said nothing.

"My friend here would, and so would I," Angela answered, emphasizing the word "friend." "We'll share a bottle of Lambrusco, if you have it."

"Of course. I'll bring it right away." The server smiled at Angela and turned.

"Oh, he's luscious," Bill murmured, fanning himself with the menu.

"You know, he smiled at me when I smiled at him. You might try it yourself. He looked at you and you missed it, silly."

Angela had met Bill in college. She'd had a crush on him for a while, and the night she decided to share her feelings for him, they went to Mama Santa's. He chose that evening to come out of the closet. Angela was so shocked that she burst out laughing. "But I have a crush on you!" she gasped in the midst of her guffaws. Bill's face went from hurt to surprised to embarrassed in one long moment, and then he began to laugh, too. They'd been close friends ever since. Mama Santa's was their favorite place to go out. They had been coming here for nearly a decade, but their server was a new sight for both of them.

"Shall we get our usual?" she asked.

"Of course."

When the waiter returned, he opened the Lambrusco, poured two even glasses of wine, and asked if they were ready to order. Bill looked at Angela and she ordered a medium pizza with cheese, pepperoni, green peppers, and anchovies on the side. The server smiled at her, then turned to Bill and asked if there was anything else they would like. "Garlic toast, perhaps?" he suggested, looking directly at Bill.

Bill met his gaze, gave a small smile, and nodded.

The server turned and Bill cursed under his breath. "I'd like to know your name, thank you very much," he sighed.

"I've never seen you get so jumpy over a boy before. You really do need some wine." Angela raised her glass, Bill raised his, and Angela offered their usual toast: "To life, love, and laughter."

After their first sip, Bill set down his glass, folded his arms, and leaned forward. "So what I want to know is, which of the places we visited spoke to you the most?"

Angela took another sip of wine and looked out the window. They had been by some abandoned factories and churches running along 55th Avenue, and then up and down residential streets in the direction of University Circle. At one point they passed the former Roman Catholic seminary in the northern part of the Hough neighborhood, a neighborhood remembered now for its racial riots in the 1960s. They drove past the Cultural Gardens on Martin Luther King Jr. Drive and visited Lakeview

Cemetery before heading back to Murray Hill.

"The cemetery, actually. I'm not sure why we went there, though. Cemeteries aren't generally up for rehabilitation, and certainly not that one."

"But why aren't they up for rehabilitation?"

Angela gave him an incredulous look. "Because they're in use."

Bill's eyes lit up. "But aren't they just filled with the dead?"

"The people buried there are people remembered by the living. People still frequent the cemetery."

"Just to see their own relatives?"

"Well, they hardly see anyone dead. They see grave markers."

"And to whom are grave markers significant?"

Angela paused. "Anyone who recognizes the name, I suppose."

"And who might recognize the name?"

Angela sighed. Bill loved to play the Socratic interlocutor. "Anyone who had passed by or visited the stone."

"So the memories don't just belong to the dead; they belong to those who still go there. In fact, the memories of the dead are honored by those who bother to show up as witnesses to those dead, even if the ones showing up didn't personally know any of the dead in the cemetery."

"I'm not sure I see your point, Bill."

Bill lifted his glass toward her. "Think," he said, and took a long sip.

"Memories belong both to the dead and the living?"

"Bingo."

Angela shook her head. "But how does that help me?"

"The cemetery spoke most to you because it represented what you're trying to capture in your proposal: a place where the dead and the living meet."

Just then their garlic bread arrived in the hands of the handsome server. Bill managed a smile before the server left. Angela tore a piece off the loaf and chewed it slowly.

"If I apply that logic," she said, "then my proposal will be most likely to succeed if I can imagine a renewed space that allows the living and the dead to meet."

"When you win, you can thank me."

Angela's dimples flashed. "I love you, Bill."

"I love you, too, sweetheart, but don't say it too loud or you'll give our server the wrong idea."

Waving her hands in surrender, Angela picked up her wine glass and cupped it, resting her elbows on the table. "I wonder which of the sites we saw today would work. I mean, it will require embracing the stories of the building. A factory building is the most obvious candidate for a renewal, but do I really want to remember the blood, sweat, and tears of factory workers in my proposal? That sounds rather depressing to me."

"Hey, don't short-change factory workers. My grandfather worked at a factory for forty years, and he was happy. He always reminded us that he earned a steady paycheck and got to leave his work at work when five o'clock came around."

Angela looked at her hands. "That makes sense. You're right, I shouldn't short-change factory workers. I just don't think I'd be very happy if I were working in a factory."

Bill noticed her embarrassment and changed the subject. "You could go the church route."

Angela sighed, but she wasn't sure if it was more from relief or dread. "I know, but as I said, turning a sacred space into a non-sacred space gives me the willies. I just don't know how that could be done."

Bill gave her a long, impenetrable look. Angela shifted in her seat.

"I suppose there's the old seminary building in the Hough neighborhood." Angela pulled her phone out of her pocket and googled the Hough neighborhood, zooming in on the seminary building. "Oh, crud. It's already in use as a rehab center." Angela showed the map to Bill, who shrugged his shoulders. "There's a whole lot more of Cleveland to see. All we saw was the East Side."

"Well, let's say we head out next weekend—are you working next Saturday?"

"No, I'm scheduled for weeknights. Next Saturday sounds fine, but do me a favor and do some mapping on your own ahead of time. You need to get moving on this thing."

Angela was thinking the same thing, and her lips pinched together as she nodded.

"Don't worry. The research is the hardest part. Once you've got that, your imagination can do the rest."

Their pizza arrived and Bill gave the server a

broad smile. *Very good,* Angela thought to herself.

Chapter 2

Angela shrugged off her coat as she shut and locked her front door. When she had moved in, the walls had been spotted with holes and all the rooms save the kitchen had been carpeted in dingy orange shag. She dealt with the walls first, spackling them and repainting them in a different hue for each room. Pulling up a corner of the carpet, she found beautiful hardwood underneath, and set about removing the carpet entirely. Now her shoes clicked as she crossed the warm brown planks of wood. The first floor consisted of her living room, a dining room and kitchen off to the right, and two bedrooms in the rear, down the central hallway. The stairs to her upstairs bedroom and office stood behind a door in the first-floor hallway. As she ascended the stairs to her bedroom, which was painted in pale blue, her phone buzzed. "Thanks for the nice night, lady." It was Bill. She smiled and responded with a heart icon.

When she reached the second floor, she headed toward her broad, cherrywood writing desk. "What do I need?" she said to herself, turning toward her bookshelves. She scanned the rows of titles to find the answer to her niggling question. Architecture and design books on the left, novels on the right. One of the spare bedrooms downstairs housed the rest of her books, which included everything from old textbooks

to notebooks to autobiographies to history books—
and more novels. *What was she looking for?*

Swiveling, she moved toward her desk where her
laptop was perched on one corner. She opened the lid,
pressed the power button, and typed in her password
when the screen flashed on. Moments later she was
looking at online maps of the neighborhoods she and
Bill had visited, her eyes illumined by the glow of the
screen.

During the first semester of her program, Angela
had gotten into an argument about the purpose of
urban development. One of her classmates—a short,
blond-haired white woman named Jessica Lyle, with
mustard brown eyes and a slight frame—had made
the claim that urban development was meant to boost
the economy by building up aesthetically pleasing
urban spaces to draw in wealthy residents. Angela
had argued that gentrification and urban
development weren't the same thing, and that
gentrification could do harm to neighborhoods,
driving established residents out of the
neighborhoods in which they had built their lives.

Jessica shook her head. "It's wealthy residents
who bring the stimulus to the local economy. The city
has to be made attractive to them so they'll want to
live and shop there," she said.

Angela stared at Jessica. "If wealthy residents
displace established residents, it isn't urban
development—it's urban displacement. The displaced
residents will end up living elsewhere, with only their
memories of the past to accompany them. Urban
development is supposed to honor memory, not make

it into a ghost."

Jessica replied, "Leaving a city to crumble under the weight of its faltering economy is no way to honor a city's memory."

"But that's the point," Angela said. "Urban development is the alternative to gentrification. Our job is to find ways to revivify what already is, not replace it with something entirely different."

"If there's no life there to begin with, there's no harm in starting from scratch."

Angela sighed as the conversation replayed in her mind. Jessica's understanding of urban development wasn't uncommon. The argument had ended with Professor Seamus McNear, a gray-haired, middle-aged man of Irish descent with half-moon spectacles, lauding points on both sides before dismissing the class. Angela had complained about the conversation with Bill later. "He cut us both off and let the class out early," she said. "Where's the academic integrity in that?"

During the next class session, however, Professor McNear asked the class to brainstorm about what the positive and negative aspects of urban development could be. "There are good ways—and better ways—to engage in urban development," he said. "Urban development consultants have an ethical responsibility to consider the short-term and long-term effects of their plans. Not all change is good or welcome, but urban development presupposes change of some kind. I want you to pair off and weigh the pros and cons of transforming an abandoned, gate-enclosed lot in a crime-ridden neighborhood into a shopping center filled with boutique shops."

Angela ended up in a pair with a man with dark skin, chestnut eyes, and closely shaved black hair in his early twenties named Ron Walker. His button-down shirt revealed toned arm muscles—he obviously worked out in his spare time. He was one of the youngest people in the group, having just graduated from Oberlin College the previous spring. He was bright and unafraid to voice his opinion, but he also welcomed the opportunity for dialogue. Angela pulled out a piece of paper and wrote "Pros" and "Cons" at the top of the sheet. "So what do you think, Ron?" she asked.

"I thought your comments during the last class were spot on." Angela stole a glance at Jessica, who was already talking animatedly with her conversation partner.

"Thank you for saying so. It got a little heated, didn't it?"

"Anything worth discussing can get heated, in my experience," he said. "I grew up in East Cleveland, so what you said about displacing residents resonated with me. East Cleveland has largely been overlooked by the wealthier residents of Cuyahoga County because it's not part of the main path between the eastern suburbs and downtown Cleveland; it's also suffered at the hands of crooked politicians, which is another story. East Cleveland is largely run-down and riddled with gang violence, and for someone like Jessica, that's the end of the story—just change it all, she would probably say. But East Cleveland is so much more than old buildings and young criminals.

East Cleveland is home to many generations of families who live there by choice, not just because they can't afford to leave. That's the side of East Cleveland that a rich suburbanite would never perceive. They'd never ask, either, which is the problem with Jessica's approach. She seems to see an old neighborhood and automatically wants to replace it all, as if the neighborhood didn't have a life of its own. All a person has to do is ask—nicely—and the stories of why people stay will well up and spill over."

Angela nodded, resting her chin on her hand. "That's what I mean. I don't know the stories of East Cleveland because I didn't grow up there or spend much time there, but if I were an urban development consultant for a neighborhood in East Cleveland, I would get in touch with residents and ask them to share their stories with me. Without the stories that already exist, any attempt at renewing a neighborhood would be a farce."

Ron nodded. "If you're ever interested in East Cleveland, just let me know. You're looking at one of its proud residents."

Angela smiled, stealing another look at Jessica. "I may just take you up on that." Ron's dimples emerged. "Let's get on with this list, shall we?"

Angela's eyes refocused on her laptop screen, drawing her out of her recollection. She turned and scanned her bookshelf again. "I need stories...." she muttered. She pulled out a sheet of paper and a pen from her desk drawer and began writing down the addresses of sites that interested her. She'd have to wait till Saturday to explore more with Bill. In the meantime, she could visit the Cleveland Public Library to do some research on the sites on her list.

A few minutes later, Angela set down her pen, stretched, and stood up. She headed down the stairs to the kitchen to put water on to boil, and then she moved into her prayer room. Her prayer room was actually the front closet of the house, but she had emptied it save for a large pillow, a candle, incense, a singing bowl, a Bible, and a prayer book her grandmother had written for her. Angela opened the octagonal window in the closet, lit the candle and incense, and returned to the kitchen to pour water over her tea. With her heavy mug in hand, she returned to the closet, set the mug down on an open shelf, tapped the singing bowl, and settled cross-legged on her pillow, just next to the window. She took several deep breaths, exhaling slowly after each one. Then she picked up her Bible.

Angela had been devoted to the Missouri Synod Lutheran Church until she was fifteen. As she was reading in scripture one day about the prophetess, Anna, Angela had the unsettling and thrilling realization that she felt a call to be a minister. She didn't know what to make of her call. She had known her whole life that she couldn't be a minister in her denomination. She pondered the contrast between her sense of call and her denomination's policies. The prophetess Anna, she knew, had announced the arrival of Jerusalem's redemption to all who visited the temple. Her voice mattered, and yet it didn't—it was Zechariah's words that were recorded in scripture, not Anna's. *Why did a named prophetess get such short shrift?* she wondered. *And why did women in the Missouri Synod get the same?* The church from which she had received her spiritual formation suddenly sent her spiraling into confusion about her identity.

When she talked to her mother about it, her mother told her to pray away her false calling — clearly she couldn't be called because she was a woman. Her mother, a black-haired, stocky woman with a bold air of self-assurance, was an obedient handmaiden of the Missouri Synod. Her mother believed in a God of the law and had taught her daughter to believe in the same. Angela had long tried — and usually succeeded — to win her mother's approval by following and even defending the rules, but her sudden sense of call to ordained ministry created a rift between them.

When she spoke with her Grandma Caroline, however, Grandma Caroline told her that ministry could take many forms; it didn't need to take the form of ordination in a particular tradition. That conversation marked the beginning of Angela's retreat from the Missouri Synod.

Angela still self-identified as a Christian, albeit an unconventional one. Her love of the Christian narrative combined with the feminism she had inherited from her grandmother placed her in a church of one. Every morning and evening, she engaged in her own prayer ritual in the closet she had transformed for that purpose. In this space, Angela was free from the rules that governed Christian denominations. She was governed solely by the rules of scripture itself, beginning with the first among the commandments: to love God and neighbor as oneself.

Angela flipped open to where her bookmark was, the second chapter of 1 Peter: "The stone the builders rejected has become the cornerstone." Angela whispered the words into her prayer space. Her prayer moved from scripture to the question of which site to choose for the urban development contest.

Grandma Caroline, a self-proclaimed flower child who had long eschewed conventional religion in favor of her own feminist spirituality, had taught Angela that sitting with questions in prayer could lead to profound answers. Angela practiced sitting with a question every time she prayed. It usually wasn't an answer that emerged, but a way-marker. In this case, the way-marker seemed to be the rejected cornerstone. Was there a site in Cleveland that had been rejected that could become the cornerstone of the city, or at least the cornerstone of one of the city's neighborhoods?

Angela lit the stick of incense and its perfume filled the prayer space. She closed her Bible, put it back on its shelf, and closed her eyes. The dim light of the candle danced across her eyelids. Memories of candles, incense, and music played gently in her imagination, inviting her past to the surface. The pain of loss tightened her chest, and she opened her eyes. She turned to Grandma Caroline's prayer book.

"Thea," she read in a whisper, "your imagination created the wonders of the world. Help me to behold the wonders that surround and dwell within me. Amen." Angela replaced the prayer book and picked up her mug, which had cooled from its original scalding temperature, and took a long sip. Orange zest, clove, and cinnamon washed across her palate, and she remained cross-legged on her pillow, pondering memories and futures in her heart. When her mug was empty, she snuffed out the incense, closed the window, and blew out the candle. She opened the door, stepped out quietly, and shut the door behind her.

The next morning, gray clouds blanketed the sky, and Angela burrowed deep under the blue covers of her bed. The smell of coffee lured her out of bed and down to her kitchen. Every evening, she ground coffee beans and filled the coffee pot with filtered water. The timer was set for 5:00am. The wafting scent of coffee was her morning incense as she greeted the day in prayer. Her morning prayer was less reflective than receptive: she asked Thea to help her perceive the extraordinary in the ordinary throughout the day.

After breakfast and a shower, Angela was on her way out her front door, bundled up in coat, hat, gloves, and scarf. Felicity rumbled awake as Angela turned the key in the ignition. She drove south toward Chester Avenue and then turned west toward downtown. She parked in the parking garage across the street from the library and headed toward the Main Library. Once inside, she loosened her scarf, removed her gloves, and headed toward the information desk.

"Could you help me find information on the history of Cleveland's architecture?" she asked. The young woman at the desk directed her up to the third floor, the Fine Arts department.

The third floor featured a white-haired librarian, and Angela headed toward her. The librarian, whose nametag said, "Peg," greeted Angela and asked how she could help her.

"I'm interested in finding information about Cleveland's history, particularly with regard to architecture. I have a list of sites in particular that I'm interested in," she said, holding up her sheet of notebook paper, "but perhaps you could also point me to books that address Cleveland's architecture in a general way?" Peg's fingers zipped across her computer keyboard and soon she was leading Angela toward the stacks.

"Here's a small section that includes books on Cleveland's architecture," Peg said. "There are additional titles available in other parts of the library on Cleveland's historic buildings. Here's a list for you." Angela took the print-out, thanked her, and began skimming the spines. She picked up one called *Cleveland Architecture, 1796-1958*, and began to read.

The clearing of someone's throat several minutes later gave her occasion to raise her eyes, and she found herself looking at a twenty-something thin, young white man with neatly trimmed brown hair and warm brown eyes wearing a black, button-down, floor-length garment that Angela recognized from her days in the Missouri Synod: a cassock. Her eyes rounded, and he smiled at her.

"I'm looking for something in this section. Pardon me," he said. Angela closed her book, her hand marking the place inside, and moved out of the aisle to a table where she could sit down. A few minutes later, the man in the cassock sat down across from her. She looked up again.

"I'm Joseph," he said, extending his hand. Angela paused before shaking his hand and saying, "I'm Angela." Who was this person, why was he was dressed in clerical garb, and why was he talking to her?

"I'm a Roman Catholic seminarian," he said, glancing down at his attire. Angela nodded, bewildered. He looked at Angela's book, and so did she.

"I'm doing some research," she offered politely.

"So am I. I'm entering an urban development contest," he said brightly.

Startled, Angela replied, "So am I."

Joseph grinned. "Happy coincidence!"

Angela looked with curiosity at the man before her. "Have you decided on a site?"

Joseph shook his head. "My bishop has asked me to look at several empty buildings owned by the diocese, but I haven't settled on anything yet. If I find something not owned by the diocese, I'll pitch it to him and see what he says."

"If you're interested in urban development, how'd you end up in seminary?" she asked.

"Men of the cloth have a wide array of interests, contrary to popular belief," he said, a smile playing on his lips. "Actually, before I entered seminary, I graduated with a B.A. in urban studies from Cleveland State."

Angela smiled with surprise. "I'm in CSU's

Master's program for urban planning, development, and design."

"Wow! Do you know Professor McNear? He was my undergraduate supervisor."

"Yes. I'm taking one of his classes now, as a matter of fact. His class is helping me figure out how to move forward with my proposal for this contest," she said.

"Please pass on my greetings to him next time you see him. My last name is Warner. Joseph Warner," he repeated.

"I'll be sure to do that," she said.

Joseph smiled. "Mind if I sit and read with you for a while?"

"Feel free," she said, gesturing toward the chair across from her.

Joseph sat, opened his book, and began to read. Angela did the same. They and Peg were the only people on the third floor. An hour passed. Angela, lost in her book, forgot she had any company; then Joseph shut his book, cracked his knuckles, and stood to leave. "Nice to meet you, Angela. Good luck with your proposal," he said.

"Thank you, Joseph. Likewise," she said. He smiled and turned to depart. She stared at his back as he walked away, musing over the strange encounter. "Grandma Caroline will get a kick out of this," she whispered.

Chapter 3

"I went to CPL and brought home a stack of books relating to Cleveland architecture. I have a few ideas about where to go today," Angela said to Bill, buckling her seatbelt.

Bill buckled his seatbelt as Angela backed her car out of the driveway. "Have you tried the Western Reserve Historical Society's Research Library?" he asked.

Angela shook her head.

"Last I checked, their collection on Cleveland's history numbered over two hundred fifty thousand books—and that's just the published manuscripts."

Angela's jaw dropped and she hit the brake, bringing the car to a full stop. "Well, perhaps I should pay them a visit soon, then, too."

The Research Library of the Western Reserve Historical Society was located in University Circle, a quick drive away from Angela's home. Bill navigated her to it.

"We drove by here last time. I used to come by here on my way to school," Angela murmured, driving on East Boulevard past the Western Reserve Historical Society, then the Cleveland Institute of Music. "Too bad one of these places isn't abandoned. Imagine if I could renovate Severance Hall."

"No, my dear—if Severance Hall is ever

abandoned, the city of Cleveland will be beyond the hope of salvaging."

"You never know. The orchestra has had budget issues for years, and they're still here. Speaking of which," Angela said, pointing out her window as they passed by the grand stone edifice that housed the world-famous Cleveland Orchestra. "But if the orchestra ever does leave Cleveland, the city will still stand. Cleveland has a lot going for it."

"If the orchestra leaves Cleveland, it will be the beginning of the end of high culture in this town."

"Nah. The art museum isn't going anywhere. The universities and hospitals aren't going anywhere. Cleveland has institutions to draw in people from all over the world. One institution's failure won't mark the end of the city. It'll mark the opportunity for reimagining the city's identity. That's where I come in, remember?" she said.

"You've got a tall order ahead of you, my friend. This city needs people to sustain it, and the ones with money are leaving. They've been leaving for a long time."

Angela slowed at a stoplight. "That's true. But hey, we're still here! There's a solution to Cleveland's problems, and it resides in the people who aren't going anywhere. I'm sure of that much."

"Yeah, but how do you figure out who those people are?"

"I can start by asking," she said.

Their drive down Chester Avenue continued in silence for several miles. Old clapboard and tile houses, brick factories, and glass and concrete business buildings flashed by their windows as they crossed into midtown and headed toward downtown.

"Want to drive by Tower City on our way over?" Bill asked.

"Sure. Want to go by the Public Square entrance?"

"That was my thought," Bill said. "I like to greet the old Higbee's building. It reminds me of Christmas. And hey, it's October — Christmas is upon us!"

Angela rolled her eyes. "My high church sensibilities are still alive and well when it comes to the calendar, even if I'm not technically a high church gal anymore. I'm putting up my tree on the twenty-fourth. Of December," she added.

"Yeah, but your tree is fake. That's not very high church."

Angela smiled. "Nope, not."

"You're just high church when it comes to the commercial world's dating of Christmas, eh?"

"Yes, but even that won't stop me from driving by what reminds you of Christmas in the middle of October. Aren't I a good friend?" Angela nudged Bill on the shoulder.

Bill nudged her back. "I guess." Angela glanced at him and he stuck out his tongue at her.

"Mature," she said. They were downtown now. Angela turned right toward Superior Avenue, then turned left toward Public Square.

Dozens of oily pigeons loitered around the square, pecking for scraps. A few jumped into Angela's path as she approached the tall stone façade of Tower City Mall's Public Square entrance. She laid on the horn and the birds flurried away.

"I love this building. I don't love what they've done to it, though," Bill said, craning his neck to see out Angela's window. The picture windows of what had once been the Higbee's store, and later the Dillard's store, were now draped by the golden curtains of the Horseshoe Casino. The 2009 vote to allow casinos in the state of Ohio had been a controversial one.

"Neither do I," Angela said. "Think they'd let me rework this site?"

"What would you do with it?"

Angela shook her head and continued driving. "I don't know. It's a monumental space. It's too big for a department store in the twenty-first century. With its lofty ceilings the electricity bill must be a nightmare, so overhead would be high. Its only hope is a place like the casino — one that has the novelty factor going for it, to draw in lots of people willing to spend loads of money. It seems to be doing that," she said.

They turned west from Progressive Field and began to cross the Hope Memorial Bridge, passing two large stone pylons that featured large carved human figures on the west and east sides. "Do you suppose those are supposed to be wings?" Angela gestured toward the design behind the figures.

"They call those the 'Guardians of Traffic.' I don't know if they're meant to look angelic, but I did read somewhere that the county engineer threatened to have them taken down back in the seventies. That's when it was placed on the National Register of Historic Places."

Angela snickered. "I like them," she said.

As they crossed the bridge, Carnegie Avenue turned into Lorain Avenue. They continued down Lorain until Angela slowed the car and pointed out Bill's window. "There's the West Side Market," she said. "Great Lakes Brewery and St. Ignatius High School are up ahead on the right."

"Did you know that St. Ignatius used to be St. Ignatius College?" Bill said. "Later it became John Carroll University and moved over to the East Side; that was when University Heights was still a long, rolling meadow."

"University Heights is sure land-locked now," Angela said.

Well-preserved edifices and swanky restaurants gave way to run-down structures as Angela and Bill continued their trek along Lorain Avenue.

"If you turn right on Randall Road, we'll hit West 44th and end up at Franklin Castle," Bill said. Angela turned at Randall and continued north. Tall trees obscured the view of the boarded-up stone building until they were right in front of it.

"Ooh, a turret," Angela purred. "This place reminds me of the houses in the Garden District of New Orleans. Grandma Caroline and I took a trip there when I was a little girl. She showed me where her grandmother's grave was—it was a stone box above ground."

"Was that when she introduced you to goddess worship?" Bill said, opening the car door after Angela parked in front of Franklin Castle.

"You know, I feel guilty even hearing the phrase 'goddess worship.' I expect my mother to pop out from the bushes and lambast me."

"Boo!" Bill screeched, and Angela jumped, hitting her head on the roof of her car as she was getting out.

"Thanks a lot," Angela said, rubbing her head. "And to answer your question, no. She didn't introduce me to the concept of God as Thea till I got my first period. She said she wanted to wait till I was a woman. I didn't start praying to God as Thea until after I left the church, though. Incidentally, that was about the time that I moved out of my parents' house." Angela peered through the iron-slatted fence that marked the perimeter of the property. "This would make a great museum—or a bed and breakfast."

"I checked on it this afternoon—it was bought up recently. No good for you, unfortunately. But it's nice to look at. Like our server from Mama Santa's."

"Oh, yes, I was going to ask you about that—did you end up going back to see him?"

Bill grinned. "Sure did. He gave me his number. We're meeting for drinks tomorrow night."

"Well, well! This is happy news. You were holding out on me!" Angela turned to walk back to the car.

"Momentous news deserves a glorious setting, no?" Bill opened his car door and sat down in the passenger seat.

"You mean my house isn't glorious?" Angela said, buckling her seat belt and turning the key in the ignition.

"Your house doesn't have a turret." Bill winked. Angela laughed.

After driving by the towering spires of St. Colman's

and St. Ignatius of Antioch, Angela got back on Interstate 90 heading east. "Want to have lunch?" she asked.

"Sure. I haven't been to Great Lakes Brewery in a while," Bill said.

"Me, neither. You know, if I ever start seeing someone, I'm not going to have room in my budget for our outings."

"You could pick up a second job."

"One plus my graduate program is plenty, thank you." Angela worked twenty hours a week as a barista at Phoenix Coffee, a local coffee chain. When Angela moved to Cleveland for her undergraduate work, she immediately went on the hunt for a part-time job. Her top job choices came down to a barista position at Phoenix Coffee and a shelver position at the Cleveland Public Library. Her final decision was an olfactory one: the enticing smell of books couldn't beat the smell of just-roasted, fresh-ground coffee beans. Angela was now a veteran among the baristas at Phoenix Coffee's downtown shop, having worked there for eight years.

When Case Western Reserve University offered Angela a full-tuition scholarship for her undergraduate degree, Angela conferred with her parents about the possibility of saving money on housing by living off-campus. "There are some really inexpensive houses in Cleveland neighborhoods. I could get a mortgage for as little as five hundred dollars a month, and then I'd have a place to live beyond my time in school. I've always wanted to settle in Cleveland anyway, and I would love to have the chance to fix up my own house," she told them.

Her parents' immediate answer, voiced by her mother, was, "No." Her mother balked at the idea of her only daughter living off-campus on her own in a big city when she was only eighteen. Her father, however, was a pragmatist. He considered his daughter's proposal in light of her excellent work ethic and outstanding academic performance. He also saw the potential in investing in a second property. After deliberating at length with his wife about it, he persuaded her to go along with it as a way of teaching their daughter financial independence. They agreed to co-sign on a mortgage under four conditions: that Angela would find a part-time job to cover the monthly mortgage and utilities, that she would use her savings to cover the down payment and closing fees, that she would live in the house for the duration of her program and for at least five years after graduating from college, and that she would take a self-defense course before starting school.

Now Angela was one year away from reaching the end of the agreement with her parents, and she had no intention of leaving. Her house was her home. She knew every neighbor on her block. She had given names to the plants in her garden. She had renovated the interior of her house almost single-handedly. Angela imagined herself staying in this house for a long time.

In front of Great Lakes Brewery, a yellow Mazda pulled out of a metered parking space just as Angela was approaching. Angela pulled into the empty space, turned off the ignition, and unbuckled her seatbelt.

Inside, a hostess led them out of the taproom and into the beer garden. Angela ordered a Burning River pale ale; Bill ordered a Holy Moses Belgian white. A breeze sent goosebumps up Angela's arms, and she stood to turn on a standing heat lamp.

"I'm probably biased having lived there my entire adult life, but I prefer the East Side," Angela said, sitting back down. She folded her hands and leaned back in her chair, her eyes sweeping the courtyard.

"So stick with the East Side," Bill said. "But first, tell me what you stood out for you from the West Side."

Angela unfolded her hands and leaned forward, setting her elbows on the table. "What stands out is how my feeling about the West Side differs from my feeling about the East Side, even though on the surface they're not terribly different. Both sides have factories and old houses, and both sides have a smattering of really beautiful buildings. I think the difference for me might be that my story is tied up with the East Side. I've walked and biked and driven those streets. The West Side might as well be Detroit for all I know about it. I don't have a sense of the place or the people at all. The West Side is a place I've only ever visited. I couldn't see myself living or working here."

"That's what people on the West Side say about the East Side."

"Yeah, probably. Point is, I think whatever site I choose is going to have to be a place that I've at least seen on a regular basis. The West Side feels too foreign."

"Spoken like a true East Sider."

Their beers arrived. The server, dressed in a crisp white shirt, black slacks, and a waist apron, asked them if they were ready to order. Angela raised her eyebrows at Bill, and he nodded. "I'll have a cheeseburger medium-well," she said. "Could you make my fries sweet potato fries, and could you hold the toppings on my burger except for the onion?" The server scribbled her order on a pad and looked up again at Bill.

"I'll have the Black and Blue, well done," Bill said, handing his menu to the server. The server wrote down his order, smiled, and hurried back inside. Angela raised her glass, and Bill raised his. "To life, love, and laughter," they said.

"So what do you think, am I being too dismissive too quickly?" Angela asked, setting down her glass.

"I think you're smart to go with your gut. You only have to choose one site—not the whole city. It makes sense to go with a site in a part of the city that you know well." Bill took a sip, and Angela sat back in her chair again, folding her arms behind her head.

"Maybe I'll go with that factory building off 61st and Euclid. There's a stop off the Euclid Corridor there."

"Do you think you could transform the whole space with ten million dollars?" Bill asked.

"To pay for the property, gut it, and refurbish it? I need to do some research, but it's possible. It all depends on how I redesign the space. I'm still letting ideas percolate."

"Well, I await those ideas with interest." Bill raised his glass, and Angela raised hers in turn.

At home, just after she finished her evening prayer, Angela heard a knock on the front door. "Angie, it's me!" cried a child's voice. Angela opened the door and was greeted by the rush of a hug. DeShawn Winters was her next-door, eight-year-old neighbor. "May I have a chocolate chip cookie, please?"

Angela patted his head, which was covered with thick black cornrows trailing down to his shoulders. "You're in luck—I just made some."

"I know, I could smell them."

"How's your granny?" Angela asked, pouring a small glass of milk for him after he'd chosen a cookie from the cooling rack.

"She's fine. She told me to tell you thank you for the eggs. Here you go." DeShawn handed her a paper bag with two eggs in it.

Angela had been visited by DeShawn's grandmother two days previous. She had run out of eggs. "I promised them pancakes for dinner, and Granny doesn't go back on her promises. I'll bring you a couple eggs next time I go to the store, okay, sugar?"

Sharon Suggs was tall and broad, with brown eyes like deep wells, light brown skin, and a hug that could crush garlic. She was the first person to introduce herself to Angela when Angela moved into her house. She knocked on the broken wooden screen door with one hand and held an enormous pecan pie in the other. "Here's something to sweeten the place for you. Welcome to the neighborhood, sugar. I'm Sharon Suggs, but you can call me Mama Sharon."

Angela accepted the pie with thanks and invited

in her new neighbor. "Let me see if I can find the plates," Angela said, but Mama Sharon interrupted her, holding up a plastic bag. "I figured you'd be swimming in boxes here, so I brought forks and plates and napkins for both of us." Angela smiled gratefully, and they spent the next half hour eating pecan pie and getting to know each other.

Mama Sharon lived next door with her daughter, Janette, and first grandchild, Desiree. Janette was a year younger than Angela. She had exotic, large brown eyes and skin just a shade darker than her mother's. She had had her baby a few months before and had just found out she was expecting another. The father of her children didn't hang around much. Janette worked two jobs and was taking GED classes three nights a week. "You probably won't see much of her," Mama Sharon said, wiping her mouth with a napkin.

Angela told Mama Sharon about how she'd grown up in Cuyahoga Falls, a small town bordering Akron, which was the first big city south of Cleveland. "There was never a whole lot of anything going on there. I took every chance I got to come up to Cleveland. Now that I'm here, I feel like I'm living a dream."

"And at a very young age, sweetheart. You're blessed. Just take care not to forget it," Mama Sharon told her.

She couldn't have forgotten if she wanted to. Mama Sharon reminded her of it often, especially when she was struggling in one of her classes or in a relationship. Mama Sharon always shook her head when Angela brought up her difficulties with her mother. "Child, your mama brought you into this world, and I'll bet she changed twice the number of poopy diapers that your daddy did. Be grateful and let the rest go. It's no use hanging onto resentment for your family." Mama Sharon was a grounding force in Angela's life, and Angela was grateful for it.

DeShawn pressed his finger into each crumb from his cookie and put it in his mouth. "This is yummy, Angie," he said.

"How about if you take some cookies home for your family? I'll even throw in an extra one for you."

"Sounds good to me!" DeShawn jumped up and down in his spot, watching Angie eagerly as she packed up half a dozen cookies in a plastic baggie.

"Okay, here you go," she said, and DeShawn took the bag and zoomed out the front door, hollering "Thank you!" behind him as he leapt from her porch. Angela chuckled. She put the lid back on her cookie tin and went to the front door to lock it. Walking through the living room, past the dining room, and down the hall past the stairs, she stepped into her bathroom to brush her teeth. The walls glimmered with green and white miniature tiles she had installed herself. Then she climbed the stairs to her room, changed into her pajamas, and switched on her desk lamp. She had planning to do.

Chapter 4

The alarm woke Angela at 5:30am. She hit the alarm clock with an open palm and blinked. She had been up until eleven working on her proposal. Now she had to get ready for her Monday morning shift at Phoenix Coffee. The smell of coffee dragged her from the warmth of her covers and down the chilly stairs. A strong wind blew through the trees outside, tearing the remaining leaves from their branches. Leaves smacked Angela's windows before sailing to the ground. Angela would have to drive in today—it was too cold for a commute on her bike.

Angela went to the kitchen and poured a cup of coffee into a heavy blue mug. She filled the mug to the brim, leaving no room for cream. She padded through her dining room and living room to her prayer room, opening the door and leaving it open. There was no vent in the closet, so the warm air would have to come in from the living room. Her skin prickled as she prayed. She wrapped both hands around her mug for warmth. It was the time of year when her meditations grew short and her spoken prayers sped forward. Tonight she would need to remember to leave the closet door open.

After her morning prayer, Angela headed to the bathroom for a hot shower. She took extra time blow-drying her hair and had to hurry through her makeup as a result. Once she was dressed in a red blouse, black slacks, and black leather ankle boots, she bundled up in her outdoor things and headed out the front door. She spotted ice on her porch steps, and then on her windshield. She groaned. Ice on the steps and the windshield meant icy roads. She was going to be late.

Angela apologized to her manager, Shelly MacDougall, as she walked in the door to Phoenix Coffee at 6:55. "Sorry, sorry, the ice slowed me down," she said. Shelly, a tall, red-haired woman in her late forties, waved her on. Angela walked quickly behind the counter and into the staff room. She stuffed her gloves in her pockets and hung up her coat, hat, scarf on a brass hook on the wall, trading them for an apron. The bell jingled just as she was walking back out. The first customer was one of their regulars, Allison Brown, a curvy, middle-aged blond woman with pale skin and light blue eyes.

"Good morning, Allison!" Angela said.

"Good morning, Angela. Good morning to you, too, Shelly," she said, nodding to Shelly who was restocking the pastry case. "I'll have my usual with an extra shot. What a morning." Allison took off her gloves and raised her hands to her cheeks. They were rosy from the cold.

"I was late getting in myself. The residential streets in my neighborhood haven't been salted yet," Angela said, tamping espresso into two pods.

Shelly chimed in. "Well, if the temperatures stay like this, we'll be free from all that lake effect snow by December!" Lake Erie always took a while to freeze over, and the snow fell heavily and frequently until it did.

"Oh, but I'm not ready for this. It's not even Halloween yet!" Allison said.

Angela poured 2% milk in a carafe and placed the carafe under the steamer. "Are you planning to dress up this year?" she asked.

"Definitely. We have a great trick-or-treating neighborhood. I was a witch last year, but I'm thinking about trying Dorothy from the Wizard of Oz," Allison said.

"I would play Dorothy just for the shoes," Shelly said.

"Exactly," Allison said. "I found a pair of red sequined shoes at the mall a few weeks ago and caved. You only live once, right?"

"Unless you're Lazarus," Angela said under her breath.

"Unless you're what?" Allison asked.

Angela blushed and looked up. "Unless you're Lazarus. From the Bible. I was just reading this morning about how Jesus called him out of the tomb. Pretty gruesome story, when you think about it. He'd been rotting for days before Jesus showed up."

Shelly blanched. "Maybe you should be Lazarus for Halloween, Ang."

"Hey, if Lazarus comes back to life, doesn't that make him a zombie?" Allison asked.

"Not just a zombie. He'd also be wrapped up like a mummy, since he's in the tomb. So maybe I could be a mummy zombie Lazarus. A cross-dressing one," Angela said. All three women began to laugh, and soon they were all doubled over.

"Oh, dear," Angela said, wiping tears from her eyes.

"'Oh, dear' is right," Shelly said, patting her right cheek with one hand and picking up a small tray of croissants with the other.

Allison unwound her scarf and fanned herself. "I think I'll have one of those croissants while I'm at it," she said.

"You've got it," Shelly said. She set down the tray on the counter between the registers and placed a croissant in a pastry bag, giving it to Allison. Angela handed Allison a no-foam, four-shot latte with sugar-free vanilla syrup. Then she rang up her order at the register. Allison put a dollar in the tip jar. "You two are a riot."

Angela and Shelly exchanged a look. "We know," they said together.

Allison laughed again, rewound her scarf, and nodded at Angela and Shelly before making her way out the door.

"One happy customer down, many more to go!" Shelly said. Angela gave her two thumbs up. "Would you help with these?" Shelly asked, nodding toward the pastry trays.

"Sure thing, boss," Angela said.

Later that morning, as Angela was ringing up a customer, the bell jingled and a young man walked in. Angela said goodbye to the customer at the register, then looked up as the next customer approached. Angela raised her eyebrows in surprise.

"Joseph Warner! We meet again," she said. She tucked a stray lock of hair behind her ear as Joseph approached the counter. Angela was tall, but he was about half a foot taller, she noticed.

"Angela! But I still don't know your last name," Joseph said, smiling.

"Bridges," Shelly offered over her shoulder as she pulled out an empty tray from the pastry case. Angela rolled her eyes. "Bridges," she confirmed.

"Well, Angela Bridges, one meeting can be called chance, but two meetings is synchronicity. It's nice to see you again!"

"Likewise. Oh, and Professor McNear told me to offer his regards if I saw you again," she said.

"He was very kind to me when I was at CSU," Joseph said, pulling off his gloves. "I'd ask you what's good here, but I already have orders about what to get. I'm meeting with my bishop at the chancery, and he asked if I'd stop for a coffee pick-up on my way."

"He puts the seminarians to work!" Angela said.

Joseph nodded. "He does. But it's all for the good."

"So what would you like?" Angela asked.

"Two medium lattes—one with one shot, and one with three."

"Is the triple for you or for the bishop?"

"For the bishop."

Angela smiled and shook her head. "And only one shot for you?"

"Caffeine revs me up. I don't handle it well. Besides, moderation is a virtue."

"For everyone except the bishop?"

Joseph's cheeks reddened. "That's not what I meant."

"I'm kidding," she said, turning her attention to the espresso. "I haven't seen you in here before. Are you going to be visiting the bishop often?"

"Maybe. He wants to talk to me about helping out with one of the ministries at the cathedral."

"Sounds like he likes you."

"He requires each seminarian to take on a four-month pastoral internship before ordination. But yeah, he probably does like me, if he trusts me at the cathedral," he said quietly.

"Don't sound so modest!" she said, pouring the shots into their respective paper cups.

"Modesty is a virtue, too," he said with a wink.

Angela chuckled. "Well, more power to you and your virtue, future Father Joseph!" She poured the frothing milk into the cups, snapped lids on, and added sleeves that featured the Phoenix Coffee logo. "Here you go! Good luck with the bishop."

"Would you pray for me, too?" he said, pulling on his gloves and accepting the steaming cups.

"I'm a heretic, but sure," she said.

"I'm sure you're not. Thanks, Angela Bridges." He nodded at her before turning to walk out the door.

"Who was the guy in the black dress?" Shelly asked, emerging from the back room as the door swung shut behind Joseph.

"That was a future Roman Catholic priest, so don't get any ideas."

"So how'd you meet him? Pick-up at a bar?" Shelly asked.

"Actually, I met him at the library when I was doing research for the contest proposal I was telling you about. Turns out he's entering the same contest." Angela picked up a rag, sprayed it with cleaning solution, and began wiping down the counter around the registers.

"He's cute. Too bad he's unavailable. He seems nice."

"Shelly, really, I'm fine. No matchmaking needed."

Shelly shook her head. "When I introduce you to the man of your dreams, you'll thank me. In the meantime, I see some tables that could use some attention."

Angela surveyed the room. Newspapers and used coffee cups littered several tables. "I'm on it."

At noon, Angela's shift ended, and she bundled up before saying goodbye to Shelly. "See you tomorrow," she said.

Shelly waved from the counter. "Stay warm!"

It wasn't as cold outside as it had been that morning. The wind had died down. Hundreds of people in business suits filled the sidewalks in search of lunch. Sometimes Angela treated herself to lunch at the Arcade, an enclosed shopping mall down the street, but today she had homemade pasta salad waiting for her at home. Angela pulled out of the parking garage and onto Vincent Street. At East 9th Street, instead of turning south toward Chester the way she normally did, she turned north toward Superior. The Cathedral of St. John the Evangelist stood on the corner of Superior and East 9th Street. Angela waited at the red light without turning on her blinker. "Thea," she said in a murmur, "help Joseph find his way. Amen." The light turned green, and she turned, heading east on Superior.

As Angela passed the Church of St. Mary Magdalene, Angela's thoughts drifted to the many Sundays she had spent at her Missouri Synod church, Emmanuel Lutheran Church. The faded brick church building was small. It had been built by the founding members of the church in 1925. At full capacity it would hardly accommodate two hundred people, and it was never full. Angela remembered the flicker of the candles, the wafting incense, the genuflections, the vestments of the clergy, the vibrant sound of the four-part choir joined with the voices of the congregation. She remembered vividly the day of her confirmation and first communion. Receiving first communion and confirmation meant becoming an adult in the church. Her mother made her her first grown-up dress, one that came down to her ankles. She used a pale blue cotton fabric as a nod to the virgin mother of Jesus. "You are becoming a handmaiden of the Lord," her mother told her. "Let Mary's perfect submissiveness be your model throughout life. That is what God seeks from his daughters."

Angela prayed that day that God would give her the grace to be perfectly submissive—submissiveness didn't always come easily to her, even though she erred on the side of following the rules more often than not. In the fervor of her initiation as an adult in the church at age thirteen, she wished and prayed for nothing but what God wanted: God's will, not her own. Two years later, still praying for God's will to guide her life, her world was thrown off its axis by her desire to take up leadership as a minister.

The early conversations she had with her mother about it haunted her. Her mother immediately dismissed her call as a temptation from the devil. If this were God's will, then God's will was leading her away from the church that had taught her to obey and love God, and how could that be? She concluded that Angela's will was asserting itself. What she had to do was pray for God's strength in resisting the temptation that had befallen her.

"I want you to pray the Lord's Prayer first thing when you wake up and right before you go to bed. 'Thy will be done,' not 'my will be done,'" her mother reminded her.

Angela did pray—she prayed harder and at greater length than she ever had in her life. But the desire to pursue ministry, instead of diminishing, grew stronger. It grew so strong that Angela came to believe that she was fallen, irreparably broken, unfit to call herself a member of her beloved church. She expected her mother to scream at her when she told her she was leaving the church. Instead, her mother gave her a stare as cold as Canadian ice. "I will pray for you," she said curtly.

Angela's father's reaction was less stern, but more vocal. "Angela, the Missouri Synod is your spiritual home. You need the wisdom of a community to guide you on your journey, or you may become lost for good. This is the time when you should rely the most on your church, not run away from it."

"I think I am lost, Daddy. This call to pursue ministry isn't going away. It's getting stronger. I can't reconcile that with the teachings of our church. Jesus went into the wilderness for forty days to be tested before he began his ministry, right? I feel like this is the time when God's testing me, and God's telling me I need to be alone for the test."

Angela's father shook his head. "You're putting yourself in danger of losing the path and never finding it again, Ang. But you're also nearly an adult, so I can't stop you."

Angela's gaze dropped to the floor. Her eyes became watery.

"Listen, honey," her father said, "I love you, and your mom loves you. Our whole church loves you. And when you're ready to come back, we're going to welcome you with open arms, and your faith will be stronger on that day than ever before. Okay?"

He wrapped her in a strong hug, and she squeezed him back. Hope shuddered through her body. Things could be okay in the end. She could come back.

Eight years later, she was still in the wilderness. She had lost sight of her former path a long time ago. She was praying to Thea now, for heaven's sake! Her whole understanding of God had changed. She could never go back. The wilderness was her home now, and her ministry was a ministry for one. *At least Grandma Caroline is camping out with me.*

At East 82nd Street, Angela turned right to head south toward her home. The dozens of children that flocked around her neighborhood in the mid-afternoon and evening were conspicuously absent. School was still in session. On a warmer day, she would have headed out to her front porch to read the newspaper on her porch swing, but it was chilly, and today she had a reflection paper to finish up before she headed off to her three o'clock class on sacred landmarks. She brought her laptop—a Toshiba she'd bought at a Black Friday sale—down to the dining room and set it on her polished, rectangular dining room table. She had found the table on someone's tree-lawn while she was on a bike-ride shortly after moving into her house. A sign marked "FREE" in bold letters was taped to the front. She rode back home, got in her car, and sped back to disassemble it before someone else claimed it. Even with the back seat folded down, the table didn't fit all the way, so she used one of several bungee cables to secure the trunk. Most of her furniture had been acquired in a similar fashion. The table had several deep scratches and mug rings on the surface when she first brought it home, so she took it to her garage and sanded the top and the rectangular legs smooth with her electric hand-held sander—a gift from her parents—before refinishing it in a dark stain.

She walked into the kitchen and padded across the wooden floor, opening one of the white cabinets with its round, spiral iron knob and pulling out a shiny Byzantium purple plate from her set of six. The refrigerator that came with the house had several colonies of mold growing in it when Angela arrived, so she had scrubbed it with bleach inside and out three times. Now the contents of the refrigerator were neatly arranged, with nary a speck of mold, dirt, or crumbs anywhere in sight. Angela pulled out the sterling silver bowl of pasta salad and scooped a ladle-full onto her plate. She filled a glass with water from the tap, left out the ice, and took her glass and plate to the dining room table, setting them on a thick, round, pumpkin-colored cotton placemat. The telephone rang as she was pulling a fork out of her utensil drawer.

Picking up the telephone from its receiver on her kitchen wall, she answered, "Hello?"

"Hello, Angela." Her mother's voice was cool and crisp.

"Hi, Mom," Angela said, looking longingly at her pasta salad.

"Did I reach you at a bad time?"

Angela turned around and faced her front kitchen window. "No, this is fine. What's up?"

"I wanted to talk to you about your father."

Angela twisted the phone cord around her index finger. "Sure. Is something wrong?"

"You may want to sit down."

Time slowed. She sat. "Okay."

"Angela, he went to the hospital last night. They found tumors in his pancreas. They had to operate immediately."

Tears stung her eyes. She swallowed hard. "Is he okay?"

"He's here at the hospital recovering. I've been with him all morning."

"Should I come right away? I mean, is he in imminent danger?"

"The doctor says he's stable, but I think he'd like to see you. When he's awake he asks for you."

Angela looked at the clock. She had ample time to

finish her paper, but there was no way she would be able to concentrate now. "I'll come right over. Can you text me the name of the hospital and his room number?"

A minute later, she said goodbye and hung up the phone. She put her plate in the sink; the pasta salad lay untouched. She took the stairs two at a time, dashed off an e-mail to her professor letting her know that she would be unable to attend class because of a family emergency, and flew down the stairs again.

Chapter 5

The drive to Akron City Hospital took forty-five minutes. It was all Angela could do to keep her body still. Thick sobs threatened to erupt from her at any moment. Her knuckles, rather than their usual golden tan color, were pale yellow from clutching the steering wheel. Her jaw was set, making her strong chin look even sharper than usual.

Jumping out of her car in the multi-story parking lot across the street from the hospital, Angela opted to take the stairs rather than the elevator. She rushed through the main doors of the hospital and approached the person at the information desk.

"You'll need to register as a visitor, ma'am. Who is the patient and what is your relationship to him or her?"

"Alex Bridges. I'm his daughter," she said quickly.

"I just need you to fill out this form and get your picture taken," the attendant said, sliding a clipboard across the desk.

"Is this really necessary?" Angela asked impatiently.

"It's to ensure the security of our patients, ma'am."

Angela shook her head and filled out her name, address, and phone number on the form. The attendant asked to see her driver's license, so she pulled her slim wallet out of her pocket and opened it for the attendant to see. The attendant took her picture using a cheap-looking webcam, and then she printed a visitor label with her picture on it for Angela to wear.

"Just go up the elevator to the second floor. Make a left, a right, and a left and you'll be there."

"Thank you," she said over her shoulder. She pushed the elevator button and it opened immediately. "Thank goodness," she muttered. Angela pushed through a set of metal doors and asked the nurse at the reception desk for help in finding her father's room.

The nurse eyed her visitor's badge. Then he checked a stapled print-out. "Go down this hall and turn left. You'll see it there."

Angela rushed down the hall, and the nurse called after her, "No running, please!" She slowed her pace to a brisk walk.

Her mother's familiar figure was visible first. Angela knocked quietly on the door and her mother looked up. Her eyes were bloodshot. She looked as if she'd been crying. Angela opened the door quietly and slid inside the room. Her father was asleep. A heart monitor beeped in the background. He was wearing an oxygen mask.

Angela turned her gaze toward her mother. She looked exhausted. Her black, gray-streaked hair was tied back in a ponytail. Stray hairs had escaped the ponytail and hung down haphazardly. Smudges of dark black mascara coated the lower rims of her eyes. Her pale face, which was soft and kind-looking despite her firm demeanor, like Grandma Caroline's, was drawn taut. Her hands were clasped tightly together. Angela walked over to her and stood next to her chair, touching her shoulder lightly. Her mother remained motionless, as if a single movement would unleash a hurricane.

"Do you want to take a break? I saw a coffee shop downstairs."

Angela's mother didn't answer. Instead, she stood up, smoothed her skirt, and walked slowly out of the room. Angela could hear her mother's pumps click down the polished floor of the hallway.

Angela approached her father, whose breathing was slow and steady. His left arm was covered in IV tubing. She moved to the other side and clasped his right hand lightly. "They picked the wrong hand, didn't they, Daddy? I'll bet they didn't even ask if you were left-handed." Angela and her father shared that trait. Grandma Caroline was left-handed, too, so Angela got it from both sides of the family.

"I prayed for you all the way over here. I even prayed the Lord's Prayer the way you taught me when I was little. Maybe God will respond more kindly to my prayers if I pray the good old-fashioned way. What do you think?"

Her father remained motionless except for the rise and dip of his chest. Angela leaned in to whisper. "You don't deserve this, Daddy. You are so good, and kind, and loving, and…."

Angela bit her lip. Tears fell down her cheeks, landing on the white blanket that covered her father. She wiped her face with the back of her hand.

"Daddy, if it would bring you back, I'd come back

to the Missouri Synod. I would, for your sake. But I know God doesn't work like that. God doesn't do special favors for people based on their actions. It's all grace, just like you and Mom taught me. But where is God's grace now? How could this be happening?" Angela's tears kept falling, and she kept wiping them away with her hand. She thought of the book of Job, and how God tested Job by taking away everything he held dear, even his family. *Are you testing me, Thea?* she asked silently. Silence was all the response she got.

Angela squeezed her father's hand, walked back to the visitor's chair, and sat down. She felt as tired as her mother had looked. The door opened, and her mother walked in, carrying two cups of coffee. Angela began to stand, but her mother waved her down, giving her one of the cups. Her generosity betrayed the gravity of the situation. Tears began to stream down Angela's face. She let them fall.

"Did you tell Grandma Caroline about Daddy?" Angela asked. An hour had passed since her arrival, and she and her mother had spent it in a weary silence. Her father hadn't woken. Her mother shook her head.

"I'll call her," Angela said, getting up. She stepped around her mother, who walked toward the visitor's chair and sat down in it, folding her hands over her lap. Angela went to the waiting room, but a sign there said "No cell phones in the waiting area," so she went downstairs to the front lobby. She punched in her grandmother's phone number from memory.

"Hello?"

"Grandma Caroline, it's me."

"My angel," she said. Angela, the only daughter of her mother, was her grandmother's only grandchild. "How are you, dear?"

"Not good. Daddy's in the hospital." Her voice caught, and she held her breath. She imagined her grandmother's soft, plump features hardening into a frown. She was probably tucking her long silver hair behind her ears the way she always did when something bothered her.

"In the hospital? What happened?"

"He's sleeping right now. I don't know what happened. Mom hasn't told me anything except that he went to the emergency room and they found cancerous tumors in his pancreas. They had to do an emergency operation"

"Oh, dear. Oh, my. Sweetheart, I'm sorry. You must be a wreck."

Angela nodded silently. People passing by her in the lobby stole glances at her mascara-streaked cheeks. She turned toward the wall. "I just sat in his hospital room for an hour with Mom and she barely said a word to me."

Grandma Caroline sighed. "Your mother goes deep inside herself when something's bothering her. She always has."

"But why is she like that? Why can't she act like a normal human being?"

"That is her normal, my angel."

"My dad could be dying and my mom doesn't have a thing to say about it."

"Honey, did you try talking to her?"

Angela put one foot on top of the other and leaned against the wall. "No."

"Well, I hate to tell you this, but she's probably up there wondering why you didn't say a word to her."

"I stopped trying to talk to her a long time ago. I talked and talked and the only time she responded was to cut me off. So what's the point of trying?"

"That's a good question. What is the point?"

Angela shook her head. "I don't see why I have to be the one to initiate conversation."

"You don't have to be. And neither does your mother. If you want to talk to her, talk to her. If you don't, don't. But there's no use being mad at someone who's acting the same way you are."

Angela's eyes welled up again. "I'm scared, Grandma."

"Thea is with you, my angel. And she's with your dad and mom, too. Did you bring your prayer book with you?"

"I didn't think of it when I was leaving."

"Nevermind. Close your eyes, take a few deep breaths, and imagine your dad being well and happy. I'm going to do the same thing."

Angela closed her eyes, inhaled, and exhaled slowly. In her mind's eye, her father woke up and saw her. He smiled and lifted his arms toward her.

"Grandma Caroline," she whispered, "I think I'm going to go back up."

"You go back up, my angel. And remember to breathe."

"Okay. I love you."

"I love you to the moon."

"Bye, Grandma."

"Bye, sweetheart."

Angela pressed the red end call icon on her phone and looked around. A bathroom was twenty feet from where she stood. She went in and washed her face. With a paper towel, she wiped around her eyes to remove the last smudges of makeup. Splotches of pink dusted her face. She washed her hands, then headed out into the hallway.

Her mother was standing next to her father's bed when Angela walked in.

"Did he wake up?" Angela asked, standing near the door.

"No."

Angela looked out the window. The tops of the evergreens outside were still. A shiver ran down her spine. Wordlessly, her mother walked over to the chair and sat down again. Angela walked softly to her father's side and took his hand. It was cold. His breathing was slow and steady. She slowed her breathing till it matched his. Her eyes closed and she squeezed his hand, willing him to be well. When she opened her eyes again, her mother was reading her Bible.

"What are you reading?"

"The Bible."

Angela bit back the first reply that came to mind. "I meant, which book?"

"John."

Angela walked over and looked over her mother's shoulder. Her mother's left pointer finger rested at chapter eleven, verse twenty-five.

"I am the resurrection and the life," Angela murmured.

"He that believes in me, though he may die, yet he shall live," her mother said.

"You don't think he's going to die, do you?"

"We're all going to die eventually. 'Yet he shall live,'" her mother quoted, "because he believes. There is no unhappy ending in store for your father."

But there is for me. Angela frowned, remembering a conversation ten years earlier in which her mother had told her she was an apostate of the faith and that she was turning from grace. "There will be no happy ending for you, Angela," her mother had said in a low voice.

Her mother's present choice of words indicated that the conversation was not going well. Thinking of her grandmother, she breathed in deeply and tried again.

"How are you feeling?"

The taut lines on her mother's face fell slack. "Tired. And hungry."

"I'll get you something to eat." Angela jumped up and scooted out the door. She could do something nice for her mother and get another break from her at the same time. Guilt and anger washed over her like silt, but she brushed them aside and continued her walk to the elevator.

Angela wondered about her mother. How did she cope with the belief that both her daughter and mother were on a surefire path to hell? She regarded life's trials as a reminder to remain humble and lowly before God. Maybe she considered the compromised salvation of her daughter and mother to be one such trial. Angela shook her head. She couldn't buy into a god of fire and brimstone. Thea was the god of love and mercy.

The sound of Angela's ringer interrupted her thoughts. She dug her phone out of her pocket and looked at the screen. It was Heidi, her best friend from high school, but Angela didn't have the energy to talk. She needed to clear her head. The call went to voicemail, and Angela walked into the coffee shop. The smell of coffee grounds sharpened her focus. As she approached the register, a blond-haired barista named Mike greeted her with a bright smile and said, "What can I get for you today?"

Eyeing the case next to the register, Angela picked up a tuna sandwich in a plastic box. She also picked up a bottle of sparkling water—bubbly beverages were a hit with her mother. She placed the items on the counter. "Any coffee or dessert for you?" Mike asked.

"I have some coffee waiting for me upstairs and I don't need dessert. I'm good," Angela said.

"Alrighty." Mike rang her up. Angela handed him a twenty from her pocket and he pulled out change from the drawer. She thanked him and headed out of the shop, clutching her purchases in her hands.

Back at her father's hospital room, Angela put both the water and the sandwich in her left hand so she could grab the door handle with her right. Inside, her mother's back was to her. She heard her father's voice.

"Daddy!" she exclaimed, rushing over to the far

side of the bed. Her father smiled weakly at her. His salt and pepper hair was trimmed neatly around his gentle, tan face. He had the same green eyes that Angela had. "Hello, Ang. Bet you didn't expect to find your dear old dad laid up in a hospital bed, huh?"

Angela leaned over and kissed his forehead. "I'm glad you're awake. How do you feel?"

"Oh, just peachy." His smile turned to a grimace as he winced in pain.

"Let's let your father rest," her mother said.

"Oh, here you go, Mom." Angela walked around the bed, rather than reaching over her father, to give her mother her water and sandwich.

"Thank you."

"Nothing for me?" her father said.

"I can go get you something if your doctor or nurse says it's okay."

"Stickler for the rules. That's my girl." Angela's father pushed a button attached to his bed. A nurse with espresso-colored eyes and black dreadlocks was there within moments. "Shandra" appeared in bold black letters on her nametag.

"Mr. Bridges, you're awake!" Shandra said. "How do you feel?"

"I was just telling my daughter that I feel great. Except for the hole in my stomach, that is."

"We can increase your medication if the pain becomes too much. It'll just make you sleepy."

"I think I'm okay for now. Talking to my two favorite ladies is a nice remedy."

Shandra leaned over him to fluff his pillows. "If you need anything, just press that button again, okay?"

"Yes, ma'am."

Shandra exited the room, and Angela's mother took her husband's hand.

"Alex, I brought my Bible along," Angela's mother said. "Would you like to read it?"

"Thank you, Susan. I would, but not before I have a chance to talk with you and Angela. It's been a while since we've all been in the same room!" It had been a long while. Angela hadn't been down to visit her parents since Christmas. She drove down after her shift on Christmas Eve. At her father's request, she joined her parents at their church's midnight service. Pleasure at the richness of the liturgy and sadness at her distance from the community settled over Angela like a heavy, stifling blanket. She could hardly breathe.

Christmas Day was a tinseled blur, and Angela felt distant from all of it. Even Grandma Caroline couldn't get through to her. On her way home that evening, Angela promised never to subject herself to her old church again. She figured that as long as she stayed away from her childhood home, she would never have to make an excuse not to go to church, and her wounded memory would scab over. Now Angela's mother looked at her husband meaningfully, and he seemed to answer her unspoken question.

Angela broke the tension. "Are you in a lot of pain, Daddy?"

"Well, I'm not ready to run a marathon. But at least the doctors were able to do what they needed to do. And I'm sitting here talking to you, aren't I? A little pain is worth it."

"I'm praying for you," she said. Her father gave her hand a squeeze and smiled. Her mother frowned and shook her head.

"I spoke to Grandma Caroline a few minutes ago. She's praying for you, too."

"Oh, would you stop it?" Angela's mother burst out.

Angela looked wide-eyed at her mother. "Stop praying for Daddy?"

"Stop pretending that your so-called faith is at the service of God. It isn't."

Her mother glared at her. Angela's face flushed red with embarrassment and anger. It was the same thing that happened anytime the subject of her faith came up: her mother yelled at her, and it turned into a shouting match. Angela couldn't do this, not with her father sick in a hospital bed.

"Daddy, I love you, but I've got to go," she mumbled. She grabbed her hat, coat, and scarf and bolted out the door. Her father's pleas followed her down the hall.

Outside, she put on her jacket and pulled her hat down over her ears. She wound the scarf around her neck and pulled her gloves out of her coat pockets. The windless chill stung her tear-stained face.

Shake it off, she told herself. *You're an adult. Don't let her get to you like that.*

But her mother had gotten to her. Here she was practically running to her car to when her father was stuck in a hospital bed, all because her mother had given voice to her already well-known views. *An adult would have stayed,* her mother's voice taunted in her head.

Angela dug her phone out of her pants pocket. A voicemail from Heidi was waiting for her. She dialed her voicemail and listened as she took the elevator up to her car.

"Ang, it's Heidi. I'm in Cleveland this weekend for a show and I thought you might like to hang out when I'm not at the gallery. Let me know if that works. Love you! Talk soon!"

Angela hung up the phone. She'd call her later.

She hadn't been at the hospital long, but it had felt like an age. *Daddy will be fine without you. You can call him.* Angela pushed the worries about her father firmly to the back of her mind, turned her radio's volume up till she couldn't hear herself think, and sped out of the parking garage.

Chapter 6

Angela pulled into her driveway just past four o'clock. Had it only been four hours since she'd said goodbye to Shelly? It was still light out, and the kids who had been in school when she drove home from work littered the streets, bundled in heavy jackets and winter caps. A few chocolate-colored faces looked up as she drove by. She turned the volume dial counter-clockwise as she pulled into her driveway.

Inside, she walked to the kitchen and pulled her plate of pasta salad out of the sink. She had no appetite, not after the blow-out with her mother. She covered the plate with plastic, put the plate in the refrigerator, and grabbed a bottle of Blue Moon.

She popped the cap off her beer and headed for the living room couch. She could flop down there and turn on the television, letting a thousand flashing images push her mother and father out of her mind. She eyed the couch, a red boxy number from IKEA, and then changed her mind, moving down the hall and into the room at the end, to the right of the bathroom. Compared with her bedroom/office, this room was small, but it was larger than the spare bedroom to the left of the bathroom. In this room, Angela had created a sanctuary for books. Three walls were covered with floor-to-ceiling pine bookshelves that Angela had designed and installed herself. The vertical windows on the south and east walls let in plenty of light, so she only had to turn on her floor lamps when dusk arrived. Each beige-gold globe lamp light hung from the top of a tall, thin, C-shaped rod that was welded into a broad metal base on the floor. The lamp wrapped vertically around the purple crushed-velvet tufted arm-chair that stood at each window. A matching ottoman stood at the foot of the chair against the south window, where Angela preferred to sit. Angela had scored the chairs and ottoman from an estate sale in Shaker Heights for thirty dollars. The original upholstery was worn, cracked, yellowing leather. She found the sturdy purple velvet fabric at a fabric store and took it and the furniture pieces to her friend Lacey's upholstery shop in Euclid Heights. Lacey used her employee discount on the order, and Angela got all three pieces back in like-new condition for less than a hundred bucks. That had been a splurge, but her library was worth it.

She set her beer on one of the bookshelves on the south wall and eyed the titles. There were hundreds. Most of them she had collected over the last ten years from her school courses, friends of the library sales, and used bookstores. Robert Pirsig's *Zen and the Art of Motorcycle Maintenance* caught her eye, so she plucked it off the shelf, grabbed her beer, and sat down to read, crossing her feet on the ottoman. She was glad to escape into the book's cross-country journey on a motorcycle for a while.

Several chapters later, Angela's phone rang, Angela pulled her phone out of her pocket to see who it was. The time read 5:43. It was Bill.

"Hey," she answered dully, putting her finger in her book as a bookmark.

"What's wrong with you?" he asked.

"My dad's in the hospital and I had a fight with my mother while I was visiting this afternoon."

"What? What happened to your dad?"

Angela put her feet flat on the round lavender rug that covered the wooden floor. She willed herself to stop trembling, but her will wasn't making much of a showing. "He went to the ER last night. Tumors in his pancreas. They had to operate immediately. He's recovering now."

"Oh, Ang, I'm so sorry."

"Thanks." Angela didn't know what else to say.

"And you had a fight with your mom?"

"Yep. It was like I was fifteen again, being put in my place. I ran out."

The hum of indistinct voices rippled over the line. "I know I've said this before, but you deserve better than that," he said at last.

"According to her, I deserve exactly what I get. That obviously includes a jerk for a mother." Angela's eyes were filling again. *Damnit.*

"Oh, honey, I'd come over, but I'm at work." *That's* what the background noise was. "Why don't I stop by afterward? Think you'll be awake?"

"I have to get up early for work, so I'd probably be asleep by the time you got here. But thanks anyway."

"How about if I drop by Phoenix tomorrow at the end of your shift? Buy you a scone!"

Angela smiled a small smile and shook her head.

"I'm a sucker for carbs. You've got a deal."

She wished Bill a good night and hung up the phone. Her stomach growled. "All right, all right," she muttered.

Several minutes later, she had the plate of pasta salad in one hand and a glass of water in the other. She set her dinner on the dining room table and turned the wall dimmer switch clockwise before sitting down in her usual chair along the east wall. From there she had a view of Mama Sharon's brick north wall, the northern corner of her west-facing porch, and what remained of the fiery foliage of her elm tree. The light from the sinking sun was dim behind Cleveland's cloudy sky. Sunset technically wasn't for another hour, but the sky would be completely dark within half an hour, from the looks of it now.

Angela chewed a bite of pasta salad thoughtfully. She still had a reflection paper to write and send off. She had her class with Professor McNear in the evening tomorrow, but no assignment due, and she had done her reading for the week already. After she was done with her reflection paper, she would have time to work on her proposal again.

She stabbed some more pasta with her fork and thought of her mother. She wondered how her father was doing. "You've got a proposal to write," she chided herself. But her father needed her. She sighed. She would head upstairs to finish her reflection paper and call her father afterward. On her way up the stairs, she dialed Heidi's number.

"Hey, babe!"

"Hey, Heidi. Thanks for calling me earlier. I'm

sorry I missed you. I was in the hospital."

"In the hospital? Are you okay?"

"I'm fine, but my dad's not. He had to have pancreatic tumors removed. It was all very sudden."

"Wow, gosh. Is he going to be okay?"

"I don't know." Angela sat down on her chair, biting her knuckle.

"Ang, I'm sorry. That must be really hard."

"Harder for Dad than for me. But yeah, it's no fun finding out your middle-aged father has cancer."

"Oh, honey. Is there anything I can do?"

"You can go dancing with me on Saturday night. I could use a Long Island and some really loud music."

"We could go to the Warehouse District! We haven't gone dancing for a long time — that'll be fun!"

"Seeing you will be great. I miss you, Heidi."

"I miss you, too. Is there anything else I can do in the meantime? I know your family is pretty conservative and Christian, but I'm happy to send him healing energy."

Angela looked up at the ceiling. Her parents didn't know her best friend from college was a witch, and she wasn't about to tell them.

"I believe in your goodness and the power of your intention, Heidi. Do what you do best. I'm sure it'll only help."

"You've got it. I love you, Angela."

"Love you, too, Heidi."

"Bye."

"Bye."

"Send," she said to her computer screen. Away went

the e-mail to her professor with her reflection paper and another apology for missing class. Now she could get on with her real work: her proposal for the urban development contest. But first, she needed to call her father.

Angela took a deep breath as the phone rang. Her father picked up after two rings.

"Hello, sweetheart."

"Hi, Daddy. I'm sorry I ran out like that."

"Things got a little tense, didn't they?"

"Yep. Listen, I've got Wednesday afternoon free—could I come see you then?"

"I'd like that very much, Ang."

"Okay. I'll do my best to keep the peace around Mom."

"She loves you, you know."

"I know. I love her, too. But I can't help thinking she doesn't like me very much."

"You two don't see eye to eye, but that doesn't mean she doesn't like you."

Angela was silent for a long moment. Her father broke the silence.

"I'll see you Wednesday, sweetheart."

"Okay, Daddy. I love you."

"I love you, too. Bye now."

"Bye."

Angela hung up the phone and ran her hands through her long hair. She wasn't looking forward to another confrontation with her mother, but she had to be there for her dad.

With that, Angela pushed her family issues firmly to the back of her mind and considered the building she had chosen for her contest proposal. After some sweet-talking and an explanation of the contest, she had obtained an electronic copy of the blueprints from the commercial realtor. The realtor told her that the asking price for the property was three million, but it could be negotiated for the right buyer. He told her to send him the proposal before submitting it for the contest. "If we work together, we can give this property the future it deserves," he said. Angela was pretty sure this realtor in the pin-stripe suit didn't care what happened to the dilapidated factory so long as he managed to sell it, but she was willing to play along.

After a quick search, Angela opened the file she was looking for: abridges_udproposal.docx. The first page was a cover sheet giving her name, her contact information, and the address of the proposed site at 61st and Euclid. The detailed description of her project began on the second page, and so far she had about two hundred fifty words. She reached for a spiral-bound notebook that was perched on one corner of her desk between two marble owl bookends. The bookends had come from the same estate sale as her library chairs and ottoman. Inside the notebook were her scrawled notes and sketches of the site. Angela held her notebook open in her lap and sat back. Tomorrow was Tuesday and her class with Professor McNear wasn't until six o'clock. She had time tomorrow afternoon to conduct interviews in the neighborhood of her site. She'd drive in and bring her notebook with her. Angela leaned forward and did a google search for "western reserve historical society" to check on their library hours. Ten to five, Thursday through Saturday, according to their website. She'd have to wait on that. It was ten dollars for admission, too. Maybe she'd spend Saturday there.

Angela turned to a fresh page in her notebook and wrote, "Interview questions." She wrote the number one with her left hand, then paused. "Are you familiar with the large factory at 61st and Euclid?" She moved to the next line and wrote a two. "What can you tell me about the work that was done there?" she wrote, then added a three on the next line. "Did you work there/Can you share any stories about people you know who worked there?"

She'd have to introduce herself in an inviting way, or no one would talk to her. She mouthed words, cobbling them together as she went along. "Hi, I'm Angela Bridges, and I'm an urban development student at Cleveland State. I'm interviewing folks from this neighborhood about one of the factories here. I'm entering an urban development contest to renew a local abandoned site." *Mention the contest first, then the interviews*, she corrected herself.

Angela stood up, put her notebook on the desk, and padded across the room to her closet. What to wear tomorrow? She pushed hangers apart and considered her options. Blue and green always suited her, and she had a periwinkle long-sleeved button-down shirt that complemented her pea coat. She could wear that with a pair of black business slacks and her pointed black leather boots. No, scratch the boots — too assertive. Better to go with a pair of flats.

That decided, Angela returned to her desk,

rehearsing her introduction under her breath. There wasn't much more she could do tonight without the interviews and more detailed historical information about the factory, so she closed her notebook and picked up her fork. Her pasta salad was a zesty mix of savory white onion, garlic, and assorted spices mixed with the sweet tang of red bell pepper. She let the contest and her proposal slip to the back of her mind as she savored each bite.

She finished her dinner and took her plate, fork, and cup downstairs to put in the dishwasher. She checked and saw there was plenty of water still in the water heater, so she clicked the on switch and pulled out a stainless steel mug from Case Western Reserve University. Orange spice tea was front and center on her tea shelf. She pulled out a teabag and waited. When the water was poured and the teabag was steeping, she walked into her prayer room and sat down and lit her candle. She began to shiver, even though she had left the closet door open after morning prayer.

"Thea," she whispered, "this has been a hell of a day."

Silence surrounded her, and she recalled one by one the events of the day as they had unfolded. She took several long, deep breaths. She could feel her heart thumping rapidly in her chest.

"I don't know what I'm supposed to do with it," she said quietly. "Daddy's in the hospital. Meanwhile, Mom's being her usual self. I don't know how to move forward, Thea. She thinks all of this," she said, raising her hand in a flourish, "is a joke. No, not a joke—she thinks my faith is apostasy. Our whole relationship seems to hinge on whether I return to her brand of faith, and I just can't. I won't. How could I?"

The silence grew heavy. Angela felt tired under its weight.

"I wish you would answer me in ordinary words, Thea. I know you're more of the strong silent type, but some straight answers from your own lips would help."

Angela closed her eyes. Several minutes passed, and her breathing slowed. She picked up her Bible and opened it to the fifty-first psalm. "Create in me a clean heart, O Thea," she murmured. "Take me not away from your presence." Another several minutes passed as she strained to listen, but no answer came. Reluctantly, she got up, picked up her cup, and blew out the candle.

Angela tipped the bartender and picked up a Long Island and an Amaretto Sour. It was Saturday night and she and Heidi had come to ANATOMY, a cocktail lounge in the Warehouse District that doubled as a dance club. "To us!" she said, handing the Amaretto Sour to Heidi. Heidi accepted the drink and said, "To us!" They clinked glasses. Heidi wore a tight, sleeveless, one-piece black dress over her slight frame that sparkled as she moved. Her long red curls glimmered over her pale skin in the lights that shone down on them. Angela wore her black leather boots, a black mini-skirt, and a purple, sleeveless, silk shirt with a plunging neckline. The scent of perfume, cologne, and sweat mingled in the packed room.

"How was your show?" Angela said, raising her voice over the beat of the sound of the thumping music.

"What?"

"I said, how was your show?" she shouted.

"Oh, it was great. My largest piece sold!" she shouted back.

"Congratulations!" Angela gave her friend a hug and grinned at her.

"Some smaller pieces sold, too, so I have enough for next month's bills plus new supplies." Angela nodded. Heidi used oils on canvas, and she knew that neither one came cheap.

"I also got a commission from the woman who bought my largest piece. She wants me to paint Mother Earth as the Goddess."

"That's wonderful! Do you have any ideas for it yet?"

"I think I'd like to have the Goddess sitting cross-legged with her eyes and mouth open in ecstasy. She'll be pregnant and nude, and her belly will resemble the earth. What do you think?"

"Sounds sexy."

"Exactly. And why not? No Puritanical bullshit here."

Angela laughed. "I can't wait to see it."

Heidi took a long sip. "How are you doing?" she said in a loud voice.

"Oh, life is crazy, what with Dad in the hospital. I visited him again on Wednesday. Things were super-awkward with my mom, but at least we didn't fight this time."

"Is your dad feeling any better?"

"He's still very much in recovery mode. He tires easily, and of course he's still at the hospital. I'm not sure when they're going to release him."

Heidi pulled Angela into a hug. "I'll do some energy work for him."

"Thank you, Heidi." Angela squeezed her back.

Heidi pulled Angela out onto the floor. "Let's dance!"

Holding their drinks over their heads, they moved to the middle of the floor and began to move to the beat. Angela put both of her hands in the air, sending all her cares up through her arms and up to the ceiling. The beat of the music gave her focus, and she pumped her body back and forth to it. Her eyes softened and closed as she moved. Her cares faded away, and she suddenly felt surrounded by the rhythm of love. Thea was with her, her voice loud and clear.

Angela opened her eyes and grabbed Heidi's hands. An irrepressible smile covered her face. She and Heidi danced through the remainder of the night.

Chapter 7

"Happy Halloween!" Angela said, waving goodbye to a toddler who was bouncing in her father's arms. Angela had just rung up a large coffee with cream for the dad, who was dressed in a business suit, a tiara, and a violet tulle tutu. His daughter, a freckled red-head with spiraling curls, wore an orange and yellow dandelion petal headband with a sequined green unitard. As the order was being rung up, Angela asked the dad if it was okay to give her an S-U-C-K-E-R, and he nodded. The toddler unwrapped her candy-apple lollipop as the dad exited the front door.

Angela normally had Fridays off, but Shelly had asked her for holiday help. They gave a fifty percent discount for those in costume, so the shop was buzzing with customers. Angela had decided to dress as Lazarus for the holiday. She was wrapped in a three-piece mummy costume made of cream-colored linen strips that covered her whole body, including her hands and feet. A long strip of linen was wrapped around her head so that only her eyes and mouth were visible; her long hair was French-braided and hung down her back, emerging from the linen wrapping at the nape of her neck. Her apparel made operating the espresso machine and the register a special challenge.

"Just don't spill anything on anyone. I can forgive

the rest, but only for today," Shelly said when Angela arrived that morning. "You look good, Ang," she added. "How long did it take you to make your costume?"

"About five hours, including the trips to the fabric store to get the linen and the thrift store to get the t-shirt and pants underneath," Angela said. "Cutting the linen into strips was what took the longest. Once that was done, the sewing itself only took about an hour and a half. Using my sewing machine was an enormous time-saver."

"You are one crafty lady," Shelly said, hands on her wide hips.

"Well, sometimes domestic skills come in handy," she laughed. "My mom taught me how to sew when I was ten. I used to sew clothes for my stuffed animals and dolls. Then I started sewing furniture coverings. That's how I became interested in design," she said. She owed that much to her mother. Once upon a time, the two of them were joined at the hip doing this project and that activity. Her mother had taught her to do many things that she thought a young lady ought to know how to do. She had taught her to weave French braids. Angela's lips curled downward at the memory, and she touched her hair.

The rest of the morning at Phoenix Coffee was colored with costumed customers entering the store. A number of people commented on Angela's costume and asked her if she had made it herself. The tip jar filled up more quickly than it usually did. At the end of her shift, Angela tapped the tip jar and nodded at Sarah Ainsley, one of her fellow baristas who worked afternoons and evenings during the week. "We've been having a good day so far!" she said. Sarah's eyes widened.

"Looks like it," she said.

On her way outside to her car, Angela wondered what Bill was doing. He had visited a week ago Tuesday as promised and bought her a cranberry-orange scone. After they sat down, she took a bite of the dense, buttery pastry. The thick dusting of brown sugar melted into the sweet tang of the orange zest and cranberries.

"This is delicious," she said through a mouthful of scone. Bill handed her a napkin and took a sip of his cappuccino.

"How are you doing?" he asked as he set his mug on the lacquered pine table.

Angela took another bite, then dabbed at her mouth with the napkin. "I'm all geared up to do some interviews in the neighborhood of that old factory. I'm going to change into some other clothes at home first."

Bill eyed her. "Feeling better than yesterday?"

"I felt better once I got to work on my project last night."

"Have you talked to your parents since you left yesterday?"

"I called Dad before I got started on my project. I'm going to see him tomorrow. Can't say I'm much looking forward to it, though." Angela took another bite.

"You could avoid going. You'd just feel terrible about yourself if you did."

"That's helpful," she said, rolling her eyes.

"Just reporting on the facts, Ang. You still feel a duty to be a good daughter, even though your mom has only given you one way to do so—and it's the one way you refuse to go."

"Are you saying I should join the Missouri Synod again?" she said incredulously.

"I'm saying that you're trying to live up to a task that's impossible. You're never going to be the good daughter your mother wants. So maybe you should decide what you want to do, rather than trying to live according to someone else's impossible standard."

"I can't not go," she repeated.

"Yes, you absolutely can 'not go.' Question is, what do you want to do?"

"My dad could be dying. It's not about what I want."

Bill conceded silently with his hands in the air. Angela rubbed her temples.

"You know I'm rooting for you, right?" Bill said.

"Yeah. I know."

Angela's father was released the day after she visited on Wednesday, so she called her parents' home number on Saturday before she met with Heidi. Her father answered the phone and asked her if she would be interested in joining them for lunch or dinner some weekend, and by the end of the phonecall Angela had given him several times and dates to choose from—all of them at lunchtime. He chose the first option, Saturday, November 1. Now their lunch-date was just a day away. Angela pushed it out of her mind. She intended to enjoy Halloween while it was here.

Nearly all the leaves had blown off Mama Sharon's elm tree and Angela's front oak tree as Angela pulled into her driveway after work. The wind had grown heavier and the temperatures had dropped steadily over the last couple of weeks. A few snowflakes by the time the trick-or-treaters came by wouldn't surprise her.

Inside, Angela dropped her keys on the kitchen counter next to the large orange pumpkin she had bought at the grocery store on Wednesday. She pulled out her old pumpkin carving kit from one of her utility drawers. Working on the pumpkin would require some finesse and some mess, so she went to the bathroom to remove her costume. She pulled on the t-shirt and PJ-pants that she had left there after her shower this morning. When she got back to the kitchen, she carved a hole in the top of the pumpkin. Scooping out the insides, Angela carved two triangle eyes and a triangle nose into the pumpkin. She carved sharp teeth in last, then placed a tea candle inside the jack-o'-lantern. Setting it aside, she pulled out an orange party bowl that she normally used for chips and filled it with Reese's peanut butter cups. She never knew how many kids she'd get at the door, so she made sure to buy candy she liked.

Angela lit the jack-o'-lantern in her prayer room, which cast an orange glow across two walls. A smile crossed her lips, and she said a prayer of blessing for the pumpkin and all the trick-or-treaters who would pass by it.

Outside, Angela wondered if the blustering wind was going to allow the tea candle to hold its flame. The light danced merrily inside the pumpkin, contorting like an acrobat. Angela put the jack-o'-lantern on the second porch step from the top. She would check on the candle again when five o'clock rolled around.

Inside, she flipped on her porch light to indicate to trick-or-treaters that she was home. Then she walked to her bathroom to put her costume back on. The doorbell rang while she was re-wrapping her head. "Just a minute!" she called.

When she was done re-wrapping her linen coverings, she rushed down the hallway to the front door and opened it. A ghost in a white sheet and a witch wearing a black cape and a purple jacket underneath yelled, "Trick or treat!" A young woman, about twenty-five years old, accompanied them in a jean jacket and skinny jeans. Angela recognized her as Gina Brown. She and the kids were a family that lived several houses north of her. Gina's smooth black bouffant reminded Angela of Rihanna, and Angela said so as she tossed Reese's cups into the trick-or-treaters' pillowcases. Gina flashed a bright smile. The young witch and ghost yelled "Thank you, Angela!" in unison, and Angela took the bowl back inside, shivering.

More trick-or-treaters trickled by as the time drew closer to five o'clock. The tea candle was still lit when Angela checked, but she pulled out another tea candle and set it inside the door just in case. Around 5:45, a swarm of little people and their chaperones lined up at her doorway, and the crowd didn't let up for nearly an hour. Angela was running out of candy. Soon she'd have to turn out her light. She checked the jack-o'-

lantern again. The candle had burned all the way down, so she went inside to fetch the other candle. As she lit the second candle, five male teens, all dressed in black shirts and blue jeans, approached her door.

"Trick or treat," a couple of them said. They all held out plastic bags.

"What are you guys dressed as?" she said.

"Black guys," answered the shortest one.

Angela thought of her classmate, Jessica Lyle. She recalled Jessica talking about "Cleveland's problem with black thugs" during a small-group discussion they shared in their first class together. Her wholesale dismissal of black people had been a total turn-off to Angela; she hadn't liked her since. Now she imagined Jessica cowering in fear at the arrival of a bunch of black guys at her door.

"You've got me convinced," she joked. She looked into her bowl. She had four peanut butter cups left.

"Well, I've got four left. One of you can be left out, or you all can come in and have some of the apple pie I made last night. What do you think?" Five pairs of surprised eyes exchanged glances. Then the youngest of the group grabbed for a peanut butter cup, and four other hands followed suit.

The tallest boy, who ended up empty-handed, spoke up.

"Don't you have any more inside?"

"Afraid not. Sorry."

"Hey, what's a white girl doing in this neighborhood anyway?" the short one asked.

Angela put the bowl on her hip and looked him in the eye. He was about fifteen, if she had to guess. "I live here. How about you?"

He ignored her question. "You married?"

Angela hesitated.

"Naw, if she was married, her man would be out here instead of her," said a stocky boy with a low voice.

"You guessed it. I'm not married."

The boys exchanged glances.

"You sure you don't have any other candy in there?" the tall boy asked.

"Just pie, but you're welcome to it."

The tall boy sniffed. "No, thanks."

Just then, another group of trick-or-treaters and several adults approached.

"Happy Halloween," she said to the boys. "Sorry, I just ran out," she said to the group of children approaching. The teenage boys jumped off her porch stairs and headed toward Mama Sharon's house. The small children made noises of disappointment as they turned to follow the teenagers. Angela shook her head, walked inside, closed her door, and turned off her porch light.

As she was walking up the stairs, she heard a knock on her front door. She paused. Immediately, there was another knock. Angela turned and walked back down the stairs. She opened it.

"Trick-or-treat!" said three high-pitched voices. Angela recognized DeShawn, his two siblings, and their mother standing at her door, all bedecked in Halloween costumes.

"You guys look awesome!" she said, admiring their clothes and vivid makeup. "I hate to tell you this, but I just ran out of treats. I have some apple pie that you could have, though."

All three kids shrieked and clambered in with their orange plastic buckets. Janette smiled and walked in behind them. "We went trick-or-treating in Cleveland Heights and then came back to our street. DeShawn insisted that we make this our last stop," she said. "Happy Halloween!"

"Happy Halloween, Janette!" Angela ushered her in and closed and locked the door behind her. "Is Mama Sharon still giving out candy?"

"Oh, yes, she bought bags and bags of it. She loves giving out Halloween candy. It's like Christmas early for the whole neighborhood."

Angela walked into the kitchen and pulled the plastic wrap off the pie.

"How are things going, Janette?" she asked.

"Things are going okay. I'm still working at the daycare. They give me a substantial discount for Jamal, so that helps both me and Mama. I have fun there, for the most part," she said.

"For the most part? Are you thinking about getting a job somewhere else?" Angela dished out three slices of pie for the kids and then prepared a plate each for herself and Janette, taking them into the living room and setting them on the coffee table.

"No, I can't afford to change jobs right now," she laughed, sitting down on the couch. "The benefits for Jamal are too good, and Mama can't chase after him like she used to chase around DeShawn and Desiree."

"Do you have plans for when you can afford to change jobs?" Angela asked.

Janette paused and looked at her hands. "Actually, I have an idea, but it's a crazy one. I want to sing."

"Professionally?"

"Yeah. It's a pipe dream, but sometimes I go down to the House of Blues to listen to their live music and I think, 'That could be me up there.'"

"Janette, that's awesome. I don't think I've ever heard you sing."

Janette smiled. "Part of the problem is that I have no band to back me up. But I've always been able to sing. You want to hear something?"

Angela nodded. Janette stood up from her seat and closed her eyes. In a velvety voice, she began to sing "Amazing Grace." Angela closed her eyes, too, and the sounds of the children died down as Janette sang, her voice filling Angela's home.

Tears filled Angela's eyes, and she drew in a breath. She had sung that very hymn dozens of times with her church choir as a teenager. She opened her eyes and saw that Janette was misty-eyed, too.

"It always gets to me. It's my favorite," Janette said.

"Janette, your voice is beautiful. I can't even describe it. What an amazing gift you have!"

"Well, if I ever do a show at the House of Blues, I'll make sure to invite you."

"I'll be there if I possibly can. Or I'll babysit so Mama Sharon can go."

Janette's smile broadened. "Really?"

"Really."

Janette sat down again and leaned over to give Angela a hug. "Girl, you're something special."

Chapter 8

Angela tapped the steering wheel as she drove. She was on her way to Aladdin's Eatery on the northwest side of Akron, which was closer to her parents' house than to hers. As she pulled into the parking lot of the restaurant, she searched for her parents' beige Ford Contour, but didn't see it. Her breath appeared as she exited her car. She shut the door quickly and kept her head down as she moved toward the back door. Inside, she walked to the front of the restaurant and requested a table for three. The pastry case caught her eye, and she scanned half a dozen large, mouth-watering cakes inside. A server took her to her table, and she ordered orange and spice tea with hummus to start after hanging her jacket up on a hook next to the table.

"Angela!" Her father's voice rang out, and Angela stood to give him a hug. Her mother stood behind him, and Angela leaned over to give her a quick hug as well. They sat down, and the server returned with Angela's tea.

"Would you like something to drink?" the server asked. Angela's mother ordered water with no lemon and no ice. Angela's father ordered the same.

"I ordered hummus for us to share," Angela said. Her father smiled appreciatively.

"How was the drive down?" he asked.

"Uneventful. You?"

"Same. I was worried last night that it was going to snow, but it held off."

"I was expecting it to snow, too! Did you get many trick-or-treaters?"

"We emptied our bowl," her mother replied.

"That's good. So did I," Angela said.

"How's your project coming?" her father asked.

"My urban development proposal, you mean?" He nodded. "I got some helpful interviews from folks in the neighborhood of my site a couple of weeks ago. I also got the chance to visit the Western Reserve Historical Society research library last weekend. My building has a strange history. Some of the folks I interviewed said it was haunted." Angela took a sip of her tea.

"What sorts of ghosts are said to dwell there?" he asked.

"According to the folks I interviewed, the stepdaughter of the original owner of the building was walking through the building one night, and a worker heard her scream. They never found her. She just disappeared. Forty years later, there was an accident in the factory and one of the workers died there. So there are a couple of alleged ghosts," she said.

"But you don't believe in ghosts," he said.

"Only the Holy Ghost," she said. "But the ghost stories aren't the most interesting part. According to my research, the stepfather of the young woman who disappeared was in the textile business; the building I'm looking at began as a textile factory. In the twenties it was bought out by a wealthy Baptist minister who wanted a place to print tracts for use across the country. It became a hub for evangelical outreach, especially during the Great Depression. They shut down in the late nineteen thirties when the Baptist minister was caught having an affair and lost all his financial support. Then it was bought up by a steel manufacturer just before World War II, and it ended up making parts for World War II—many of the workers at the time were women. The worker who died was a woman, in fact. The steel company closed its doors in the mid-eighties, and then another textile company moved in. They shut down in 2004, and the place has been unoccupied ever since."

"That's quite a history," her father said.

"That's what a day at the Western Reserve Historical Society will get you," she said.

"You mentioned that you were going to see Heidi Saturday night. How was your visit with her?" her father asked.

"It was great. She had a show that day, and she sold her largest piece."

"Good for her!"

Angela picked up her water glass. She considered telling her parents about the rest of the evening, but decided against it. What they didn't know wouldn't hurt them. And they would certainly be scandalized if they knew their only daughter had gone out dancing and drinking for a night.

The hummus plate arrived, and after the server took the rest of their order, Angela's father lifted his hands toward his wife and his daughter. Angela's mother clasped his left hand in her right and extended her other hand to Angela. Angela took her parents' hands, took a deep breath, and closed her eyes. Her father presided over the table blessing, as was their family custom.

"Heavenly father," he said, "we thank you for this food and the hands that have prepared it, and we ask that you bless our time and conversation together. In Jesus' holy name we pray."

"Amen," all three said in unison. Angela's voice was softer than her parents'.

She pushed the hummus plate across the table. Her mother took it, spooned some hummus onto her plate and picked a piece of pita out of the basket. Her father did the same, then handed the hummus back to Angela. As she was putting hummus on her plate, Angela's mother spoke up. "I remember the first time we went to Aladdin's. It was for your graduation dinner, and we went to the one near your house."

Angela looked up. "Yep. It was the three of us and Grandma Caroline. Mom, you ordered spinach salad. Dad ordered a chicken shawarma, like me. Grandma Caroline ordered V8 soup with chicken on top."

"Your memory is as sharp as ever," her father said. Angela smiled and dipped a piece of pita in her hummus.

"Speaking of memory, I wanted to remember to talk to you two about the house. We're coming to the end of our agreement next summer."

"Indeed, we are," her father said. "What are your plans, sweetheart?"

"I want to stay. In fact, I'd like to take sole

ownership of the house."

Her father sat back in his chair and folded his hands. Her mother sat very straight. "Taking sole ownership is a big move, Angela," she said.

Angela nodded. "I'm happy in my neighborhood. I've made this house my home. I've been paying the mortgage this whole time anyway—the only thing that would change would be the title, and I can cover the cost of that."

"It would also mean refinancing the mortgage under your name only," her mother said. "Do you think they'll issue you a loan on your income?"

"Well, the loan wouldn't be for very much—we only owe about ten grand on the house now. I can manage that."

"You've been very responsible over these last eight years, Angela," her father said. "I don't see any reason not to let you put the house in your name. What do you think, Susan?"

"I think this idea merits more consideration than we can give it over lunch." Angela's mother picked up a wedge of pita and bit off a small piece, chewing it slowly and staring at her daughter.

Angela looked back at her mother, then her father. Her father's smile was strained, and her mother wore no smile at all.

Angela turned her head and caught sight of the server coming with their food. Her stomach rumbled as she caught a whiff of the scents coming off the plates and bowls.

"Yum," she said as the server set the first plate in front of her.

Saved, she thought to herself.

Angela took I-77 home. The trees on either side of the highway looked naked and forlorn as she made her way north. She turned the heater up to full blast, waving her fingers in front of the vents to shake the chill.

The conversation between her and her parents replayed in her mind. After the short-lived discussion about Angela putting the house in her name, they had talked about her father's latest visits to the doctor. He was doing better, he said, although he still looked wan to Angela. Her mother had also talked about things that were going on at the church. Angela nodded politely, even smiling when her mother told her that the pastor's daughter had had her first baby. She could still remember when Mary was born, and how she and the other kids had cooed over her when her mother brought her into church for baptism. Now she was married to a young man several years her senior who was in seminary to become a Missouri Synod minister. The wheel kept turning.

Felicity was getting uncomfortably hot, so Angela turned off the heater and cracked open her window. The skyscrapers and towering baseball stadium lights of the Cleveland skyline came into view as she rounded a bend on I-77. Soon I-77 merged with I-90, and she exited at Chester Avenue, taking the outer turn lane to enter street traffic.

At home she prepared herself a cup of black tea and sat down on the living room couch, tucking her legs underneath her. The steam swirled around her fingers, and she took a long, scalding sip.

Angela considered what she had left to do this weekend. There were two interviews left to transcribe out of the seven interviews she had conducted. She could start that this afternoon and finish up after evening prayer. Tomorrow she would do her usual Sunday morning worship, and then she could brainstorm about her proposal with all the interview transcripts in front of her. She also had several hundred pages of reading to do and a paper to write for her Monday afternoon class. Angela looked at her watch and looked out the window, wondering if she could get a walk in at the Cultural Gardens before she started on the transcriptions.

Angela finished her tea and got up. Minutes later, she was bundled up and out the door.

"Bless Thea, my soul, and bless her holy name," Angela sang in a soft voice. "Bless Thea, my soul, who leads me into life."

Angela sat cross-legged in her prayer space. Several candles flickered around her. A picture of her paternal grandparents lay in her lap. Her eyes were closed, and she rested her hands on her knees with her palms up. Her voice grew in intensity as she sang the words again and again. Then she tapered off, till she was nearly whispering.

"May the grace and peace of Sophia Christ, the love of Thea, and the fellowship of Holy Ruach be with you all," she murmured, beckoning unseen presences to surround her. Then she opened her eyes and turned to her prayer book, which she had prepared that morning.

"Let us pray," she said. Silence filled the space. "Thea, you are the midwife of both life and death. As we remember all those who have died to this life, we ask you to walk with them as they continue their journey in the next life. Amen."

Angela turned the page in her prayer book. Today was All Souls' Day, which always fell two days after Halloween and happened to fall on Sunday this year. The Missouri Synod would have looked down on her celebration of this Catholic holiday, but they would have looked down on a lot more than that, she thought.

"A reading from the book of Sophia," she said, then paused. "The souls of the just are in the hand of Thea…." Angela read the passage about trust and hope in a strong voice, ending with, "Thanks be to Thea." Then she turned to some music she had tucked inside her prayer book.

"The Lord is my shepherd…" she began. Instead of masculine pronouns for the shepherd, however, the music indicated feminine ones. Angela continued singing the words of Bobby McFerrin's "Twenty-Third Psalm," imagining a choir of voices surrounding her own. She had heard the piece many times in Bobby McFerrin's voice, and she'd even heard it sung by a female choir on WKSU, one of the local NPR stations. McFerrin had dedicated his rendition of the famous psalm to his mother. What would it be like to compare Thea to one's mother? She shuddered at the thought. Thea couldn't be anything like her mother, could she? And for her mother, there was no such thing as Thea. There was only God, perfectly and eternally male.

Angela sang McFerrin's closing doxology, slid the music to the side, and continued with the second reading. "A reading from the letter of Paul to the church at Rome." She paused again. "Sisters and brothers, do you not know that we who were baptized into Sophia Christ were baptized into her death?" Angela sometimes wondered what her parents would say if they could hear her pray to Jesus as a she, but today she was caught up in Paul's exposition of baptism as dying and rising. Goosebumps crawled along her arms. "Thanks be to Thea."

She stood. The alleluia she sang after the second reading was one of her favorites—it was written in a minor chord, laced with yearning and hope.

"A reading from the Good News according to John," she said, crossing the reading with her thumb. She paused. "Jesus said to the crowds: 'Everything that the Mother gives me will come to me, and I will not reject anyone who comes to me....'" *Even an unorthodox woman like me?*

The reading ended with an echo of what Angela's mother had been reading at the hospital: anyone who believes in Jesus will be raised up on the last day. Angela shook her head at the implied exclusivity of the passage. The Gospel of John wasn't her favorite, although it had been once. She paused, lingering on memories of her parents, and particularly her mother. Thoughts of her mother were like daggers to her heart. She shook her head and returned to the rhythm of her liturgy. "The Good News of Thea," she said. "Praise to you, Sophia Christ."

Now it was time for her homiletic meditation. She set the prayer book next to her on the floor and picked up her grandparents' photograph. She gazed at the image with soft eyes. Memories of her grandparents flooded her imagination. She let them wash over her, and imagined them sitting at Thea's banquet table, surrounded by countless others.

After about ten minutes, in a quiet voice, Angela began to murmur prayers, adding silence and "Thea, hear our prayer" to each petition: for the wellness and fertility of all creation; for all nations, that they might learn to live in peace together; for all leaders, that they might lead with wisdom and justice; for all who seek Thea and her call in their lives; for those suffering from grief, despair, or illness; and for the beloved dead, especially Grammy and Grampy Bridges.

Angela wiped tears away. Her grandparents had both died last February. The funerals took place at Angela's old church. She hadn't attended either one. Her father was hurt and her mother was furious, but Angela couldn't bear to be back in that place again, not after Christmas, and especially not while she was mourning. She had held a memorial service for each of them at home, instead.

Angela chanted the words of her abbreviated Eucharistic prayer, singing the parts that belonged both to the presider and congregation.

"Thea be with you.

"And also with you.

"Lift up your hearts.

"We lift them up to Thea.

"Let us give thanks to Thea, our Goddess.

"It is right to give her thanks and praise.

"On the night before he died, Jesus took the bread, said the blessing, broke the bread and gave it to his friends and said, 'Take this all of you and eat it. This is my body, which will be given up for you.'"

Angela took a deep bow, then continued.

"When the meal was ended he took the cup, again he gave you thanks and praise, gave the cup to his friends and said, 'Take this all of you and drink from it. This cup is Thea's covenant sealed in my blood. When you do this, remember me.'"

Angela bowed again.

"Bring us into the everlasting heritage of your daughters and sons, with Mary, Theotokos; Mary Magdalene; Miriam; Anna the Prophetess; and all who have done your will throughout the ages. Now may we praise you with them and give you glory.

Angela ended with a flourish of crescendoing amens before beginning the Lord's Prayer in a tune she had written herself.

"Our Mother, who art in heaven, hallowed be thy name. Thy wisdom come, thy will be done on earth as it is in heaven. Give us this day our daily bread, and forgive us our trespasses as we forgive those who trespass against us, and lead us not into temptation but deliver us from evil."

She picked up the glazed stoneware that held the homemade bread and blush wine and said, "The gifts of Thea for the people of Thea." Holding up the bread, she broke it apart, saying, "Body of Christ" before eating the broken bread. She held up the cup in the same way, saying, "Blood of Christ" before swallowing its contents.

Silently, she set aside the cup and plate and raised her hands again.

"Go in peace to follow the good road and may Thea's blessing be with you always," she said, eyes closed. "Thanks be to Thea."

When she was finished in the prayer space, she walked out with the photograph pressed against her chest and entered the spare bedroom across from her library. It had taupe walls and a cream-colored round rug to cover the hardwood floor. A cinnamon-colored futon stood on one wall. Next to it stood a wide, free-standing bookcase, and across from it stood an armchair and a small table. Behind the armchair, covering the wall, were dozens of framed photographs, almost all of which Angela had taken herself. She walked over to the left side of the wall and hung the picture of her grandparents, touching their faces with her fingers before letting her hand drop away.

Angela used to visit their house nearly every Saturday as a child. They kept a trunk filled with toys for her to play with, and her favorite was a tea-set that had belonged to her father's sister, Norene. During each visit, Angela set the living room table with care, including folded paper napkins, Lorna Doone shortbread on plates, and apple juice in teacups. Each piece of the set bore a fleur-de-lis, and Grampy would always point one out and ask her if she knew that it was a symbol of the Trinity. She would nod her head, and he'd tell her stories about the three persons of the Trinity, and Grammy would chime in with details he forgot. Sometimes they were biblical stories, and sometimes they were personal stories. Once he told her a story about a dream he had in which God the Father appeared to him as God the Mother, and Mother God invited him to bake bread with him. "I passed along the recipe to your Grammy, and that bread has won blue ribbons at the county fair more times than you can count!" When Angela graduated from high school, Grammy gave her the recipe for her award-winning bread. It was the same recipe she used for her Eucharistic bread.

They were both still young when they died— Grammy died in her sleep at age seventy-two, and Grampy died the same way a few weeks later at age seventy-four, two weeks shy of his birthday. *Too young to die*, she thought, staring at their photograph.

Angela's eyes moved to a black and white picture of a young Grandma Caroline standing with her husband, Ralph, and their then-ten-year-old daughter, Susan. Grandpa Ralph had died a year after Angela was born. She didn't remember him, but she had his long, sharp nose. Grandma Caroline told her that she had a difficult time talking to God after Grandpa Ralph died, and eventually she turned away from Lutheran Christianity altogether. That was the beginning of the end of her relationship with Angela's mother, who had found special comfort in reading scripture, especially the resurrection narratives, after her father died. *The stories we weave form the web of our lives.*

Angela gazed at a picture of herself and her parents on her confirmation day. Her mother's smile was as wide as her father's. All three of them looked as if it was the best day of their lives. If only things had been different—or rather, if only things had stayed the same. If she hadn't felt a call to ministry, she probably would never have left her church. She'd probably be married with children by now if she had stayed. Everything would be... simpler. She'd still be the model daughter, rearing model children with her model husband.

Angela shook her head and turned from the wall of photographs. Things hadn't gone the way she or her mother had planned. Now she was making her own road, one cobblestone at a time. She wasn't sure where she was headed, but she knew that any other path would be the wrong one for her.

Angela turned from the photographs and walked out, closing the door behind her.

Chapter 9

"Joseph Warner, we meet again." Angela smiled up at Joseph from behind the counter. He was carrying a book, and he handed it to her.

"I thought of you as I was reading this. Thought you might like to borrow it," he said.

Angela looked at the spine of the hardback book: *Ghosts of Cleveland: An Architectural History, 1847-2013* by Marjorie Hewett. It had a white library sticker at the bottom of the spine.

"Don't you need this?"

"I have it out for another two and a half weeks. I can always come back and pick it up."

Angela nodded. "Thank you! Was there anything in particular that made you think of me?"

"The author weaves social history into her discussion of Cleveland sites. I thought the site of your proposal might be mentioned in it, but even if it isn't, you may find the book useful."

"Well, thank you. It's very kind of you to think of me! What can I get for you?" she asked, setting the book aside. "Another two medium lattes, one with one shot, one with three?"

"You have a good memory."

"I don't make coffee for bishops every day," she said, grinning.

"Same as last time, then, yes. I hope you don't

mind my asking: are you Roman Catholic?"

"You may ask. And no, I'm not. I grew up in the Missouri Synod Lutheran Church."

"I'm not familiar with the Missouri Synod."

"They're a small branch of the Lutheran Church. Very socially conservative, and at least the parish I grew up in took the smells and bells approach to liturgy."

"So we grew up in similar churches, it sounds like."

"Yes, but I'm not part of the Missouri Synod anymore. I'm not sure what you'd call me these days."

"You seemed to think I'd call you a heretic last time I saw you," he said, eyeing her.

Angela laughed. "That's what the Missouri Synod would probably call me. I have a prayer space that I pray in twice a day, and I do my own liturgy on Sunday mornings."

"Wow. You sound like a person of faith, not a heretic," he said earnestly.

Angela looked away from Joseph and into the milk carafe. She avoided his gaze as she finished steaming the milk. Then she poured it into the two cups that had shots of espresso waiting. She put lids on and handed Joseph the cups, reading a look of concern on his face as she met his eyes again.

"I'm sorry. I didn't mean to upset you," he said. "I imagine your separation from the Missouri Synod was pretty traumatic." He handed her a ten-dollar bill.

Angela nodded again and rang him up. "My mother thinks I'm going to hell."

"That must be difficult for you," he said,

sympathy etched in his eyes.

"Family gatherings tend to be awkward, yes. Anyway, thank you for the book. I'll read it within the week, so you can pick it up anytime after that." She handed him his change and a receipt. He put two dollars in the tip jar.

"Oh, and here's my card, in case you ever want to chat. I'm available to listen," he said, offering her a business card.

She took his card with a look of surprise and tucked it inside the library book. "Thank you."

"You're welcome, Angela. See you next time."

She watched him walk out, then shook her head.

"Take a break."

Angela turned to face Shelly.

"Go on. You look like you could use some fresh, icy air."

Angela smiled gratefully, took off her apron, and exited the front door without taking her jacket. Outside, she braced against the wind and walked around to the side of the building. She thought about Joseph and his offer to listen. She had plenty of people who already listened to her. She had support. Then she considered the book he had given her to borrow. She already knew about the ghosts of her building—the stepdaughter of the original owner and the female worker who had died when the building was a steel factory. Angela wondered if there were anything more available about them at the Historical Society. She shivered in the chill of the outdoors. *Focus, Angela.* Today, after her afternoon class, she would print the transcripts of her interviews and begin making notes.

This weekend, she'd head back to the Historical Society and dig around for information about the two women who had died in her building. Armed with a plan, Angela headed back toward Phoenix.

Inside, Shelly handed her her apron. Angela took it and put it over her head, tying a knot behind her back.

"You okay?" Shelly said.

"Yeah, I'm fine. Sometimes church stuff just gets to me, and Joseph was asking me about my religious background."

"I couldn't help overhearing," Shelly admitted.

"Isn't it your job to hear everything?"

Shelly smiled. "I try to excel in all things job-related," she said.

"Don't worry, you succeed," Angela said back.

"Are you sucking up to me, Bridges?"

"I try to excel in all things job-related."

Shelly narrowed her eyes, a pursed smile on her lips.

Angela whistled and began wiping down the counter.

At five minutes to two, Angela slid into her seat and set her messenger bag next to her legs. Her Neighborhood Planning course was taught by Dr. Starla Jones, a tall, slim, broad-shouldered black woman who worked for HUD, the U.S. Department of Housing and Urban Development. Dr. Jones was writing on the whiteboard when Angela came in. Now she looked up at Angela and gestured for her to come to the front of the class. Angela got up and moved forward.

"Angela, since you missed a couple of classes ago, I wondered if you'd like to make up for it by being my volunteer in class today?"

Angela shrugged. "Sure. What do you want me to do?"

"We're going to pretend we're in a townhall meeting, and you're going to be the mayor, leading the meeting. I want you to answer questions that come in from the citizens about a neighborhood plan that's in the works."

"Without any preparation?"

"You're one of the most articulate people in the room. You'll do fine. It's a classroom experiment."

Angela blanched. Why did she get the feeling that she was the frog about to be dissected via the scalpel of her classmates?

"I'll do my best."

"Thank you, Angela. I'll call you up when it's time to begin."

Angela sat down again.

"Hey, Angela, how are you?" Beth Weaver asked. Beth had long, silky black hair and wide, light brown eyes. She often sat next to Angela in Neighborhood Planning. They had gotten to know each other last fall in their Intro to Urban Planning course when they worked together as part of a group. Their assignment was to put together a proposal for the renewal of a local neighborhood. Beth managed the financial side, which included calculating costs and finding a grant to cover said costs. Angela put together the details of the neighborhood proposal: where it would take place, what changes would be made, and whom it would impact. They aced the project.

"I'm doing fine, Beth. How are you?"

"Panicked. The site I wanted to use for the urban development contest was razed to the ground. I drove by this weekend and all that was left was an empty lot. Now I have to start all over again."

"What luck," Angela said sympathetically.

"I know, right? How's your proposal coming?"

Dr. Jones raised her voice. "Good evening, everyone. Let's get started."

Angela leaned over and whispered, "I'll tell you later."

Beth nodded and looked up at Dr. Jones.

"Tonight we're going to conduct a classroom experiment. We're going to have a townhall meeting to discuss the neighborhood plan that was given as an example in your assigned reading for today. I'm going to pass out cards with details about where you live in relationship to the site. Angela," Dr. Jones gestured toward her, "has volunteered to be mayor of the city and head of the townhall meeting. I want the rest of you to come up with questions to ask her during the meeting. I'll give you ten minutes to review the neighborhood plan and form your questions, and then we'll get started."

Angela opened her course reader and scanned the article containing the hypothetical neighborhood plan. A large paid parking lot would be purchased and converted into a neighborhood park, complete with a man-made pond. Angela pondered the issues that her classmates might ask her to address. Soon the ten minutes were up, and Dr. Jones called Angela to the front of the room. Angela took her place at the whiteboard where Dr. Jones normally stood, and Dr. Jones took a seat on a window-ledge to observe the class.

Angela looked out at the class and realized she was the one in charge of starting the role-play, so she thought for a moment and then introduced herself. "Good evening, everyone. I'm Mayor Bridges and I've called this townhall meeting to facilitate discussion about the proposed renewal of the Thornwood neighborhood. Please go ahead with your questions."

Jonathan Thomas, a large, tall, thirty-something man with brown hair and hazel eyes raised his hand first. Angela called on him and he stood. "I live in the Rosemont neighborhood that borders Thornwood. One of the counter-proposals for this area is to build a highway through Rosemont and Thornwood creating easier access from the outer suburbs to downtown. With exits to each neighborhood, this highway would draw new folks into our neighborhoods and increase local business. How does this park proposal compete with the highway plan?"

Angela drew a deep breath and thought for a moment. "Thank you, Mr. Thomas. The park plan seeks to revitalize the Thornwood neighborhood by making it more resident-friendly. By focusing on the unity of the neighborhood, the neighborhood will become attractive to new residents and visitors alike, which will boost the local economy. The attractiveness of the neighborhood will draw visitors in through the Rosemont neighborhood as well, increasing car traffic and foot traffic and very likely increasing business there."

Elaine Parker, a fifty-something woman with graying hair in pulled-back dreadlocks, raised her hand next.

"You say that this park will draw in new residents. Are you suggesting that it will displace existing residents?"

"As you probably know, there are nearly fifty houses on the market in the Thornwood neighborhood. The hope is not to displace current residents, but to add new ones, especially those with young children. The hope is that empty houses will be filled with families who are committed to living in the neighborhood in the long term."

Jessica Lyle raised her hand next. "Do you really think new residents, especially young families, will want to move into this crime-ridden neighborhood? There were fifteen violent crimes there last month alone, according to police records."

Angela frowned. That hadn't been part of the article. She looked at Dr. Jones, who raised her hands and shrugged.

"By building this park, the hope is to increase community bonding and a shared sense of safety —"

"But who would want to put their children at risk just because a new park has been built?" Jessica interrupted.

Angela attempted a polite smile, but she didn't think she was pulling it off. "I understand your concerns, Ms. Lyle. Crime is a reality that every neighborhood must face. With the building of this new park—"

"And what families will want to visit a park that's infested with drug dealers, prostitutes, and thieves?" Jessica interrupted again.

Angela paused, angry at the second interruption. *She's goading you,* she thought. *Keep your cool.* "The strength of any neighborhood lies in its residents. The new park will strengthen community ties between existing residents and will draw in new residents.

"You haven't answered my questions, *Mayor* Bridges," Jessica said, sarcasm dripping from her voice.

Angela gave her an icy stare. "I believe we see things differently, Ms. Lyle. Next question, please?"

No one raised a hand. Tension prickled through the room. Dr. Jones looked around and raised her hand.

"Perhaps you can give us a picture of the features this new park will bring," she said.

Angela smiled gratefully at Dr. Jones. "Certainly." In a calm voice, Angela described the details of the park. More questions followed. Jessica raised her hand multiple times, but Angela ignored her. After about fifteen minutes, Dr. Jones stepped in.

"All right, I believe everyone has had a chance to ask a question," Dr. Jones said. "Thank you, Angela, for playing mayor in our little experiment. You may sit down." Most of her classmates applauded. A small smile crossed her lips as she took her seat. Beth nudged her arm with a closed fist.

"Now," Dr. Jones said, walking to the front of the room, "what did we learn from this experiment?"

Beth raised her hand. "I learned that Angela's got my vote whenever she decides to run for mayor of Cleveland." The class laughed, and Angela turned red. Then she raised her hand.

"Yes, Angela," Dr. Jones said.

"I learned that even a sound plan has both pros and cons, and not everyone will see eye to eye."

"Excellent point. From the very beginning of the townhall meeting, we were presented with viewpoints that favored other plans. As urban development specialists, you'll be called on to answer these sorts of questions at public meetings, and you're likely to encounter a wide range of emotions and ideas about the plans you've poured your time and effort into. It'll be your job to address each voice with equanimity. Angela, you showed us exactly what that looks like. Thank you."

Angela imagined Jessica rolling her eyes, but she wouldn't dignify her reaction by looking at her. She folded her hands and stared straight ahead as Dr. Jones continued her remarks about the townhall meeting.

At the class break, Beth leaned over. "So, how's your project coming?"

"Slow but steady. I interviewed a bunch of folks from the neighborhood where my site is located. I also found some interesting information about it at the Western Reserve Historical Society. You should check that place out when you figure out your new site."

Beth shook her head. "If I find one. I can't believe my original site is gone, just like that. Talk about lousy timing!"

"You'll find one. I found lots of places as I was searching. If you want me to pass along some of the sites I found, just shoot me a note."

"Really?"

"Of course."

"You don't have to help me, you know," Beth said. "You're trying to win this contest, too."

"Competition makes the contest more exciting," Angela said, smiling.

Beth raised her eyebrows. "I think it makes it more nerve-wracking, but I'm sure not going to turn you down your help. You're a pal, Angela."

Angela tapped Beth's desk with her fingers and got up. She walked out to get a bottle of pop from the vending machine outside the classroom. Jessica followed her out.

"You're really helpful there, Angela, offering to share site ideas with Beth. But is it really help when you know she has no shot at winning?"

Angela put her money in the pop machine and pressed the button for her selection. "I'm pretty sure that conversation was between Beth and me, not you and Beth and me, Jessica."

"You know I'm right," she continued. "You don't mind looking like the good guy when you know your competition has no chance of beating you. I don't see you offering to help the people who actually have a shot of winning."

"Is that your way of asking for help?"

"I'm all set, but thanks, anyway."

"I'm sure you are," Angela said flatly.

"'Competition makes the contest more exciting,'"

she mimicked. "What a crock. You're full of yourself, Bridges."

Angela stared at Jessica coldly. "Someone here's full of it, but I'm pretty sure it's not me."

Jessica smirked. Angela walked past her and back into the classroom. She could feel heat rising up her neck. *What the hell?*

At home, Angela finished transcribing the last of her interviews. She sat back in her desk chair and clicked the "Ctrl" and "S" buttons simultaneously. With that done, she was ready to print and start making notes. She leaned forward, pressed "Ctrl" and "P," and waited for the interviews to print. She had twenty-one pages in all.

As her interviews printed, Angela thought of Jessica's remarks in the hallway. *Who does she think she is?* Angela wondered if Jessica felt threatened by her.

Memories of middle school floated up in her consciousness. Brandy Levine was tall and blond and one of the most popular girls in the sixth grade, and she thought it was a great game to bully Angela. Angela cornered her in the gym one day and said in a shrilly voice, "Why do you keep picking on me, Brandy?"

"Because you think you're better than everyone else," Brandy spat.

"No, I don't!" she exclaimed.

"Yes, you do—you walk around with your nose in a book ignoring everyone, and you have an answer to every question the teachers ask. You think you're better than the rest of us, when the truth is you're just a nerd with no friends."

Brandy spun on her heels, leaving Angela speechless. At home that afternoon, her mother asked her what was wrong. "One of the girls in school is picking on me. She says I think I'm better than everyone else."

"Do you think you're better than everyone else?"

"That would be pride, Mommy."

"Yes, honey, it would be."

"I just try to do my best. I can't help it if the answers come easier to me than to the other kids."

"Just remember that God gave you gifts so you could use them for his glory, Angela—not for your own. If others persecute you for using your gifts for God's glory, then you are blessed indeed."

"I'm blessed if people pick on me?"

"Suffering for the sake of God is a martyr's honor, Angela. That's what you need to remember. Suffer silently, and turn the other cheek. That is what God wants for you."

Anger boiled up in her as she remembered her mother's words. It was as if she were defending her daughter's bully, rather than protecting her bullied daughter.

Angela had no interest in being a martyr. She would stand her ground. *So I'm smart and I'm generous,* she thought. *So Jessica's jealous. That's her problem, not mine. I'm going to continue being who I am whether she likes it or not.*

She picked up the printed pages and began making notes with a highlighter and a pen. An hour ticked by, and she got up and stretched. Time for prayer. She headed down the stairs and into her prayer space. Lighting a candle, she sat cross-legged on a soft purple pillow. Wind rattled the window, and she relaxed, breathing in and out slowly.

"Thea," she said softly, eyes closed, "I feel bright, burning anger in my belly. Release me from it. Soften my hardened heart, and help me to hear the music of your voice, so I may be an icon of your love in the midst of hatred and violence. Amen."

She sat quietly for several minutes, feeling the breath pass in and out of her body. Then she opened her eyes, blinked away tears, and blew out the candle. Had she prepared the coffee yet? *No.* She groaned inwardly and got up to finish her evening routine. As she moved into the kitchen, she thought about her plan for tomorrow. She had work in the morning, then a break in the afternoon before her six o'clock class with Professor McNear. She had done her reading for the class this weekend, but she hadn't yet written her reflection paper. She would do that after work tomorrow. In the kitchen, Angela checked the veggie drawer in the fridge for salad ingredients. Red-leaf lettuce, romaine lettuce, sprouts, carrots, snap peas — check. She checked the pantry for garbanzo beans. There were two cans left. Satisfied that she had everything she would need to make lunch tomorrow, she pulled out a bag of whole-bean Phoenix French roast and began grinding coffee. She put a filter in the coffeemaker and poured the ground beans inside it. Next, she pulled out her jug of filtered water and filled the coffee maker to the eight-cup mark. Pressing the "on" button twice to set the timer, she left the kitchen and trudged down the hall to the bathroom.

A look in the mirror told her she was exhausted. She had dark half-moons beneath her eyes and her skin looked wan. She shouldn't have stayed up this late on a work-night. At least she had finished sketching her proposal. She had almost two months left before the proposal was due—plenty of time to research the remaining costs of her proposal.

As Angela brushed her teeth, she thought of Jessica again. Then she thought of her mother. They were two sides of the same coin—so much like Angela, and so much not like her at the same time. *How could the world look so very different just by standing behind another pair of eyes?* Suddenly Angela had a vision of disembodied eyes floating in front of her, and she spit toothpaste as she burst out laughing.

Chapter 10

"Morning, Shelly," Angela said as she walked in the front door of Phoenix.

"You look like you could use some coffee," Shelly said, eyeing her.

"Guess I've come to the right place, then!" Angela quipped. It was going to be that kind of morning. Angela hadn't yet recovered from staying up late on Monday night, and it was already Thursday. At least it was her last day of the workweek.

Angela went to the back room, put on her apron, and brought a box of pastries out to place in the pastry case. Shelly was finishing up with the first three urns of percolated coffee. They worked quietly, at ease in each other's company. At seven, Shelly flipped the "closed" sign to "open." Snow fell outside in fat, wet flakes, giving the ground a thin white sheen.

"Not even Thanksgiving," Shelly said in a displeased voice.

"What are you doing for Thanksgiving, Shelly?" Angela asked, stifling a yawn.

"I'm going up to my mom's. She's seventy-three, but she still loves putting on big family dinners. My brothers and sister will be there with their families, too."

"Sounds like a big event. Does everyone bring something to share?"

"No, Mom likes to cook everything herself. I'll go up early to help her out, but she's very clear that she's in charge of the kitchen."

"She sounds like she has a lot of energy."

"Where do you think I get it from?" Shelly grinned, and Angela laughed. "What are you doing for Thanksgiving, Ang?" Shelly asked.

Angela blushed slightly. "Staying home."

Shelly didn't say anything for a moment, but looked at Angela with concern. "You want a place to go? There's always room at my family's table."

Angela gave a small smile. "Thanks, Shelly. That's very sweet of you. I want to stay at home this year. I've been meaning to master the art of turkey-basting anyway, and it'll give me leftovers for weeks."

"Well, the offer stands if you change your mind, sweetie."

"Thank you for offering," she said with feeling.

Shelly nodded and smiled, heading to the back room. The tables were still clean from last night, so Angela checked the untouched pastries to pass the time. She let her mind wander to memories of last Thanksgiving. She had made a pumpkin pie from scratch, mixing the dough and rolling it out at home the way Grandma Caroline had taught her when she was eight years old. When she arrived at her parents' small colonial house, she leaned over, picked up the pie, and opened the door to get out of Felicity. The street was icy, but the front walk had been salted and cleared, undoubtedly by her father. Grandma Caroline's car wasn't there yet.

She headed up the front walk and rang her

parents' doorbell with a gloved finger.

Two customers walked in, interrupting her recollections. Angela recognized them both as early-morning regulars.

"Good morning, John. Good morning, George," she chirped.

"Good morning, Angela" they said, nearly in unison.

"Usual?" she said.

"Yes, please," John said, removing his gloves. He had salt and pepper hair, tan skin, a hefty gold ring on his right hand, and boxy glasses on his nose George gave a thumbs-up. He was bald and wore small hoops in his ears. Angela pulled two large paper cups off the top of the stack and tamped espresso into two pods. Just then, a tall, muscular black man in dark gray slacks, a mauve button-down shirt, and a matching silk tie walked in. He had on a leather shoulder holster with a sleek black gun tucked inside, and he was wearing a badge. Angela greeted him and said she'd be with him in just a minute. She finished the two large espresso drinks, rang up George and John together, and said goodbye as they exited.

"May I help you?" she asked, after a quick glance at his gun.

"I'm Detective Omar Winston of the Cleveland Police Department. I'd like to ask your staff some questions about yesterday morning."

Angela stared openly at him. "Sure," she said. "Let me get my boss." She went to the backroom. "Shelly? There's a detective here from the Cleveland Police Department. He wants to ask some questions."

Shelly hurried out to the counter and greeted Detective Winston, inviting him to come to the backroom. He followed her in, and Angela returned to the counter. *What was that all about?* Angela wondered if he was going to question her next. Not ten minutes later, Detective Winston said, "Ms. Bridges?" peeking his head out from the back. Shelly took her place at the counter, and Angela followed him into the backroom.

Detective Winston took Shelly's blue rolling office chair and gestured toward another similar chair, originally black but now graying with wear. Angela sat down and waited. Detective Winston pulled out a pad of paper.

"Ms. Bridges, I'm investigating the alleged rape of one of your customers. I'm hoping you can tell me who came in yesterday morning and whether you noticed anything out of the ordinary."

The blood drained from her face. *Rape?*

"Detective, may I ask who the rape victim was?"

"Cassidy Henner," he said brusquely.

"Oh, my god," she said.

Cassidy Henner was another one of the Phoenix regulars — she was a thin black woman with light skin and big brown eyes. She worked downtown as a mortgage banker.

"Did you notice anything or anyone unusual yesterday?" he asked.

Angela thought. There had been a steady stream of customers, but no one stood out to her.

"I remember Cassidy coming by around eleven o'clock. I looked at the clock when she came in —

eleven o'clock is when she usually comes by on her lunch break."

Detective Winston nodded, scribbling notes in a yellow legal notepad that lay in a leather binder.

"I don't remember seeing anyone out of the ordinary," she continued.

"Did you have any new customers?"

"Yes, there were several, but I don't remember much about them. It takes three or four visits before I really remember someone."

"Can you give me the names of the men you remember who came in?"

"Gosh, there were a lot." Angela closed her eyes, trying to remember. "I remember Josh Winstead coming in first thing in the morning, then Brian Halforth. Then there was Adam Smalls, Jake Leonard…" Angela squeezed her eyes shut and pressed her index fingers against her temples. "I'm pretty sure I saw Devon Williams, then Joseph Warner. Then I took a short break outside. Then… um…" Angela took a deep breath, trying to remember the faces that had come through the door yesterday. "When I came back in, there was a young man with dark hair that I didn't recognize. He was tall. That's all I remember about him. And he paid with cash. He came in right before Cassidy, actually."

Detective Winston scribbled notes rapidly across his legal pad.

"Do you remember anything more about the young man with dark hair? What he was wearing, perhaps?"

"Let me think. I think he was wearing blue jeans

and a dark polo—a black polo. He had blue eyes. I remember thinking that his pants matched his eyes and his shirt matched his hair."

"Anything else you remember about him?"

Angela shook her head.

"Okay. Let's keep going with the male customers you remember seeing yesterday. Who came in after him?"

"Brooks Stone came in after him, then came another guy I don't remember really well…"

"What did he look like?"

He was pretty non-descript. White guy. Khakis. I don't remember what kind of shirt he was wearing. He had short brown hair, but I don't remember what color eyes."

"Tall, short? Thin, fat?"

"He was average—average height, average weight."

Detective Winston flipped a page and began writing again.

"Anyone else?"

"I don't think I saw any more men after that. My shift ended at noon."

Detective Winston read through the list of names Angela had given, and asked her if she had left anyone out.

"I don't think so."

"As for your regular customers, did any of them do anything out of the ordinary? Anything unusual? Even if you think it might not be significant?"

Angela looked at her feet, thinking. Then she looked back at Detective Winston. "One of them let me borrow a library book. That was Joseph Warner. He's in training to become a Roman Catholic priest."

"What is your connection to Mr. Warner?"

"He and I met at the library. We're entering the same urban development contest, and we have people in common at CSU."

"Can you remember the name of the book?"

"I think it was called *Ghosts of Cleveland.*"

"A ghost book?"

"An architectural book."

Detective Winston looked deadpan at Angela, then looked back at his legal pad. "Anything else you can remember about any of the male customers you saw?"

Angela thought some more. "No, I think that covers it."

"Ms. Bridges, thank you for your time. We'll be in touch if we need anything further, and please don't hesitate to contact me if you remember anything else. Anything at all."

"Oh, Detective?" she said, as she took his business card. "Doesn't Cassidy remember anything about her attacker?"

"I'm not at liberty to discuss the details of the case, ma'am."

Angela blushed. "Of course. I'll let you know if I think of anything else."

"Thank you, Ms. Bridges." Detective Winston shook her hand firmly and gestured for her to walk out to the front. Angela began moving out of the backroom, and he followed her.

"Thank you, Ms. MacDougall," Detective Winston

said, shaking Shelly's hand with the same firm grip he had given Angela.

"Would you like any coffee, Detective?" Shelly asked.

"No, thank you, ma'am. Have a good day."

"You, too," she said as he walked out the door. Shelly turned to Angela. "*That* was bizarre."

"I feel so bad for Cassidy," Angela whispered. Shelly nodded and squeezed Angela's left shoulder. Just then, the bell on the door jingled. It was the young man from yesterday with the dark hair and blue eyes.

"Welcome back to Phoenix!" Angela said. *Is this Cassidy's rapist?* she wondered with alarm. She tried to keep her composure. She was managing surprisingly well

"My name is Angela. What's yours?" she asked casually.

"Luke," he said, smiling.

"Well, Luke, I do my best to remember repeat customers. It's nice to meet you," she said, amazed by the calm in her voice. "Do you work around here?"

"I just started working as a waiter at Cleveland Crossroads."

"Where is that? I've never heard of it."

"It's the restaurant at the House of Blues."

Angela raised her eyebrows. "That must be a nice gig."

"I'd be happier if I were singing and playing instead of waiting tables, but I figure I can get an in this way."

"Nice. What can I get for you?"

"Do you remember my drink from yesterday?"

More quizzes. Great.

"Let me think—did you order a large coffee, black?"

"Well done!" he said with a broad smile. Angela thought of telling him his coffee had matched his hair and his shirt, but she simply smiled and went to the coffee urn to fill up a large cup with coffee. As she waited for the cup to fill, she thought of Janette and wondered if Luke could help her get a spot on stage at the House of Blues. *But he might be a rapist!*

Angela handed the coffee to him. He gave her a five. "You can keep the change, he said. "Nice to meet you, Angela."

"Bye, Luke."

She watched him leave. If he had parked here, he hadn't parked nearby, because he walked beyond the windows of Phoenix Coffee.

"Who was that handsome guy?" Shelly said in a quiet voice.

"I think I'm going to call Detective Winston," she whispered, and headed to the backroom. Shelly's eyes followed her in alarm.

Angela typed the number from Detective Winston's card onto her phone and pressed the green send button. The phone rang several times, and then his voicemail came on. "You've reached the voicemail of Detective Omar Winston. Please leave a detailed message with your name and phone number and I'll return your call as soon as possible. Thank you."

"Detective Winston, this is Angela Bridges from Phoenix Coffee. I wanted to follow up and let you know that the tall, dark-haired man I mentioned to you came back to Phoenix just after you left. His name is Luke and he works at the restaurant at House of Blues. I'll let you know if the brown-haired man comes by, or if I think of anything else from yesterday. Thanks."

Angela hung up and went back out to the register where Shelly was waiting for her. "Do you think that was…" Shelly whispered.

"I don't know," she whispered back. "But he was in here yesterday. I thought I'd give Detective Winston some more information about him, just in case. But if he were, he wouldn't show his face here again, would he? I mean, if he abducted her just outside of here…"

Chills ran down Angela's spine.

"Listen," Shelly said in a low voice, "let's just get back to work. We'll do our jobs and Detective Winston will do his. He'll find whoever the guy was."

Not if Cassidy didn't see who her attacker was, she thought.

"All right, why don't we stop here and take a break. Ten minutes?" said Dr. Rene Moore, the professor of Angela's Conservation Techniques for Historic Preservation class. Ron Walker, sitting in the chair next to Angela's, stood up and put his things in his dark blue backpack.

Angela turned and gazed at Ron, who was stacking his things in a pile before putting them in his rucksack. She loved the way his eyes sparkled as he concentrated. "Ron, how's your contest proposal coming?" she asked, stepping toward him as she stood from her chair.

"I just submitted it," he said, gazing up at her with a smile.

Angela's jaw fell slack. "You don't believe in the power of procrastination then, I take it?"

Ron chuckled and slid between his desk and the one behind it, stepping behind her, his chest brushing her back for a moment. "No, I don't. My mama taught me well."

Angela led him out into the corridor. "I think I remember you mentioning that you picked a church. Is that right?"

"Yes, a church on the East Side."

"It wasn't the former Church of St. Mary Magdalene, was it?"

"No, my site is a former Lutheran church."

"Lutheran? Do you know what branch of Lutheranism?" Angela watched as Ron inserted two dollar bills in the pop machine.

"As a matter of fact, I do know," he said, pressing the button for water. "It was an ELCA church. Why? Are you Lutheran?"

The ELCA, or Evangelical Lutheran Church of America, was the largest branch of the Lutheran Church in the United States. "I used to be," Angela said. "Missouri Synod."

"I'm not familiar with the Missouri Synod. I'm African Methodist Episcopal, myself."

"I've never been to an AME church, but I've read about them."

Ron opened his water bottle and took a sip. They were standing a touch closer than Angela might stand with someone else, and she had to admit that she was enjoying it. "You're welcome to join me some Sunday if you want. Unless you have church obligations somewhere else, of course."

Angela was surprised by the invitation. Her cheeks flushed a light shade of pink. "I do church at home these days, so my Sunday schedule is flexible."

It was Ron's turn to look surprised. "How does one 'do church at home,' praytell?"

Angela hesitated, wondering how he would respond to the truth. "I'm my own minister. I walk a rather unconventional spiritual path, actually. I'll tell you about it sometime, if you're interested."

"Well, why don't you join me for worship this Sunday, and you can tell me about your unconventional spiritual path over brunch afterward. My treat." He looked at her earnestly, and she searched his eyes. Angela wasn't sure, but she thought the invitation sounded suspiciously like a date. She hadn't dated since she'd started the program at CSU. A smile formed on her lips. "Sure thing. I'd love to."

"I'll pick you up Sunday at 10:20, then—is that all right?"

"Yes, that's fine. Let me write down my address and phone number for you," she said, pulling a pen out of her pocket. She wrote down the information and tore the sheet of paper from her notebook, handing it to Ron. He looked at it before pocketing it. "Hough neighborhood?"

"Yep. I've lived there almost ten years now."

"You are full of surprises, Angela," he said, holding her gaze for an extra moment before following her back into the classroom.

Angela didn't know what to say to that, so she sat down without saying anything. He sat down next to her.

"How's your day been so far?" he asked, turning his legs toward her and taking another sip of his water.

"Unusual," she said quietly. "I went to work this morning and ended up being questioned by a Cleveland police detective."

"Really?" Ron cocked his head, his eyebrows raised. "Why?"

"One of our customers was raped," she said in a low voice.

"How unfortunate," he said with a deep frown.

"I'm guessing it happened right after she left our store. I work at a coffee shop," she explained. "I keep wondering if I served coffee to her rapist yesterday. I didn't notice anything strange about any of my customers, but you just never know, right?" Ron shook his head. "Anyway, the detective stopped by first thing this morning and I spent the rest of the morning in shock. Then I came to class. How about you?"

"Nothing as exciting as all that. Like you, I worked this morning, then came to class."

"Where do you work?"

"I work at an antique shop in East Cleveland."

Angela imagined working in the midst of dusty relics and their forgotten stories. "I'd run myself out of business if I worked in an antique shop—I'd want to buy everything for myself."

"That's one of the hazards of the trade," he laughed. "I content myself with making up stories about the items I sell. I'm a writer," he said.

Angela grinned. "Really? What sorts of things do you write?"

"Mostly short fiction, but I dabble in poetry, too. I love the art of word-weaving."

"If you're a writer, how'd you end up in this program?" she asked.

"Writers have to make a living somehow, don't they?" He leaned toward her, setting his left shoe against the tips of her feet. "And as much as I like working at the antique store, I don't feel like I'm contributing much to society by working there. Armed with the degree I earn here, I'll be able to use my power of storytelling for the good of whole cities, particularly East Cleveland. I'd really like to see my city turn around," he confided.

"Makes sense," Angela nodded. "What was your major at Oberlin?"

"History."

"Okay, everyone, let's get started," Dr. Moore said.

Ron opened his notebook and began to write. Half a minute later, he offered Angela a piece of paper, brushing her hand with his as he slipped it into her hand. Angela read what he had written. "More on Sunday. Looking forward to it."

Angela slipped the paper inside her own notebook and stole a glance at Ron. He looked back at her out of the corner of his eye. She grinned. He smiled back.

As Dr. Moore talked, however, Angela's thoughts

wandered back to the incident from this morning. Angela thought of Luke. He didn't *seem* like a rapist. He seemed like an open, friendly guy. There was also the other young man to consider. Angela tried to remember his face, but it just hadn't been that remarkable. Or she had been too busy to notice. Or both. He hadn't returned to Phoenix today. If he was Cassidy's rapist, and he had come with the express purpose of following her, he probably wouldn't be back. Angela wondered if Cassidy would be back to Phoenix. She doubted it.

Dr. Moore asked the class to form groups of three or four for a discussion of the readings. Angela turned her desk toward Ron, and Jamal White, who was sitting in front of Ron, turned his desk around to face both of them.

"So, what'd you think?" Angela asked.

"Bill, you would not believe the day I've had," Angela said, raising her voice to compete with the background noise at Nighttown.

"I'm all ears for the next ten minutes, and then I'm off my break," he said.

Quickly, Angela filled him in on the visit from the detective this morning and her recollections from work yesterday.

"Do you have any idea who it might have been?" he said.

"There were two male customers I didn't recognize. One of them came back to Phoenix today. He doesn't strike me as a rapist—but I suppose a rapist could look or act like anyone. The second guy didn't return, at least not during my shift. My bet is on him—that's assuming the rapist even came into the shop. I hope Detective Winston figures it out. I imagine we won't be seeing the rape victim anytime soon, unfortunately."

"The whole thing is dreadful. Let's hope the guy gets caught. So, apart from serving soon-to-be-convicts and their victims, what have you been up to? We need to catch up. It's been at least a week, missy."

"I know, I know, things have been busy on my end. But hey, I don't have to work tomorrow, so I can stay up. Want to treat me to wine at your place after your shift ends?"

"As a matter of fact, I have a dry Riesling with your name on it. Literally."

"You bought a wine called Angela?"

"Couldn't resist."

Angela rolled her eyes. "Dry Riesling sounds interesting. Okay, I'll come over at eleven fifteen."

"See you then, lady."

"See ya."

A board of names and accompanying buttons stood to the left of the main entrance of Bill's building. Angela pressed the button next to "W. Kinsman." Bill didn't answer except to buzz her in. She entered the red-carpeted foyer and ascended three flights of stairs. Bill's apartment was near the end of the narrow hallway, on the left. The door was ajar; she let herself in.

"Thieves and murderers could be at your door," she called, shutting the door behind her.

Bill peeked his head out of the kitchen. "My apartment is too fabulous to draw in people like that."

Angela snorted. Bill, like Angela, had made his dwelling his home, but where the rooms in Angela's house varied in style, united only by the common hardwood flooring, everything in Bill's apartment was coordinated. He had started with the black and white tile kitchen floor and worked his way up. His living room had a large framed reprint of Tamara de Lempicka's "The Musician." "The Musician" prominently featured a woman wearing a thin, nipple-accentuating blue dress. She was playing the sort of stringed instrument one might find in a classical painting, but her hair was styled in a flapper's coif, and behind her rose a black, charcoal, and white skyline of art deco high rises. Bill's couch and living room rug matched the musician's dress. His glasswear, apart from the clear wine glasses, was the color of charcoal, and his dishes were a careful mix of black and white. All his furniture was black. His coasters, on which he set empty clear wine glasses before opening the bottle of dry Riesling, were solid white squares. Bill's bedroom, which was visible from the living room couch, featured a king-sized bed with a deep blue bedspread with black and white throw pillows.

Bill poured Angela four ounces of wine, then poured another four ounces for himself. Angela picked up her glass and held it up to her nose, inhaling deeply. It had light, citrusy notes. Bill sat down across from her on the couch, and they held up their glasses.

"To life, love, and laughter," they said. Each of

them took a sip. Angela had only tasted sweet Rieslings in the past. The dry Riesling was delicate, but still a delight on the palate.

"I think I prefer dry Riesling to sweet Riesling," she murmured.

"I had a hunch you'd like it. All the flavor without the sweetness, which is perfect for your non-sweet tooth," he said. It was true that Angela didn't have much of a sweet tooth.

"So fill me in," he said.

She told him again about the interview with Detective Winston, in greater detail this time.

"Who is this Joseph guy?" he asked with raised eyebrows, when she told him about the library book he'd let her borrow.

"I met him at the library—didn't I tell you about him?"

"Uh, no."

"I told someone about him. Maybe it was Grandma Caroline. Yes, it was—she thought it was a hoot that a guy in a cassock came up to me."

"And you forgot all about little old me. Details, Ang, I need details!" he exclaimed. "So, is he cute?"

"You and Shelly are on a mission to set me up with unavailable men, aren't you? It's a conspiracy, right?" She nudged his leg and he stared innocently at the ceiling. Then he looked back at her.

"So is he?"

Angela groaned. "He looks fine."

"You're not giving me much to go on."

"Fine. He's taller than me and has brown hair. Satisfied?"

"Absolutely not. What more can you tell me? Come on!"

"He gave me his business card," she said, pulling her wallet out of her pocket. She gave the card to Bill to examine.

"'Joseph C. Warner – Seminarian.' That's informative. But hey, it has his phone number. Have you called him yet?"

"No. I might, though. He offered to listen after I told him about my falling out with the Missouri Synod. He doesn't think I'm a heretic based on what he's heard. That's gotta count for a lot coming from a Roman Catholic, right? Especially one who's in training to become a priest."

"You're thinking about calling him? But you're not attracted to him?"

Angela took a sip of wine and measured her words. "I wouldn't say I'm attracted to him, but there is something compelling about him. He listens without judgment. He's the polar opposite of my mother. I think I could use a deeply religious person in my life who isn't convinced I'm going to hell, you know?"

"What about me?"

"Of course there's you, but religion isn't the center of your life. I mean, there are plenty of kind people in my life, but there are so few who are as ardent about their faith as I am who are also non-judgmental."

"Well, what about your grandma?"

"Grandma Caroline certainly qualifies as a deeply religious person, but she's in the same boat I am. It would be nice to have some validation from someone mainstream."

"So you want to use him for validation," he said.

"Hey, he's the one who gave me his card—he offered. Is it wrong if I take him up on it?"

Bill leaned back. "Hey, it's your life. Do what you want to do."

Angela took a sip of wine, pondering. "Oh, and that reminds me—I'm about to go out with another religious person."

"How many religious people have you got up your sleeve?" he asked incredulously.

She told him about Ron's invitation to go to church with him this Sunday.

"He's taking you on a date to church?"

"Well, that's not the date part—but brunch afterward is. At least, I think it's a date. He definitely seems interested in me, and I think I may be falling for him."

"And Ron is who again?"

"He's a recent Oberlin grad. African-American guy from East Cleveland. He has some of the finest brown eyes I've ever seen."

"Younger guy? Work it, girl!"

"He's not more than five years younger than I am. And he was a history major. He's got some stories up his sleeve."

"Oh, I know about you and your fetish for stories. Sounds like he's got you hooked."

Angela laughed. "He's pretty fine. I will say that."

"Well, I think we should plan a phone date for Sunday afternoon. I want to hear all about Ron and his charms."

"Deal."

Angela changed the subject, telling Bill about her Wednesday clash with Jessica Lyle.

"She was all over me—she interrupted me several times. I don't know what her deal is, but she's a nightmare. Thea help me if I ever have to work in a small group with her. You never know."

"Sounds like you need some more wine. Here," he said, picking up the bottle of Angela and tipping it over her glass.

"Hey, I still need to drive tonight."

"You're going to be driving the couch tonight, sweetheart—you might as well make the most of it."

Angela grumbled but let him continue pouring the wine till her glass was nearly full.

"Anything else you haven't caught me up on?" he asked, pouring the remaining wine into his wine glass.

"Hmm. Oh, I didn't tell you about having lunch with my parents. It was awkward as hell. That's about it."

Bill took a long sip of his wine. "Have you come to any resolution about how to deal with your parents?"

"I'm going to keep in touch with Dad by phone and e-mail and go to see both of them on ordinary days. I won't be going back to their house or their church for Thanksgiving or Christmas, though. The holidays are too much."

"Wow. That sounds like avoidance."

"It is, isn't it?"

Bill slid over to Angela's side of the couch and gave her a side hug. Angela squeezed him back, fighting back the urge to cry. Tears welled up, threatening to spill over. Bill took her glass and set it down on the black coffee table. Then he wrapped her in a hug and let her bury her tears in his shoulder.

Chapter 11

Angela awoke, and for a moment she didn't know where she was. She looked around and realized she was in Bill's apartment, on his couch, covered by a black and white crochet blanket. *I must have cried myself to sleep*, she thought.

Angela rubbed her eyes and sat up, looking in the direction of Bill's bedroom. His door was cracked open, and she could hear him snoring. She got up and trudged to the kitchen, fighting off a headache. Before long she had coffee brewing in the coffeemaker, and she was tossing together ingredients for veggie and ham omelets. Behind her she heard a low moan.

"You're making breakfast," Bill said, ecstasy in his voice. "Thank you, Ang."

"You deserve a treat after the pathetic show I put on last night."

"I won't argue with that," he said, and she swiped at him with the egg-covered spatula.

"Hey, the floor!" he protested, as egg remnants dripped on the tile.

"Make yourself useful, *sous chef*," she replied, pushing the roll of paper towels in his direction.

"She makes a mess on my floor and I have to clean it up. Women," he muttered.

"I think you've forgotten who wields the spatula," she said, glancing at him over her shoulder.

"Fine, fine," he grumbled, bending down to wipe up the mess. The egg mixture sizzled as Angela poured it in the hot frying pan. After throwing the paper towel away, Bill pulled a blue over-sized mug out of the cupboard and poured himself a cup of coffee.

"So you're going to hang out up here for Thanksgiving, eh? You're welcome at my parents' house."

Angela looked over and gave a small smile. "Thanks, Bill, but I've already decided I want to do Thanksgiving at home."

"Do you know what you're going to make?"

"I was thinking of a small turkey. I want to brine it myself, rather than getting a pre-brined turkey. I'll also make cranberry sauce from scratch, maybe some homemade bread, stuffing, and cheesy potato casserole. Oh, and pumpkin pie from scratch. Can't forget dessert."

"Sounds like you're going all out for yourself. Good for you," he said. He took a sip of coffee.

"I want my first Thanksgiving in my home to be memorable," she said. "Besides, I do church alone. No reason I can't do holidays alone. Just call me 'Hermit Angela.'"

"Well, if you change your mind about wanting to celebrate alone, just let me know."

"I will. Thanks for offering, Bill. That's very sweet of you."

When she got home from Bill's, Angela set her keys on the dining room table and headed up the stairs. She wanted to do a search for some architects and contractors. For the rest of the morning, she looked at websites and gathered phone numbers. At lunchtime she headed down the stairs and realized she'd forgotten her morning prayer. She opened the door to her prayer closet and a cool draft of air spilled out.

"Brr." Angela shivered. She sat down on a cold throw pillow and rubbed her arms for warmth. She lit a candle and held her fingers above the flame, warming them. Then she sat back and breathed deeply with her eyes closed.

"Thea," she whispered, reading from her prayer book, "may I welcome all the challenges of this day with your strength, wisdom, and courage. Amen."

After several minutes of silent meditation, Angela blew out the candle and got up. In the kitchen, she opened her refrigerator before realizing that she was still full from this morning's omelet. She poured water in the water heater instead and turned it on. Once the water was ready, she poured it over tea in her teapot. Armed with the teapot and her favorite striped mug, she headed back up the stairs.

For the next hour and a half, Angela drank increasingly lukewarm tea, talking to architects about her project and asking them for a sense of how much their work would cost. Contractors were next on her list. They wouldn't have all the information they needed without blueprints from the architects, but they could still give her an idea based on the information she provided — she hoped.

As it turned out, two of the five contractors she called were willing to talk to her about pricing.

Between the costs of the architect, the contractor, and the purchase of the building, she was looking at about eleven million dollars.

Angela looked at her computer's clock. It was already 3:30, and now she was hungry. She got up and headed down to the kitchen, where she pulled out a nearly-empty tray of butternut squash and gorgonzola casserole.

As she ate a bowl of warmed-up casserole, her conversation with Bill last night replayed in her head. Ron came to mind, and she paused, lingering over the memory of his face. Her skin tingled at the thought of him. Then her parents came to mind, and she frowned. As if on queue, the phone rang.

"Hello?" she said, after swallowing her last bite of food.

"Hello, sweetheart. It's your dear old dad."

Her stomach dropped as if a brick had fallen on it.

"Hi, Dad."

"Ang, we just wanted to call and confirm plans for Thanksgiving. Is there anyone you'd like to bring with you?"

"Dad, I'm not coming to Thanksgiving this year," she said quietly.

"Er… what?"

"I said I'm not coming to Thanksgiving this year," she said with a bit more force.

"Honey, why not?"

"For the same reason I didn't come to Grandma and Grandpa's funerals. I can't."

"But I still don't understand *why*," he said. This time his voice was impatient.

"Because being there makes me sick to my stomach. I can't deal with going to church."

"Well, you don't have to go to church. You can just come for dinner."

"No, Dad. Mom and I will fight just like we always do, the whole thing will be tense, and I'll wish I were anywhere but there. I'm doing Thanksgiving at my house this year."

Silence pressed against her ear.

"If that's how you feel about it…" His voice trailed off. Then Angela heard her mother's voice in the background. She was shouting.

"Angela Bridges," her mother spat into the phone, "you ungrateful little brat, how dare you skip Thanksgiving when your father is sick?"

Angela heard her father say, "I'm fine, Susan" in the background.

"No, you're not," she hissed. "Angela, you *will* come to Thanksgiving at our house, and you will honor your parents by joining us at church. Have I made myself clear?"

This time it was Angela's turn to be silent.

"Angela?" she said, her voice shrilly.

"I'm not coming to Thanksgiving, Mother. I'm not coming to Christmas, either. I won't ruin the holidays for everyone, including me, by setting myself up for yet another argument with you. Don't you see that it's just not worth it? If we can't get along—and we can't even get along now—then I don't want to be there."

"Angela Bridges, how dare you defy your parents? We didn't raise you this way. We raised you to be obedient and respectful, and now all you can do is act like an apostate. All you seem to want to do is dishonor us in whatever way you can."

"Mom, don't you see? It's the same thing over and over again between us. I don't want any part of it. Not when we're supposed to be celebrating the joy of the holidays."

"Now, wait just a minute…."

"Goodbye, Mom."

And she hung up the phone.

The phone rang again almost immediately, but she didn't answer. Instead, she pulled on a jacket and shoes and walked out the front door, locking it behind her. She needed a walk.

By the time Angela returned to her house, it was nearly dark. Her legs were stiff and sore, and her face was bright red from the cold. When she got in the house, she pulled off her coat and rubbed her hands together. *What now?*

Angela pulled her wallet out of her pocket and opened it. Joseph's card was tucked inside behind several other cards. She pulled it out, walking to the phone in the kitchen. She dialed his number. It rang several times, and then his voicemail picked up.

"Hello, you've reached Joseph Warner. I'm sorry I missed your call. Please leave any message after the beep. I look forward to speaking with you. God bless."

Angela's breath caught as the beep sounded. "Joseph, this is Angela Bridges from Phoenix Coffee. You invited me to call you if I wanted to talk, and I think I do want to. Feel free to give me a call anytime. Thanks." She hung up with a sigh, then went to her prayer closet to pray.

On Saturday afternoon, armed with a mug of piping hot black tea, Angela walked to her desk and reviewed her notes. Her search this morning at the Historical Society had turned up nothing about the female worker who had died during World War II. It did, however, lead her to the journals of the stepdaughter of the original owner of the building. She'd pored over them and made notes, since photocopies weren't allowed. The journals were falling apart and she had to handle them with white gloves. What she had read in the journals surprised her. The young woman, Adeline Parker, wrote eloquently about her desires to help lead the family business. Her stepfather welcomed her to take her place among the leaders of the textile factory, but the other men in leadership rejected her, telling her her place was in the home, not on the job. One man in particular, Ebenezer Jones, threatened her, saying he would keep her out of the hierarchy of the business if it was the last thing he did.

Was he her murderer? Angela wondered. She dug around in newspaper microfiche from the weeks after she died, and the police questioned Ebenezer Jones, but they ultimately didn't charge him with anything, since Adeline's body was never found.

Another man in leadership had been kind to her, however. Jeremiah Winslow encouraged her. It appeared as though they were all but courting. They even had a special place they went to in the factory, a secret nook that no one else knew about. Angela wondered if the police had read her journals and if they had found the secret nook. There wasn't any obvious place where one could hide away, given the open floor plans. Could there have been a trapdoor to a basement room? Angela wondered if the real estate agent would meet with her at the factory one more time so she could look around.

As she left the Historical Society, she called the commercial real estate agent and asked if he could show her the building again. He agreed, and they headed over together. Angela walked carefully around the first floor. She didn't find anything. She searched the second and third floors more quickly, but nothing gave her clues as to Adeline's fate.

Angela was disappointed she hadn't been able to find more clues about Adeline Parker's fate, but the history she had gathered from the Western Reserve Historical Society, the information she had gleaned from the interviews, and her visits to the factory building were beginning to gel into a picture of the factory's past. With that, she could begin to frame the factory's future.

The factory contained 20,000 square feet and three floors, with the main entrance on the east wall of the southeast corner of the building, just off the narrow parking lot. Each floor was tall, about fifteen feet high, and had glass pane windows running along all the outer walls. Inside, the floor plans were open. Leftover work tables and large looms from the textile business littered each floor, and a smattering of offices stood at the north end of the first floor.

According to her interviews, this mill had been *the*

place to work in the neighborhood from the time it opened. Many of the neighbors she spoke to had worked there or had a relative who had worked there. The first step was to make the building into a community center again. There were several ways she could do this. For the first floor, she imagined getting rid of the existing offices to open up the space for a permanent indoor flea market and farmer's market, not unlike the West Side Market on the other side of town. She could call it Adeline's Flea Market. It would be a place where locals could sell goods they had produced. Money would go directly into the pockets of vendors, boosting the local economy. One of the advantages of having a permanent indoor market was that it didn't require much structural modification. Building vendor booths would be relatively inexpensive both in terms of parts and labor. *So far, so good.*

For the second floor, Angela wanted to have a neighborhood museum sponsored by the Western Reserve Historical Society. There would be displays about the history of the mill itself, including the stories about its ghosts, as well as displays pertaining to the broader neighborhood. Angela's interviews could be expanded and incorporated into the displays. There might be a section reserved for contemporary exhibits of local art and activities happening around the neighborhood. For the rest of the second floor, Angela imagined several ways of dividing up the space. There could be a local restaurant on the southwest corner, complete with a sports bar for those who just wanted a drink and appetizers. An arcade for kids and teenagers would stand next to the restaurant, and a community gym would stand next to that against the northwest corner of the building. Along the east wall, office space and meeting rooms would be available for lease and rent.

The third floor would be the most expensive to renovate. Angela envisioned six units of housing: two for regular-income families, two for low-income families, and two for artists. Each unit would have a full bathroom, a kitchen, one or two bedrooms, and a living room. The new residents would give the building new history, new memories; they would also ensure that the building was constantly occupied. Angela liked the idea of the old mill being in use twenty-four hours a day, rather than shutting down after business hours. There would be life inside the building at all times, not just sometimes. After years of standing empty, the building deserved that, she thought.

The parking lot outside would be repaved and expanded to include the south side of the property. The west side of the property would include a playground, a walking path, a community garden, benches, and trees throughout. This would make the property accessible to all who wanted to enjoy it, not just those who had money to spend.

Angela sat back. Her thoughts drifted to the photograph of Adeline Parker that had been featured in the *Plain Dealer* after her disappearance. Her hair was probably light brown or dark blond, and in the portrait it was pulled up in a tight knot at the nape of her neck. She had penetrating eyes of a light color. She reminded Angela of herself, in fact. Angela shivered. *What happened to Adeline?*

Angela buckled up in Ron's red Ford Ranger and he pulled out of her driveway. She had done her own usual liturgy at seven this morning, and then she had gotten showered and dressed to visit Ron's church. She was wearing a black, sleeveless, knee-length, form-fitting dress with black flats. Her green pea coat kept her warm.

Ron was wearing a dark gray suit and matching skinny tie with a light gray shirt. He looked sharp. Angela folded her hands in her lap and smiled at him, fully aware of how close their shoulders were in the truck.

"Thanks for picking me up," she said.

"My pleasure," he said.

They arrived at St. John AME Church on the corner of 40th Street and Central about ten minutes later. Greeters at the main doors greeted Ron by name and welcomed Angela. Ron led her down the main aisle to one of the dark, shiny pews near the front. The pews sloped downward toward the pulpit. A robed choir was currently seated behind the pulpit, and the pastor was nowhere in sight. The ladies and men in the choir were chatting with one another. Ron shook hands with more church members as they entered the pew, and they sat down together.

"So this is the guest you were telling us about," a female voice said behind them. Angela turned and met the mahogany eyes of a short, wide black woman. Her hair was short with a thousand miniature corkscrew curls, and she had red glasses perched on her nose.

"Hello, Mom. This is Angela Bridges, one of my classmates."

"Welcome, Angela. I'm Mrs. Walker, but you can call me Rhoda." Rhoda shook Angela's hand warmly.

"Nice to meet you, Rhoda," she said.

"This is my husband, Mr. Walker," Rhoda said, touching her husband's shoulder. He was tall and well-built. Ron got his looks from him, Angela thought, except for his eyes, which matched his mother's.

"Timothy," Ron's father said, extending a hand. "You're very welcome here, Angela."

"Nice to meet you, Timothy. Thank you. I've never been to an AME service before."

"I think you're in for a treat," Rhoda said, smiling.

They all sat down in their pews, and the service began a couple of minutes later. For the next hour, Angela listened to the rich voices of the four-part choir and the commanding voice of the pastor who preached about Jesus' teaching that we forgive others as we would be forgiven. Angela thought of her mother. *I may be able to forgive you someday, Mom, but I'll never be like you*, she thought to herself.

Afterward, Ron led her out of the pew and up the aisle to the main doors. He opened the passenger door for her, and she slid in. He got in several moments later.

"Hungry?" he said.

"Very," she said.

"Well, you're in for the best brunch in East

Cleveland."

"Can't wait!" she said.

Twenty minutes later, they parked across the street from a two-story house with a large front porch and pale blue siding.

"Welcome to my parents' house," he said, nodding his head toward the eastern-facing house. Just then, a silver Ford Taurus pulled into the driveway. Angela recognized Ron's mother's hair peeking up above the passenger side seat.

"Nobody cooks better than my mama," Ron said with a grin.

"Not that you're biased or anything," she said, smiling.

"Not at all!"

They headed toward the front door. Ron unlocked it with a key on his keyring and ushered her inside. Angela stepped into a living room with beige carpet and white walls. Stairs stood directly across from the front door, and the rest of the living room stood to the left, with a green couch along the west wall and lounge chairs in front of the picture window. There was no television in this room. Instead, black bookshelves lined the entire southern wall from floor to ceiling. It reminded Angela of her library at home. Beyond the couch, an entryway led to the kitchen, and Angela heard the bustle of Ron's parents entering through the back door.

"Make yourself at home, dear," Rhoda called. Angela looked at Ron, who pointed a hand toward the couch. She shrugged off her jacket, which he took from her and carried into the kitchen.

"Would you like some coffee?" he asked, peeking his head back in the living room.

"Yes, I'd love some," she said.

"It'll just take a few minutes," he said.

"Ron, get yourself in the living room—I'll take care of the coffee, boy!" Rhoda said. Angela caught herself before she snorted. Ron walked in, blushing.

"Thanks for bringing me to your parents' house. That's a bold move for a first..." Angela swallowed her words.

"For a first date?" he offered. Angela's cheeks burned.

"Good, I'm glad I'm not the only one turning red around here," he laughed. Angela rolled her eyes at him and got up from the couch to look at the bookshelves.

"These look like history books," she remarked as she scanned the titles.

"Yes. Many of them are histories of African-American people. A number of them are general American histories, and the rest are histories of various nations around the world. We're a history-loving family," he said.

"Hence your major."

"Indeed."

"I imagine your proposal for the contest is history-rich."

"Yes, I was able to find out a lot about the church I chose. You're welcome to take a look at my proposal, if you want."

Angela turned to look at him. "Really?"

"Sure. I have it at my apartment. I'll e-mail it to

you."

"Don't mind if the competition has a look, then?"

"I don't think it'll do any harm. I have faith in your integrity," he said.

Angela stepped closer to him till she could breathe in his scent. He wore Old Spice. She gave him a long, appreciative look. "Thank you."

Rhoda emerged from the kitchen with two cups of coffee. "Here you are. Would you like cream or sugar, Angela?"

"No, thank you."

Angela and Ron took their cups of coffee and sat down on the couch. Angela took a sip. It was earthy and rich, without any bitterness. Perfect.

"You like it," Ron said. It wasn't a question.

"I do. Where does your family get its coffee?"

"Phoenix Coffee. Best coffee in town."

Angela paused, her eyes meeting his. Then she took another sip, smiling.

"What is it?" he asked.

"I work at Phoenix."

"Really? Which one?"

"The one downtown."

"My parents visit the one in Cleveland Heights, usually. Parking's a little easier there."

"Well, if you happen to be downtown some morning, you can catch me at the downtown store. I work there every morning, Monday through Thursday."

"I'll make a point of it," he said, holding his cup to his lips.

They chit-chatted about Cleveland sites they liked

to frequent until Timothy called them into the kitchen. An oblong wooden table for four was set with red placemats and a red table liner. On the liner stood a bowl of grits, a bowl of scrambled eggs with cheese, and a plate stacked high with pancakes. Butter, syrup, salt, and pepper were also clustered on the table liner.

"Before we sit," Timothy said, "it's our custom to say grace holding hands."

Angela took Ron's hand on her left and Timothy's hand on her right and bowed her head.

Timothy spoke the table prayer. "Heavenly Father, we ask you to bless this food and the hands that prepared it. We remain mindful of those who go without enough to eat this day. May they be blessed with your abundance, and may we who are gathered here become your generous hands. Amen."

"Amen," Angela said.

Rhoda began passing food around the table, and brunch passed in cheerful, light conversation. When Timothy asked how Angela liked the service at St. John, she said, "I liked it very much. The music especially moved me."

"We do have a fine choir," Timothy said. "Ron sang in it as a teenager."

Angela looked at Ron with interest. "You sing?"

"I'm a baritone," he admitted.

"I'm a singer, too. I'm an alto," Angela said.

"I'll bet you two would sound mighty fine together," Rhoda said.

Angela and Ron's eyes met, and they grinned.

"Thanks for having me at your church, Ron. And

please thank your parents again for me for brunch. It was delicious," she said as Ron walked her up to her front door.

"Thank you for coming. And I will. I'm just sorry we didn't get a chance to talk about your spiritual path. I was looking forward to hearing more about it." They arrived at her front door, and Ron took her hand and kissed it lightly. Her hand was charged with the touch of his lips. She swallowed.

"Maybe we can go out sometime, just the two of us," she suggested quietly.

"That sounds like a plan to me," he said, his eyes gazing softly at her.

"Goodbye, Ron," she said.

"Goodbye, Angela." He reached forward to touch her shoulder and turned around, walking down the steps toward his truck.

She unlocked her door and stepped inside to watch him. She waved with a warm smile as he drove away. Then she looked up, took a deep breath, and shut the door behind her.

Chapter 12

Angela shut her eyes. Candlelight played on her eyelids. She thought of Ron with long breaths of gratitude. Then she thought of her mother. The distance between her and her mother—the distance that she contributed to—hurt. Her breaths came more rapidly.

"I'm sorry things aren't better between my mother and me, Thea. I'm sorry for my bitterness toward her. I just can't let her walk all over me—and I don't believe you're the sort of god who'd want me to let her walk all over me. Help me let go of my resentment so I can move on with my life." Angela breathed deeply. "Amen."

Angela blew out the candle and stepped out of the prayer closet. Her cell phone rang from inside her coat pocket as she shut the door. She walked over to the couch where she had deposited her coat and fished the phone out of her pocket. She didn't recognize the number.

"Hello, this is Angela," she answered.

"Hello, Angela. This is Joseph Warner."

Angela sat on the couch. "Hi, Joseph. Thanks for calling me back."

"Of course. So what's up? You mentioned in your message you wanted to talk. I'm here to listen."

"How long have you got?" she joked.

"As long as you need," he said seriously.

"That's kind of you. Thank you." Angela sat back and looked at the ceiling. "I was just praying about this, actually." Angela measured her words. Joseph was still a stranger. But he was in training to become a priest, and priests were trained to listen.

"Take your time," he said gently.

Encouraged, Angela began at the beginning. "I grew up in the Missouri Synod Lutheran Church, as I mentioned to you. My mother taught me to be an obedient handmaiden of the Lord, and I was. But then, when I was fifteen, I was reflecting on scripture when I realized I felt a call to ministry. The Missouri Synod, like the Roman Catholic Church, doesn't ordain women." Angela hesitated, wondering if telling a future Roman Catholic priest about her call to ministry was a mistake.

"When I told my parents—well, my mother, particularly—my mother was furious. She said my calling was false. She told me to pray it away. But the more I prayed, the more certain I became of my calling. It was a difficult time in my life, because suddenly the faith that had shaped me and taught me about the God I loved suddenly seemed to be at odds with God's calling for me. I ended up leaving the church when I was eighteen. My dad told me I could come back to the church when I was ready and I'd be welcomed with open arms, but since then, I've grown too far apart from it to have any hope of returning.

"Now, encouraged by my grandmother, I call God 'Thea' and imagine God in the feminine. That must sound terribly odd to you," she stammered.

"Not at all," he said quietly.

"Really?"

"Really."

"But you're a Roman Catholic. You're in training to become a priest."

"And one of the things I've learned is that God transcends every image we might have of God. No image is sufficient, but many images bear unique truths about God. God as mother hen, God as *sophia*, God as *ruach*—all these are feminine images of God. They are not the totality of God, but they are revelations of God."

Angela's voice caught in her throat.

"Angela, are you still there?"

Her voice broke. "I'm still here."

Joseph was silent for several beats, then spoke. "As for your calling to ministry, there are many mainstream Christian denominations that ordain women. My personal feeling on the subject is that the Roman Catholic Church—and the Missouri Synod, for that matter—just haven't caught up yet. They will eventually. But maybe not in time to appreciate the God-given gifts you bring to the table. And if God is calling you to ministry, your first duty is to obey that call, wherever your gifts are welcome."

"That's the thing. My faith has shifted so much since I left the Missouri Synod that I don't think I'd be welcome in any Christian church."

"Then maybe God is calling you to start your own church," he said.

"That's more or less what I've done," Angela murmured. "I worship in a church of one. Two, if you count my grandmother, whose beliefs more or less mirror mine."

"Sounds to me like you're doing just what God has in mind for you," he said.

Tears flooded her eyes. She wiped them away with the back of her free hand.

"Thank you, Joseph."

"You're welcome," he said softly.

Angela shook her head to clear it. "So what about your parents—are they on board with you becoming a priest?"

The line was silent. Angela held up her phone to make sure she was still connected. Then she put it back to her ear, and Joseph spoke. "My mother died when I was two. My father died three years ago."

"Oh, wow—Joseph, I'm so sorry." *Good going, Angela.*

"Thank you. Everyone carries burdens—losing my parents is mine to bear."

"Do you have brothers and sisters?"

"No, I was my mother's first and only child. She had complications with me, and her health was never the same afterward."

"Joseph, I'm so sorry. I don't know what to say."

"There's nothing that needs to be said. I will say that the holidays are pretty hard now that my dad is gone. Professor McNear was very kind to me when my father passed away. He was like a grandfather to me. All my grandparents have passed as well, so having him to talk to was a godsend."

"I can imagine." Angela thought of Professor McNear with new appreciation. Timothy's prayer from that morning came to mind: "May we who are gathered here become your generous hands." An idea sparked.

"Hey, you know, I'm celebrating Thanksgiving at my house this year and I'll be on my own. Would you like to join me? I'm already planning to make a full feast, so there will be plenty of food for both of us. I'm planning to do a special table blessing, so you'd have a chance to see what my prayer life is like."

The line was quiet for a moment. "I'd have to get permission from the rector of the seminary, but I would be honored. Let me ask him and let you know."

Thanksgiving's loneliness could be cured for two people at once. *Maybe this is an occasion of synchronicity.*

"Angela, I want to thank you, not only for the invitation to share your Thanksgiving meal, but also for your trust in me. I imagine it wasn't easy to share the story of your calling with someone who belongs to the Roman Catholic Church—especially someone who's about to become part of that hierarchy. I don't take your trust for granted. Thank you."

"Thank you for listening. You are very kind, Joseph. I'm glad our paths crossed when they did."

"I'll give you a call when I've had a chance to talk to my rector, okay?"

"Sounds good. Talk to you then."

"God bless, Angela."

"Bye."

Angela pressed the end button and sat for a while, dazed. Then she walked back into her prayer closet.

"Thea," she said, after she had settled cross-legged on the floor, "did you bring Joseph into my life so I could experience the affirmation my mother cannot offer? Because that was a hell of an affirmation."

Angela sat quietly, steadying her breath. She was crying.

She pulled the box of matches from its shelf, opened it, struck a match, and relit the candle. For several minutes, she gazed into its piercing light. Then she blew out the candle, left the prayer room, and walked up to her bedroom to get ready for bed.

Monday morning was a chilly fifty degrees—perfect for biking. Angela pulled her green mountain bike out of her garage and hopped on, snapping her blue helmet over her head. She was dressed in long black yoga pants, a white long-sleeved shirt, and a heavy feather-lined silver jacket. Her muscles felt strong as she pushed the pedals, propelling herself north on 82nd Street and then west down the stretch of Superior Avenue. She preferred taking Superior on days she rode her bicycle to work because it was less crowded than Chester.

As she made her way downtown, she could see her breath in front of her. She waited at Superior and 55th for the light to turn green, then continued on her way. The former Church of St. Mary Magdalene came up on her left. It looked bleak against the gray skyline. *If only those stones could speak.*

When she arrived at Phoenix Coffee, she unlocked the door and rolled her bicycle inside, taking it to the backroom. Shelly was there at her desk.

"Hey," Angela said.

"'Morning," Shelly replied. "Rode your bike in

today? Aren't you freezing?"

"I feel great. My muscles are all warmed up and I'm full of energy."

"You're nuts," Shelly muttered.

"That's why you love me," Angela called over her shoulder as she walked up to the front. A large white box sat on the counter. Angela opened it and began transferring pastries to the pastry case.

At seven o'clock, Angela unlocked the front door. A familiar figure stood just outside.

"Ron!" Angela said, opening the door. His cheeks were flushed from the cold, and he wore a broad smile. He reached for her hand.

"You invited me to stop by some morning. Is this too soon?"

Angela accepted his hand, looked in his glittering eyes, and grinned. "Your timing's just right. Come on in." She stood aside and he walked in, squeezing her hand lightly as he walked toward the counter.

"I'm supposed to get to the antique shop by 7:45 to open at eight, so I have just enough time for some coffee," he said, unwinding his scarf.

"What can I get started for you?" she asked, moving to the register.

"A large cup of your darkest roast."

"You've got it." Angela set a large paper cup underneath the urn of French roast coffee and held down the knob. Steaming coffee poured out of the spout.

"You don't need room for milk, right?" she said, turning her head toward him.

"You have a good memory."

"That's what people tell me," she said, smiling. She snapped a lid on top and slipped a sleeve around the cup. As she handed it to him, their fingers touched.

"Hi, there," Shelly said brightly, bustling out of the backroom.

Reluctantly, Angela lowered her hand. "Shelly, this is Ron. He's one of my classmates from CSU. Ron, Shelly is my manager."

"Very nice to meet you, Ron."

"Nice to meet you, Shelly," he said. He transferred his coffee cup to his left hand so he could shake her hand with his right.

"Would you like a cookie or anything for the road?" Shelly asked.

"Actually, those wedges of baklava caught my eye. I'll have one of those," he said.

"Fan of Mediterranean food?" Shelly asked.

"Absolutely," he said.

"Angela's a fan of Mediterranean food, too."

Ron looked at Angela with interest. "Are you?" he said to her.

Angela cast a pointed glance at Shelly before looking back at Ron with a smile. "I am. I enjoy Aladdin's and the Mad Greek up at Cedar-Fairmount."

"Hm. I'll keep that in mind," he said with a wink. "I've got to run, but I'll see you at class tomorrow, Angela."

"See you then, Ron."

Ron gave her a warm smile before he walked out the door, and Shelly turned to Angela.

"Wait just a second," Angela said, holding her

hands up. "As it turns out, you don't need to set me up with him. He took me out for a date yesterday. At least, I think it was a date."

"I want to hear the whole scoop," Shelly said, folding her arms.

Angela told him about their visit to Ron's church. Shelly raised her eyebrows at the mention of church. Then Angela talked about brunch at his parents' house, and Shelly leaned in. "You see what he did there, right? He's introduced you to his parents already. He must like you."

"That much seems clear. But we'll see. I'm in no rush to make a big thing out of this. He's just… nice."

"And handsome," Shelly said.

"And smart," Angela admitted.

"Sounds like your kind of guy, Ang."

"He does, doesn't he?"

Shelly looked her over. "You like him."

"Yeah… I do. I like him a lot, in fact," Angela said.

"Well, you happen to be one of the pickiest people I've ever met when it comes to romance. You've never once taken one of my suggestions."

"Hey, I can afford to be picky. Like I said, I'm in no rush."

"That biological clock is ticking, sweetie."

Angela rolled her eyes. "Please."

The door opened with a jingle, interrupting their conversation. Shatika Carson, one of their regulars, walked in.

"Good morning, Tika," Angela said.

"Large mocha for me, Ang. I'm kind of in a hurry."

"Sure thing." Angela got started with the espresso,

and Shelly tapped her on the shoulder on the way back to the backroom.

The bell sounded again as Angela was ringing up Shatika. This time it was Cassidy Henner.

"Good morning, Cassidy," Angela said, her eyes lingering for a moment on Cassidy's face. Dark circles ringed her eyes. She looked gaunt, as if she hadn't eaten for a week. *Maybe she hasn't*, Angela thought.

Cassidy approached the counter as Shatika hurried out the door.

"What can I get for you?" Angela said.

"A large coffee with room for cream," she said. She didn't make eye contact with her. Angela thought of mentioning what had happened, but thought better of it.

Angela poured a cup of medium roast coffee into a large cup and saved room at the top. Cassidy took her cup to the condiments counter for half and half as Angela ran her credit card.

"Thank you," Cassidy said, keeping her eyes down as she took her receipt. She walked out, coffee cup in hand.

Angela's heart ached for Cassidy. She couldn't imagine the horror of being raped, much less the humiliation of returning to regular life afterward as if nothing had happened. Angela wished there were some way to communicate to Cassidy that she knew, and that she was on her side, but she was sure it wasn't her place to do so. Was it?

Angela wondered if Detective Winston had discovered anything yet. She hadn't seen the nameless brown-haired man since the day of Cassidy's rape. If he came in again, she would ask for his name. And she hoped she wouldn't be wielding anything sharp just then. *No vigilante justice, Angela.*

The bell over the door rang again and two regular customers walked in. Angela didn't have a chance to think about Cassidy or her rapist for the next couple of hours because Phoenix was inundated with customers. By the time a lull came in the morning rush, Angela had put the subject out of her mind.

The brown-haired man didn't show up for the rest of that week. Cassidy came in a couple more times, looking just as withdrawn the latter two times as the first time — but at least she was coming in.

Angela saw Ron twice in class — first in Professor McNear's class, and then in Dr. Moore's class. Angela admired the clear, assertive way he answered and posed questions in class. He was sure of himself in a tempered way, without the air of arrogance that Jessica Lyle exuded. The more she thought about him, the more she thought he was a good fit for her. And she certainly felt attracted to him. Her stomach had butterflies at the thought of him.

"What are you thinking about, Ang?" he asked her in a whisper at the end of Dr. Moore's class.

"I'm thinking about how much I'd like to take you out for Mediterranean food," she whispered back. No reason for her to wait to ask him out — she was as self-assured as he was. His eyebrows shot up in surprise.

"Well, I wouldn't want to disappoint you. How's a week from Saturday night look for you?"

"It looks like I have a dinner-date that night." She

grinned. His eyes twinkled.

"Seven o'clock?" he said.

"The Mad Greek?" she said.

"Sounds good," he said. He waved goodbye, and she gathered up her things, happy at this turn of events.

By Friday morning, the recent snows had melted, leaving two yards full of overgrown grass. Angela went out in the cold to her garage where she got out her non-powered push mower. She went up and down the small front yard first, going over it twice to get all the grass. Once with her mower was never enough, but it made for a good workout. She moved to the back when she was done with the front. Her heart rate was up; she breathed hard as she made her way down the yard.

Her phone rang in her pocket, and she stopped to pick it up. It was an unfamiliar number.

"Hello, this is Angela," she said.

"Hi, Angela. Joseph Warner," the voice on the other end responded.

Angela let the handle of the mower rest against her side. "Funny, I thought I plugged your number into my phone, but your name didn't come up."

"Oh, I'm calling you from one of the seminary phones, not my cell phone," he said.

"I see."

"You sound out of breath. Are you okay?"

"Just mowing the lawn. The snow melted and left my yards looking like the jungle."

Joseph chuckled. "Well, I wanted to let you know

that I spoke to my rector and he gave me permission to share Thanksgiving dinner with you."

"Wonderful! I'm looking forward to it."

"So am I. Is there anything I can bring?"

"Just yourself. I have the whole menu planned out."

"Okay. If you're sure."

"I'm sure."

"I'll see you next Thursday then. What time should I arrive?"

"How about five o'clock?"

"You've got it. See you then. Take care, Angela."

"Bye, Joseph."

"Bye."

Angela put her phone back in her pocket and began to push her mower again. Thoughts of Thanksgiving weighed on her mind, and she thought of her parents. She stopped, pulled out her phone again, and dialed her parents' home number. Her dad picked up on the second ring.

"Hi, sweetheart."

"Hi, Daddy. How are you?"

"I'm doing fine. I've been tired lately—still haven't fully recovered from surgery, I don't think."

"Have the doctors given you any more news?"

"I'm supposed to go in Monday for tests. They should be able to tell me by Thanksgiving whether the cancer is all gone."

"I'm praying for you, Daddy."

"I know you are. And I appreciate it."

Angela's face flushed with pleasure at his affirmation and sadness at his predicament. "How's

Mom?" she asked.

"She's keeping on. She's upset that you're not coming to Thanksgiving."

"Are you upset?"

"I'd be happier if you were coming, but I understand," he said.

"Well, about Thanksgiving — I thought I'd make it up to you by taking you two to lunch some weekend in December. What do you think?"

"Let me check in with your mother and see what she thinks, okay?"

Angela shivered as a gust of wind blew against her body. "Sure thing, Daddy."

"I love you, sweetheart."

"I love you, too. Bye, Daddy."

"Bye."

She put her phone back in her pocket for the second time, then raised her hands to her face to warm her cheeks. The thought that her parents might say no to meeting with her hadn't crossed her mind. Angela grasped the handles of the mower again and pushed. If the choice was between allowing her mother to mold her into someone she wasn't or not seeing her parents, she would choose the latter. She couldn't, wouldn't, live a lie — not for her mother, and not even for her father.

By Tuesday it was snowing again. When she got home from work, Angela kicked the snow off her shoes before walking in the front door. Cleveland would be in for a white Thanksgiving at this rate. Angela went to the kitchen, made herself a peanut butter sandwich, and took it and a glass of water up to her room.

Angela looked at the time on her computer's clock. She owed Professor McNear a research paper that she hadn't quite finished. She also had to get ready for Thanksgiving, but she would do all her shopping tomorrow after work. Phoenix was closed for Thanksgiving and classes were canceled that day at CSU, so she'd have all day Thursday to prepare for dinner. She would work on finalizing her contest proposal after Thanksgiving.

Armed with a mental priority list for the next few days, Angela opened her file for her class paper and got to work.

Chapter 13

On Thanksgiving morning, plump snowflakes fell lazily to the ground. Angela stood at her kitchen window and watched the snow fall with both hands cupped around a mug of coffee. *Today will be a good day*, she thought.

The night before, Angela had put a ten-pound turkey in a cooler in the garage to brine. She had also put together the ingredients for the cheesy potato casserole and put the casserole dish in the fridge to chill overnight. Bread dough, which she'd started from scratch with yeast, sugar, flour, and salt, was rising for the second time in the oven. Now she could get started on the rest of the preparations.

She removed the Pyrex container of bread dough from the oven and turned on the oven to preheat. Then she began mixing together the ingredients for the pie crust. When that was done, she pulled out her rolling pin and rolled the pin back and forth across the dough, flattening it. When the dough was thin and even, she grabbed a pie plate from the drawer beneath her oven. She folded the dough into quarters before picking it up and laying it on top of the pie plate. Then she unfolded the dough and carefully cut off the excess around the edges. She crimped the dough with a fork.

Next, she emptied a can of pumpkin puree into a

bowl and mixed in sugar, evaporated milk, eggs, a pinch of salt, ground cinnamon, ground ginger, and ground cloves. Once that was mixed, she poured the filling into the pie crust and put the pie in the oven to bake.

Angela grabbed her jacket from the living room couch and headed outside to check on the turkey. Ice was still floating inside the cooler alongside sliced oranges and lemons, bay leaves, and a variety of spices, so she shut the cooler lid and left the turkey to continue brining.

She didn't need to make the cranberry sauce or the stuffing until later, so with one last peek at the pie in the oven, she took off her apron and headed up to her desk to print the script for the table blessing. She pulled two sheets of buff-colored card stock out of her desk drawer and inserted them in the paper tray of her printer. The two sheets were warm when they came out of the printer. Angela examined them. They were printed in her favorite font, Metamorphous, which reminded her of cavernous medieval cathedrals.

Angela took the two sheets downstairs with her and got the table ready. Most of the food items would go on her sienna table runner. On top of the table runner she put two crystal taper holders with beeswax tapers. She set the table with two large plates, two small plates, wine and water glasses, and stainless steel knives, forks, and spoons. She placed the copies of the table blessing on top of the large plates and stepped back to examine her work. *Nice.*

The timer in the kitchen went off, and Angela took the pie out of the oven and put the bread pan in the oven. Out her window, she could see the neighbor kids playing in the snow, so she set the timer for the bread, took off her apron, put on her jacket, and went outside.

"Hey, guys," she said.

"Hey, Angela!" they cried. A snowball hit her square in the chest. DeShawn giggled. Angela bent down, patted a snowball together, and lobbed it under-handed at DeShawn. The snowball hit his stomach and fell apart. Soon snowballs were flying in every direction, with shrieks of laughter to accompany them.

"Okay, okay, I'll be right back—I need to take some bread out of the oven," Angela said, holding up her hands in surrender.

When Angela returned, the kids were rolling three big balls for a snowman.

"Want some help?" She jogged over to Desiree and helped her push the largest of the snowballs through the wet snow. When it was big enough, she and Desiree helped the DeShawn and Jamal transfer their snowballs onto the biggest snowball, forming a three-tiered snowman.

"What should we put on him?" DeShawn asked.

"I think I have some charcoal and a carrot, if you want," Angela said.

"Can I go get them with you?" DeShawn asked.

"Sure, buddy." She and DeShawn walked to Angela's garage for charcoal, which she piled into his arms. Then Angela ran inside to grab a carrot. DeShawn and Desiree were putting the coals on the snowman when she arrived, carrot in hand.

"Jamal, do you want to put the carrot nose on?" Angela said. Jamal nodded shyly, and Angela picked him up so he could place the nose in the middle of the top snowball.

"What's going on out here?" Mama Sharon called out, appearing at the front door.

"Look, Granny, we're building a snowman!" DeShawn shouted.

"I see that. Looks like you picked up a helper along the way. How you doing, Angela?" Mama Sharon nodded at her.

"I'm having a grand old time with these three youngsters, Mama Sharon."

"I'm not a youngster," Desiree protested.

"Oh—my apologies. I'm having a grand old time with these two youngsters and this young lady, Mama Sharon."

Desiree gave a toothy grin, which Angela promptly returned.

"Are you going home for Thanksgiving, sugar?" Mama Sharon said.

"I am home for Thanksgiving," Angela said, gesturing toward her house.

"What about your mama and daddy?"

"They're doing their usual thing at their house. I thought I'd try something a little different this year."

"Child, you should join us instead of doing Thanksgiving in that big old house all by yourself."

"Thank you, Mama Sharon. I actually have a guest coming, so I won't be alone." Angela smiled up at her neighbor. Mama Sharon shook her head.

"All right then," she said. "Okay, kids, come on

inside and dry off and I'll give you a Thanksgiving treat before dinner."

All three kids clambered up the stairs to the front porch.

"Take off your boots before you come inside!" Mama Sharon said.

Angela laughed and began to move toward her house, but then she stopped. "Mama Sharon?" she called.

"Yes, sugar?"

"I'm thankful for you and your family."

Mama Sharon's face melted from seriousness into a generous smile.

"We're thankful for you, too, sugar."

Angela blew her a kiss and walked around to her garage to fetch her turkey.

At 4:45, Angela took the turkey out of the oven and set it on the counter to rest. On the table, the runner was covered with food. The homemade cranberry sauce was ready in a bowl from Angela's tableware set. The bread was on a wooden cutting board next to a small tray of softened better. The cheesy potato casserole was cooling off in its Pyrex dish on top of a trivet. The pie was in the kitchen; Angela would bring it out when it was time for dessert. She headed upstairs to change clothes.

At five o'clock sharp, the doorbell rang. Angela had just finished applying makeup and was brushing her long hair. She set the brush down and walked down the hall to open the door. Joseph stood before her, wearing a crimson sweater and beige slacks and carrying a pot of marigolds.

"This is a new look," she joked. He smiled as he offered her the flowers.

"I don't wear my cassock everywhere—just most places," he said.

Angela took the flowers. "These are lovely. Thank you."

"You're welcome." Joseph stepped in and looked around. "You have a lovely home."

"Here, let me show it to you," she said. She set the flowers on the sideboard in her dining room and ushered him into the kitchen, where he sniffed appreciatively at the aromas that greeted him there. She took him to her library, which made his eyes round with wonder. She also showed him the other bedroom featuring her wall of photographs.

"The upstairs is my office-slash-bedroom, and the basement is just a basement," she said. "But I saved the best for last." Angela walked to the door of her front closet and waited a moment before opening it. When she pulled the door open, Joseph's jaw dropped.

"May I?" he asked.

"Of course."

He entered the closet and lowered himself onto a pillow. He closed his eyes and breathed deeply. "This room smells like prayer—just like a church."

"This is my church," she said. "My church for one. I pray here twice a day and do my own liturgy on Sunday mornings and some holidays."

Joseph looked around the room and got up. "This is a wonderful space. Thank you for sharing it with me." He touched her shoulder as he walked out. His hand felt warm and secure. She smiled to herself, grateful for the presence of this kind person in her home.

"Everything's ready except the turkey, which I just need to put on the table," she told him. Angela hurried into the kitchen and eyed the turkey before transferring it carefully onto a large white platter. She spooned the remaining stuffing onto the platter and carried it into the dining room, where Joseph was standing behind a chair.

"Please, sit down," she invited him. He pulled out his chair and sat as she laid the platter in between the two tapers. She went to the kitchen to grab the carving knife and grill fork and laid them next to the turkey. The matches for the tapers were in her prayer closet, so she went to fetch them and lit the candles.

"There, I think we're ready. Your copy of the table blessing is in front of you. I'll start, and you can chime in where the text is bold."

Joseph nodded and picked up his copy of the table blessing. Angela closed her eyes and began to sing.

"Bless Thea, my flesh, and bless her holy name. Bless Thea, my flesh, who leads me into life." She started softly and crescendoed gradually. Joseph joined her after she had sung through the lilting melody twice. His tenor voice followed her alto voice in bright confidence. Their voices blended and rose together. After several minutes, Angela began her decrescendo and Joseph followed suit, softening the words with each repetition. Angela held the final repetition in a ritard, signaling the end of the singing;

Joseph held the final note with her.

"The eyes of all wait upon you, Thea," Angela said.

"And you give them their food in due season," Joseph replied.

"You open your hand and satisfy the desires of every living thing," Angela said.

"Thea is righteous in all her ways and faithful in all she does." Joseph replied.

Together they said, "My mouth will speak in praise of Thea. Let every creature praise her holy name, forever and ever."

Angela lifted her hands in the *orans* prayer position and said, "Thea, bless us and this food, the fruit of your creation. We offer you our earnest thanks, and we remember those who go without enough to eat this night. Nourish our bodies, that we might have the strength to nourish others."

"Amen," they said in unison. The silence hung around them for a long moment.

"Now I invite you to share what it is you're thankful for," Angela said, setting aside her copy of the table blessing.

"Let me see," Joseph said, setting his copy of the table blessing on the table next to him and resting his hands in his lap. "I'm thankful for the hospitality you've shown me. I'm also thankful for my many brothers in Christ at seminary for their companionship."

Angela wondered what his fellow seminarians were like. It was her turn to express thanks, however, so she had to put her wondering on hold.

"I'm thankful to be celebrating Thanksgiving in my own home for the first time, and I'm thankful for kind, accepting company at my dinner table. I'm also thankful for my dear friends, my coworkers, my professors, my fellow students, and my neighbors." She had a lot to be thankful for, she realized.

"My best friend and I have a toasting custom," Angela said. She stood, uncorked the wine, and poured two even glasses of pinot noir, which she had opened just before she took the turkey out of the oven so it would have time to breathe.

She set the bottle to her left and raised her glass.

"To life, love, and laughter," she said.

"To life, love, and laughter," Joseph said. They clinked glasses, and they each took a sip of the red wine. Light, fruity flavors crossed Angela's palate. She looked at Joseph for his assessment of the wine.

"Delicious," he said.

"Oh—I forgot the water. Hang on a moment." Angela walked quickly into the kitchen and rummaged around for a water pitcher. She had one around here somewhere. There—in one of the bottom cupboards. She pulled a full ice tray out of the freezer and emptied it in the pitcher, then filled the pitcher with filtered water from her fridge.

"Here we go," she said, returning to the table with the pitcher. "Help yourself."

"Thank you," he said. Joseph took the pitcher from her and poured himself a glass of water.

As he was pouring, Angela picked up the carving knife and grill fork. "This is my first time carving a turkey, so consider yourself forewarned," she said.

Joseph smiled. She made her first cut along one of the breasts of the turkey with a swift, sure motion. She offered the first cut to Joseph, and he held up his plate for her. She cut a piece for herself next and place it on her plate. Angela sat down and dished some cheesy potato casserole onto her plate. Joseph picked up the bread knife and cut a thick slice from the loaf.

"Is this homemade bread?" he asked as he returned the bread knife to the table.

Angela nodded. "It's my father's mother's recipe. Well, technically, the recipe was passed on to my father's father first, in a dream." Angela told him the story Grampy Bridges had told her about the divinely inspired bread recipe. "It's the same recipe I use for Eucharistic bread," she said.

Joseph took a bite. "It's delicious."

Angela smiled and spooned cranberry sauce onto her plate. She passed the cranberry sauce to Joseph and then slid the bread toward her, cutting a slice for herself.

When her plate was full, Angela took a long sip of wine. Then she cut off a small piece of turkey with her knife and fork and put it in her mouth. Spices and citrus tang accompanied the juicy turkey. Her brine had done the job.

"Wow, this turkey is amazing," Joseph said. "How did you make it?"

"The trick is to get a non-brined turkey and then brine it yourself," she said, taking another sip of wine. She tried the cheesy potato casserole next. The blend of cheddar, sour cream, and potato was one of her favorites, and it tasted as good as ever.

Joseph continued to comment on the tastiness of each dish until he had tried every one. After another bite of turkey, he held his napkin to his mouth and wiped his lips. "So this is your first Thanksgiving in your home?"

Angela looked up from her forkful of turkey. "Yes. For years I went to my parents' house for the holidays, but last Easter was my first major holiday at home. Last Thanksgiving didn't go all that well, and Christmas was even worse."

"What happened last Thanksgiving?"

Angela thought back. "I arrived as usual with a pumpkin pie, and we all bustled into my parents' car to go to their church."

"You and your parents?"

"Yes. My grandmother always joined us for Thanksgiving, but she never joined us for the Thanksgiving liturgy. She has no attachment to the Missouri Synod. My mom was actually a convert to the church—she joined after she met my dad."

"Converts tend to be more zealous than their counterparts."

"Funny that you should use that word. Mom would always talk about having good zeal."

"So what happened last Thanksgiving?"

"Oh, the usual. We went to church, and I felt simultaneously uncomfortable and nostalgic. Then we got back to their house, and the Thanksgiving dinner conversation turned to religion. My mother started in on my grandmother, and they bantered back and forth.

"My grandmother took it all gracefully. My

mother, on the other hand, looked like she was keeping her cool for a while, but she was really just building up steam. She exploded at my grandmother for her 'unconventional' faith life. She accused my grandmother of leading her granddaughter astray with her unorthodox ideas. It was all I could do to sit there and say nothing."

"Sounds like your mother has some strong feelings about faith. What happened at Christmas?"

"I joined them for their Christmas service and had a panic attack. I spent the rest of the day on edge, and by the end of the day I was determined never to go back to my old church—or my parents' house—for the holidays." Angela sipped her wine, then speared a cranberry with her fork.

"Tell me more about how you came to worship God as Thea," he said.

Angela met his curious, kind gaze.

"It's a long story," she said finally.

"I've got time," he said, holding his wine glass to his lips.

Angela put down her fork and sipped her wine. "Well, I've already told you why I left the Missouri Synod, so perhaps I should start with my grandmother, my mother's mother. My grandmother and my mother couldn't be more different, as you can imagine by now." She talked at length about Grandma Caroline introducing her to Thea when she was eleven, and about the emotional estrangement between Grandma Caroline and her mother. "It's hard to believe that someone as straight and narrow as my mother could have been raised by someone as forward-thinking as my grandmother. I think my mom took after my grandfather, though." She got up to fetch her prayer book. She felt a little dizzy as she stood, so she paused before heading to the prayer closet. When she returned to the table, she showed the book to Joseph, explaining to him that Grandma Caroline had written it for her.

"So Thea was your Grandma Caroline's idea?" he asked after several minutes of reading through the pages of her prayer book.

"Yes," she said after a sip of wine, "although Thea is more than just an idea to either me or my grandmother. Thea is who I imagine God to be.

"God has many names," Joseph said, closing the prayer book and handing it across the table to Angela.

"So she does," Angela said, taking the book. "I figure that God transcends all the images we could ever have of her, so it's no harm imagining God for oneself."

"Apart from the feminine language you use for God, your faith still seems to be very much steeped in Christian tradition," he commented.

"It is. I pray regularly with a Bible—I just change all the pronouns." Angela smiled tentatively at Joseph, and he smiled warmly back at her.

"I hope you don't think I'm prying too much," he said. "Your faith is so original and traditional at the same time. I'm in awe of you."

Angela smiled. "Even though I'm a heretic?"

"I don't think you're a heretic."

"Your church might have a thing or two to say about that."

As she took another sip from her wine glass, Angela felt dizzy again. The room began to spin. She put down the glass and put her head in her hands.

"What's wrong?" Joseph said, concerned.

"I don't know. I feel dizzy," she said. She reached for her water, but it blurred in her vision. *What's happening?*

"Can I help you?" Joseph said. He was standing beside her now.

"Maybe I should lay down," she said, pointing in the direction of the couch.

He helped her to her feet and put an arm around her shoulder to steady her. They crossed the room. Just before they reached the couch, she turned toward him, saw his concerned look, and slumped in his arms.

Chapter 14

Angela opened her eyes. Darkness surrounded her, and her head throbbed. She was laying down. When she tried sitting up, she became dizzy, so she laid down again.

Where am I?

Angela felt around her. The soft fabric of her bedspread met her fingers. *Why am I in bed?*

Angela tried to remember what had happened. She'd been having Thanksgiving dinner with Joseph. They'd been talking, and then… what?

She turned slowly and reached for the lamp on her bedside table. She switched it on. The light hit her body and cast a large shadow across the opposite corner of her room. *Where is Joseph?*

Gingerly, she pulled herself into a sitting position. Her abdomen was sore. *Did I eat something bad?*

She placed one foot, then the other, on the floor. A wave of nausea hit her, and she put her head down. Half a minute later, the wave passed, and she sat up again. Now she stood and shuffled, very slowly, across the room to the stairs. She descended the staircase and went into the hallway.

The whole house was dark except for the light she had turned on upstairs. She walked in the direction of the wall dimmer in the dining room and turned it clockwise. Light illuminated the now empty table.

"Joseph?" she called.

No answer. She checked the kitchen, and then the back bedrooms, but they were empty. She went to the stairwell to the basement and called Joseph's name, but there was no reply.

He was gone.

Why am I so sore?

Angela put a hand on her stomach and grimaced. But this wasn't a regular stomachache. The pain was lower, like cramps before her period.

But it's not time for my period.

Angela's mouth opened as realization slowly dawned on her. *No.*

No, no, no.

Disbelief crowded her brain. Stunned, she walked step by step to the bathroom. She removed her pants. She removed her underwear. They were spotted with blood.

It's not *time for my period.*

Mechanically, she put her underwear and pants back on. Tears stung her face. She looked in the mirror.

I trusted him.

The truth confronted her in her mirror image, and she screamed with anguish.

Half an hour later, Angela pulled into the parking lot of the Cleveland Clinic. She got out and walked slowly, awkwardly, to the doors to the emergency room. She walked in, and the blaring lights made her squint.

She approached the registration desk.

"May I help you?" The attendant, whose nametag read "Martha," looked up at her.

Angela leaned forward and spoke in little more than a whisper. "I've been raped."

Martha's eyes flashed. "You need a rape kit," she said. It wasn't a question. Angela nodded. More tears threatened, but she held them back.

Martha handed her a clipboard. "Fill out this information and bring it back to me, and we'll get you in here as soon as possible."

Angela took the clipboard and sat gently on a chair. Her abdomen screamed at her. She looked at the paper in front of her. The lines blurred. She blinked, and realized the tears had come again. She wiped her eyes with the back of her right hand and picked up the pen with her left. She began to write.

A few minutes later, Angela took the clipboard back to Martha.

"It'll just be a minute, okay? Why don't you come on back and wait for the nurse?"

Angela obeyed wordlessly. Martha took her through a door in the registration room to a smaller room with filing cabinets and two chairs. Angela sat.

"Would you like some water?" Martha asked.

Angela shook her head.

"It'll just be a minute, okay, sweetie?"

Angela nodded as she stared at her feet. Her eyes were still fixed there when someone came into the room.

"Angela Bridges?" a low female voice said.

Angela nodded again, still staring at her feet.

"Angela, I'm so sorry. Come with me, okay?"

When Angela looked up, she saw a short, thirty-something black woman with straight hair pulled back in a tight bun. Her name tag read "Joyce."

Joyce led her to a curtained partition in the emergency room.

"Have you ever had a rape kit before?"

Angela shook her head and sniffed to keep her nose from dripping.

"Well, the first thing you need to know is that we'll only do as much as you're willing to do. The goal of the rape kit is to collect samples of tissue and fluids in order to gather evidence against your rapist. The more you let me collect, the stronger your case will be — but you have the right to say no to anything that feels uncomfortable to you. Okay?"

Angela nodded, her eyes glued to the ground.

"The first thing I'd like you to do, if you're willing, is put on this gown." Joyce handed her a heavy cloth hospital gown. Angela took it with trembling hands.

"I'll be back in a couple of minutes, okay? Take your time."

Angela undressed and carefully folded her clothes into a pile. She was grateful there was no mirror; she couldn't face herself. She slipped the hospital gown on and reached behind her to tie the strings, but suddenly she felt trapped, like she was pinned against a rock and couldn't breathe. She left the gown open at the back and sat down on the hospital bed. Joyce returned a minute later.

"Okay, Angela, I'm going to talk you through the process. Take as much time as you need to answer my questions. Are those the clothes you were wearing before the rape occurred?"

Angela looked dully at her neat pile of clothes. "Yes."

"With your permission, I'd like to take these clothes as evidence. We have spare clothes you can wear home. Is that okay?"

Angela blinked tears. "Yes."

"Okay. The next steps are critical for gathering evidence. With your permission, I'm going to draw a blood sample. Is that okay?"

Angela nodded.

"Thank you. The next step will be for the on-duty doctor to perform a pelvic exam and swab you for fluid and tissue traces. This will involve inserting a speculum into your vagina, just like you were receiving a PAP smear. Is that okay?"

Angela's body shook as she imagined being probed with a foreign object. *He violated me!* she screamed inwardly. Outwardly, she answered with a shaky "Yes."

"Thank you, Angela. I'll be right here with you when the doctor examines you, okay?"

Angela nodded.

"Sit tight and I'll be back shortly, okay?"

Angela sat and waited. Joyce returned with a hypodermic needle attached to a test tube. She wrapped up Angela's arm in a tourniquet, told her to squeeze her fist, found a vein, and inserted the needle. Angela flinched. After a minute, the test tube was full, and she withdrew the needle. Joyce left again, and after what seemed like an eternity, Joyce re-entered the partition with a doctor in scrubs. Angela stared at the doctor's shoes

"Hello, Angela, I'm Dr. Oakley. I'm so sorry about your experience."

Angela's heart raced. *A male doctor?*

"Angela," Joyce said soothingly, "I've worked with Dr. Oakley many times. He's safe. He won't hurt you. Okay?"

Joyce extended her hand and Angela gripped it, squeezing hard. Nevertheless, Angela hesitated when Dr. Oakley asked her to lay down. Putting her feet in the stirrups sent waves of rage and humiliation rushing over her. When Dr. Oakley inserted the speculum, she began to sob violently. Anger, regret, and shame poured out of her eyes and down her flushed face. Joyce stood next to her, still holding her hand.

"Okay, that part's all done," Dr. Oakley said as he withdrew the speculum. Angela flinched at the sensation of the metal sliding out of her.

"I'm done. I want to leave," Angela said.

Dr. Oakley looked at Joyce as he removed his gloves; Joyce looked at Angela. "We've got a lot to go on here, Angela. Thank you so much for letting us go through these procedures. I know you've been through hell, and this is part of that."

Angela looked up at her. "Yes."

"I'm going to bring in some clothes for you. Are you about a size eight? Ten?"

"Ten."

"What about your bra size?"

"C."

"Okay, I'll be right back," Joyce said. She slipped

behind the curtain, and Angela watched her white shoes pad away. Angela put her arms around herself and held on tight, willing the pain to go away.

"Here you are," Joyce said a couple of minutes later, sliding the curtain aside. She handed a stack of clothes to Angela: jeans, a long-sleeved green turtleneck, underwear, and a size C bra.

"I brought you a pad to wear, too," she said, handing her a thick, plastic-covered sanitary pad.

"Okay."

"I'm going to be right down at the end where the nurse's station is, okay? Come find me when you're ready and I'll walk you out."

Angela looked at the floor without answering. Joyce exited the partition. Slowly, she slid on the underwear and inserted the pad; then she pulled on the jeans. She tried to put on the bra, but felt the same panic she'd had when she tried to tie the laces of the hospital gown, so she left the bra aside and pulled on the green turtleneck. She wiped her eyes with the back of her hand and walked out, looking down the wide corridor to the nurse's station. Joyce was sitting at the desk, so she walked toward her. Joyce heard her shuffling across the floor and got up to join her.

"The exit is this way, Angela," Joyce said, moving toward a pair of double-doors. Joyce held one of the doors open as Angela walked through.

"Have you been in touch with the police yet, Angela?"

Angela looked at Joyce, wide-eyed. "I haven't gotten that far yet."

"Do you want a phone number of someone to

call?"

"Actually, I know someone from the Cleveland PD who investigates rapes. I'll call him."

"Are you okay to drive?"

"I got myself here," she said. She turned to walk toward the exit.

"Angela."

Angela turned.

"I'm sorry."

Angela turned back again and headed out the automatic door, tears running down her face.

When she reached her car, it was nearly 1:00am. Angela pulled Detective Winston's number out of her wallet and dialed his number with a shaky hand. He answered after the third ring in a groggy voice.

"Detective Winston."

"Detective Winston, this is Angela Bridges from Phoenix Coffee. You came in and asked me questions regarding Cassidy Henner's case."

"Hello, Angela. How may I help you at this late hour?"

Angela swallowed and took a deep breath. "I was raped tonight."

"You were raped?"

"By one of the men who was at Phoenix Coffee the day Cassidy was raped."

Angela heard a scratching noise in her ear. It sounded like he was sitting up. "Can you meet me at the police department in half an hour? It's at 1300 Ontario Street."

"I know where that is."

"See you soon, Angela."

It took Angela less than fifteen minutes to arrive at the police station. She parked in front of the large drab building. Long horizontal windows stretched across each story of the building like a hundred eyes, as if Orwell's Big Brother were on the watch. The street was deserted except for police cruisers. She got out, double-checked to make sure her doors were locked, and went to the door.

The door was locked, and there was no one sitting at the reception desk inside. Angela would have to wait. She returned to Felicity and climbed in, rubbing her arms for warmth. Time ticked by slowly, and the horror of waking up replayed itself in her mind over and over, drumming in her mind with a loud, terrible beat. Eventually a dark Chevy Impala pulled up, flipped a U-turn, and parked behind her. Detective Winston got out of the car. Angela did the same.

"Detective Winston," she said, shutting her door and locking it.

"Ms. Bridges," he said formally, extending a hand. She didn't take it, and he dropped it at his side.

"We're going to head up to an interview room so we can talk, okay?"

"Okay."

Detective Winston held a card up to a scanner at the door and the door unlocked. Detective Winston held the door open for Angela and she walked inside. The hallway was brightly lit. Plaques shone on the walls as they made their way to the elevator. They rode up in silence.

"Right this way," he said, as the doors slid open.

He took her down a hallway past some cubicles where a number of detectives were at work. He led her into a windowless room with white walls, a particle-board table with a dark finish, and three chairs. She sat down in the chair to the left of the table.

"Would you like some coffee?" he said.

"No, thank you."

Detective Winston took one of the chairs on the right.

"In your own words, please tell me what happened tonight."

Angela looked him over. Detective Winston of all people could make this situation right if she told him everything. *So I'll tell him everything.*

Tears threatened again. Angela spoke anyway. "I was raped by Joseph Warner, a Roman Catholic seminarian in the Diocese of Cleveland.

"He came over for Thanksgiving dinner. We had wine, and after pouring the wine I went to the kitchen to fill a jug of ice water. He must have spiked my wine with a drug while I was in the kitchen, because twenty minutes or so later, I felt dizzy, and I passed out. I woke up in my own bed on the second floor, and my abdomen was sore. I discovered blood spots in my underwear when I went to the bathroom, but I just had my period two weeks ago."

Detective Winston leaned back. "So you don't remember him raping you?"

"No, I was passed out."

"And you were sore afterward?"

"Yes. It felt like menstrual cramps, but again, it's not time for my period."

"What did you do after you discovered the blood spots in your underwear?"

"I drove myself to the emergency room at the Cleveland Clinic and they collected a rape kit."

Detective Winston scribbled a note on his notepad.

"Then what happened?"

"I called you from my car, and drove here to meet you."

Detective Winston scribbled something else on his notepad and looked up.

"Let's recap. You were having Thanksgiving dinner with Joseph Warner. Was there anyone else at the dinner?"

"No, just the two of us."

"And you say you felt dizzy after about twenty minutes and passed out? What room were you in?"

"Joseph was helping me get to the couch in my living room. I blacked out before I reached the couch."

"And you woke up in your bed in your bedroom?"

"Yes, on the second floor."

"Were you clothed?"

"Yes, I was wearing the same clothes I'd had on for dinner. They took my clothes as evidence for the rape kit," she added.

"What is the nature of your relationship with Mr. Warner?"

"I met him at the library a few weeks ago. We're both entering the same urban development contest. He happened to come by to Phoenix Coffee to pick up coffee for him and his bishop, and I saw him at Phoenix several times after that. He offered me his business card and said if I ever wanted to talk about religion, I could call him."

"So you called him?"

"Yes, I called him, and we talked, and I found out that his parents are both dead and he had nowhere to go for Thanksgiving, so I invited him to my house, since I was already planning to make dinner for myself."

"And he accepted?"

"He said he'd ask his rector for permission and let me know. He called me back a few days later to say his rector had given him permission."

"What time did Mr. Warner arrive at your house for Thanksgiving dinner?"

"Right around five o'clock."

"Did he do or say anything suspicious?"

"No, nothing at all. We were having a pleasant time."

"Now you said that Joseph Warner was one of the ones who was at Phoenix the day of Cassidy Henner's rape, is that correct?"

"Yes. I remember telling you about him specifically because he had come by that day to let me borrow a book that he had checked out from the library."

"And what was that book again?"

"*Ghosts of Cleveland.*"

Detective Winston wrote something on his notepad and put down his pen. He looked at her, but she couldn't read his face.

"Please tell me about your sexual history, Ms. Bridges."

Angela flushed. "I have none."

"You've never made sexual contact with anyone before?"

"Not before tonight." Angela put her hands over her face. Her hands grew wet as they caught her tears.

"Thank you for this information, Angela."

Angela waited for him to say something more. When he didn't, she did. "Are you going to be able to do anything about it?"

Detective Winston hesitated, and her eyes grew wide.

"Since you don't remember him raping you, we'll have to wait on the rape kit to see if a DNA sample other than your own appears. If there is DNA other than your own, we may have probable cause to get a search warrant for Joseph Warner's DNA."

"And if not?"

"Then we probably won't be able to get a judge to sign a search warrant."

"Can't you call him in for questioning?"

"Yes, we can, but if he really did rape both you and Cassidy, chances are, he's not going to admit anything. Neither you nor Cassidy saw your rapist during the act itself, so the evidence around Mr. Warner is circumstantial."

"Did any useful DNA evidence come back from Cassidy's rape kit?"

"No."

Angela's mouth hung open. *He raped two women and he might get away with it?!*

"Look, Angela, we're going to do everything we can. I'll call you when the results of the rape kit come back. We'll go from there."

Angela nodded numbly.

"Would you like some coffee for the road?"

"I don't think I'll be sleeping tonight no matter what I do," she said. "But thanks anyway."

Angela exited the way she'd come in and went to her car. The wind was blowing off Lake Erie, cold and damp. Angela jumped in Felicity, turned the key in the ignition, and turned the heat up full blast.

When she got home, she stopped before entering her front door. The image of Joseph standing here, right in this spot, offering her flowers, made her tremble with rage. She unlocked the door, picked up the flower pot, and took it outside. She lifted the lid on her garbage can, but hesitated. *Maybe they can collect prints off this*, she thought. Furious at the thought of having this gift in her house any longer, she opened her garage door and set the flowers on the garage floor. *They can rot.* She'd tell Detective Winston about them later.

She returned to her house and went to the kitchen. She looked inside the fridge. Everything was wrapped up and put away. Dishes were stacked up inside the dishwasher, and they were already clean. Angela felt sick. *He raped me and then did the dishes?*

Angela couldn't bear to return to her bed, and there was no way she would sleep on the couch, so she went to the spare bedroom and unfolded the futon. She lay down and stared into the dark until daybreak, when she finally fell into a fitful sleep.

Chapter 15

Angela spent the next couple of days ignoring her phone, except to see if Detective Winston's name popped up. Bill called several times and her parents called once, but she didn't call them back. She texted Ron to let him know that she wasn't going to be able to meet him at the Mad Greek, after all, and she was sorry, but she'd explain later. Her contest proposal went untouched. She drank water, but ate nothing. For the bulk of Friday, Saturday, and Sunday, she stared at the walls or slept. The door to her prayer closet remained shut, the room unused.

Sunday marked the first day of the liturgical season of Advent, but Angela didn't have the energy or the desire to set up her Advent wreath. On Sunday afternoon, a knock came to her front door. Angela's eyes opened. She was laying on the futon in the spare bedroom. She had been staring at the photos on the wall, but she'd nearly drifted off. The knock came again. She didn't get up.

"Angela?" a voice called through the door. It was Bill. Still, she didn't get up.

"Angela, I can see your car parked in the driveway. You haven't answered any of my calls. Please come to the door."

Angela closed her eyes and hugged a pillow to her chest, squeezing it hard.

A couple of minutes later, the sound of the door unlocking made her eyes fly open. *He knows where the spare key is. Damn.*

Footsteps sounded on her wooden floors. She could hear him checking various rooms, including her bedroom upstairs. At last, he found her in the spare bedroom.

"Angela? Why didn't you answer the door? Is something wrong?"

Angela didn't answer, but stared at Bill's shoes. They were black, well-polished leather.

Bill crouched down. "Hey, what's wrong?" he said, touching her arm. She shrank back.

"Don't touch me," she hissed.

Bill withdrew his hand as if he'd been electrocuted.

"Did something happen with your parents? Is it your dad?"

Angela shook her head.

"Did something happen to you?"

She nodded, trembling.

"Did someone hurt you?"

She nodded again, clutching the pillow hard against her chest.

"Can you tell me what happened?"

Angela paused, then shook her head slowly. Bill sighed. He took a seat on the end of futon, well clear of Angela so he wouldn't touch her.

"Honey, whatever happened, you're safe now. I'm here, and I won't hurt you. Okay?"

Angela nodded. Tears fell freely from her eyes, dripping on the pillow, the futon, and her clothes. She was still wearing the clothes she'd received at the hospital.

"Hey, I saw some bananas in the kitchen. How about if I get you one?"

He stood up without giving her a chance to answer. A minute later, he came back in the room and handed her a peeled banana. She took it, but didn't eat it.

"I'm going to run a bath for you so you can soak in the tub, okay?"

Angela didn't respond. He left and turned on the bathwater. She heard him climb up the stairs to her room. A few minutes later, he returned with a stack of clothes. He took her uneaten banana and gave her the clothes.

"Go get in the bath, honey. You'll feel better. I'll wait in the living room." And he marched off down the hall. Angela looked at the clothes in her hands. He had included jeans, a blue flannel shirt, and white undergarments. Angela blanched at the thought of a man touching the contents of her underwear drawer—even Bill.

She moved into the bathroom, locked the door, and undressed. She felt sticky and ripe from days without a shower. She put one foot in the tub, then the other, and sat down slowly, letting the water envelop her. Her tired, aching muscles relaxed. She wept.

Angela washed her long hair and dived underwater to rinse out the suds. She stayed in the bath till the water was lukewarm. Then she got out, dried off with a thick terry-cloth towel, and looked in the mirror.

She looked like hell. And she was hungry.

As quickly as she could manage, she pulled on her clothes and exited the bathroom toward the living room. Bill stood up from the couch and offered her the banana. She ate it in three bites.

"Can I make you breakfast?"

"Denny's," she said.

Bill and Angela headed out to Bill's car, a black nineties Volvo. He drove them to the Denny's near University Circle, off Bellflower Court on the Case Western Reserve campus. They sat down in a red booth, and a red-haired waitress named Jenny took their order. It wasn't long before Jenny sat a carafe of coffee on the table. Bill poured coffee for each of them and held up his mug.

"Not this time, Bill," she said quietly.

Bill frowned and put his mug to his lips.

"You want to tell me what happened?" he said, after he'd taken a sip from his mug.

"No, I don't want to tell you what happened."

"Are you going to tell me what happened?"

Angela sipped her coffee and set it on the table. She gazed at it, then looked out the window. The trees were bare and the wind was dancing with their branches.

"I had company for Thanksgiving," she said at last.

"Really? Who?"

"Joseph Warner."

"The priest?"

"Future priest."

Bill waited. Angela took a deep breath.

"We had a nice dinner conversation. Everything was going fine. And then I passed out."

"You passed out?"

"I woke up in bed. He was gone. And I was sore."

"Sore?"

"I had blood in my panties."

"Did you get your period?"

"No."

Recognition dawned on his face. His pale face turned red, like a plump tomato.

"Did he…?"

She nodded.

"Did you report it to the police?"

"Yes. And I went to the ER so they could collect evidence."

"Oh, my god, Ang. I'm so sorry."

Bill reached for her hands, then withdrew them.

"Is that why you didn't want me to touch you?"

Tears threatened to spill again. She nodded, clasping her mug tightly in her hands.

He remained silent. She didn't look at him. They sat wordlessly together as thoughts raced through their minds. Jenny interrupted their silence several minutes later.

"Here you go. French toast for the lady and buttermilk pancakes for the gentleman." Jenny placed the main plates and the side plates on the table and asked if they wanted more coffee.

"Yes, thank you," Bill said.

French toast was Angela's favorite dish at Denny's. It was comfort food when nothing else seemed comforting. She took a bite, and the buttery, slightly sweet toast melted in her mouth. She took another bite, and another.

Bill watched her all the while.

"You haven't eaten since Thanksgiving, have you?"

Angela shook her head and took another bite.

"What did the police say?"

Angela took another bite and chewed before swallowing. "Detective Winston said they have to wait for the testing to be done on the rape kit. They need DNA evidence before they can get a judge to sign a search warrant for his DNA."

"Why?"

"Because I didn't actually see him do it."

"Well, that's fucking stupid," he said in a loud voice, spearing a piece of pancake with his fork. Several faces turned toward their table.

"If there's no DNA evidence, it would be pretty useless to ask him for his DNA, wouldn't it?" she said.

"He was the only person in your house besides you when you passed out."

"But so far the only evidence of what happened is how I felt afterward. They could say I was just bloated."

"But you were bleeding, for chrissakes," he said. More faces turned toward them. Angela lowered her right hand toward the table, gesturing for him to lower the volume.

"Are they going to question him?"

"I think so. But he's sly. He had me completely fooled," she said. Her left hand trembled, and she put her fork down.

Bill folded his arms and leaned forward. "Listen, Ang, they're going to get this guy. They've got to."

"There's one thing that might help my case," she said. "I think he may have been the rapist of my customer at Phoenix. Remember me telling you about that? Joseph was there that day, right around the time she was."

Bill let out a low whistle. "A serial rapist? And this guy's going to be a priest?"

"Not if I can help it," she said.

After they'd finished their breakfast, Bill dropped her off at home and asked her if she needed anything.

"I need to erase what happened on Thanksgiving. Can you do that?"

"I don't have that kind of skill. Nor do I know anyone who does." He sounded apologetic.

"This is between you and me, okay?"

"Sure, Ang. You can call me anytime if you want to talk about it, or talk about anything. You know that, right?"

"Yeah, I know. Thanks, Bill."

As she shut the door, though, the weight of her memories settled on her stomach. Angela held her hand to her mouth and ran to the bathroom. She made it to the toilet just in time.

Monday morning, Angela called off work.

"Are you not feeling well?" Shelly said.

"I'm really sick," she said. It wasn't entirely untruthful. The sight of food had made her sick for the rest of the day Sunday. That most of the food in her refrigerator was left over from Thanksgiving might have had something to do with it.

That morning at home, Angela threw out all that remained of the Thanksgiving leftovers. She hauled the heavy trash bag out to the garbage can. As she lifted the door to the garage, she noticed the potted marigolds. She shivered in disgust. She made a note to herself to call Detective Winston about the flowers, put the trash in the garbage can, and closed the garage door.

Detective Winston called her first.

"Hello, Angela?"

"Hello, Detective Winston. Do you have news?"

"Yes. I'm afraid the rape kit didn't come up with any DNA other than your own."

"*What?*"

"I'm sorry, Angela. Consequently, we don't have probable cause to secure a search warrant, much less an arrest warrant. We spoke with him over the weekend, and he insisted on bringing a lawyer, so we got nothing out of him."

So he knows I know.

And he's denying it to the police.

"Angela?"

"I'm still here, Detective."

"Look, Angela, we're going to keep an eye on this guy. I'm afraid our best shot is to wait for him to do it again and hope he messes up."

"Surely there's something more you can do. There's got to be."

"There isn't. We have no solid evidence linking him to either your rape or Cassidy Henner's, and we also have no solid evidence that links the two rapes together. Cassidy wasn't drugged, but you think you were. Neither of you saw your attacker. Cassidy didn't know Joseph Warner, but you did. As far as we know, the two cases could be completely unrelated. There's even less to go on in your case because you don't remember the attack — only the after-effects. The rape kit didn't turn up any evidence of a drug in your system, so we don't even have that to go on.

"He brought me flowers."

"Excuse me?"

"He brought me a pot of flowers. You could probably get his fingerprints off it."

"He's already admitted to being at your house on Thanksgiving, so unfortunately that wouldn't do much good."

Angela's eyes welled up with tears for the umpteenth time since Thanksgiving night.

"Angela, we'll do what we can. I promise."

"Okay," she said meekly.

"Goodbye, Angela."

"Goodbye."

Angela heard the click of Detective Winston's phone as the phone call ended. She put the phone on her couch and walked gingerly up the stairs to her desk, where she composed an e-mail to Dr. Jones, letting her know she would be missing class that night. According to the syllabus for the class, if a student had more than two absences, she would fail the course automatically, and this would be her second absence. But Angela couldn't do this. Not today.

Angela called in sick Tuesday morning as well.

"Do you have the flu?" Shelly asked.

"I don't know. I feel awful," she said. Again, not a complete lie.

"Do you want to take the rest of the week off?" Shelly said.

"I think maybe I should," she said quietly.

"I'll see if I can get some of the other employees to step in for you. Feel better, Angela."

"Thanks, Shell."

She went upstairs to e-mail Professor McNear and Dr. Moore, letting them know that she would be missing class this week. She had assignments due for both her Tuesday and Thursday classes, but she shoved them into a dark compartment in the back of her mind and shut the door. She'd deal with them later.

For now, she bundled up in her coat, gloves, and scarf and headed outside. The air was cold and the sky was overcast, but there was no snow or ice on the streets today. It hadn't snowed since Thanksgiving, and the plows had done their job, moving snow and salting the roads. Now the streets were dry. She got out her bicycle, put on her helmet, hopped on her bike, and went for a ride.

Angela rode through the Hough neighborhood and down into the Cultural Gardens on Martin Luther King Jr. Drive. The gardens were still covered with Thanksgiving's snow. She pedaled hard along the flat, winding road, and images of Joseph flashes through her mind. *How did I fall for it?* she asked herself. She searched her memories for clues of what Joseph was. He was pretty forward when they first met at the library, but she hadn't thought it was unusual. When he came into Phoenix, it had to have been a coincidence, right? Or was it? Had he looked her up somehow? Angela wondered what would turn up if she googled herself. She had no idea. She knew that she wasn't mentioned on the Phoenix website, though. No, it had to be a coincidence. But beyond that?

He had listened to her as she talked about her religious background, and she had fallen for his kindness. Had she been too eager to regard him as sincere? Was she so desperate for approval with regard to her faith that she had missed obvious signs of what was to come?

She wondered if his parents even were dead. She wondered if he had gotten permission from his rector to come to Thanksgiving. *What kind of rector would let a seminarian go by himself to a young woman's home for a holiday dinner?*

Angela's face burned, and not just from the cold. *She* had let this man into her life, and he had taken advantage of her. It happened like clockwork. What made her think that inviting someone she barely knew to Thanksgiving was a good idea?

A thousand of her own accusing questions battered her, and she began to cry. Her tears turned to ice on her face as the chilly air blew past her at twenty miles an hour. She was riding hard and fast. *Time to turn around.*

On the second Sunday of Advent, Angela bought a white pine wreath at Giant Eagle, a local grocery store, and laid it on her dining room table. She set four white tapers around it and lit two of the candles. She couldn't pray yet—not when she felt so extraordinarily abandoned by Thea. But she could light candles.

Advent was her favorite liturgical season—it was the one season that invited joyful anticipation of light being birthed in darkness. In the northern hemisphere, at least, it was a celebration of the return of light. If she had ever experienced a time in her life when she yearned for illumination, it was now.

Thanksgiving Day replayed in her mind over and over again. The weeks leading up to it replayed in her mind as well. She searched her memory for clues to Joseph's true character. He had been pretty bold in coming up to her at the library—but anyone with an extraverted personality might have done that. He followed her to her place of work—but surely that was a coincidence? He couldn't have known where to find her. He didn't even know her last name until he visited Phoenix for the first time. And he had reason to keep returning to Phoenix. He had appointments with his bishop. Right?

Angela realized that all of it might have been a lie. Maybe it was a coincidence that they met at Phoenix, but his return trips may very well have been calculated, especially if he had raped Cassidy. He must have known Cassidy's schedule, if he was her rapist.

Then there was the phonecall when he told her his parents had died. Would she have invited him to Thanksgiving if he hadn't made it sound as though he had no place to go? Probably not. He might have lied about his parents to encourage an invitation—but how could he have known she would ask?

Maybe he assumed I was desperate.

Had she been desperate? She thought she was being generous. But she had sought his companionship when she realized he wasn't going to judge her for her religious propensities. She had wanted him in her life—and he sensed that. She invited him into her life, and he accepted the invitation.

Maybe he thought he deserved me.

Bile rose in her throat. She had to get her mind off what had happened, off *him*, but her memories screeched like fingernails across a blackboard, demanding attention. She wondered despairingly if there would ever be a day when he wasn't the first thing she thought of in the morning and the last thing she thought of at night. She hated him. And she had never hated anyone—not even her mother.

"And what about you, Thea?" she said aloud as she paced across her living room Sunday afternoon. "Where were you when I started to trust him? Where were you when he drugged me? Where were you when he *raped me*?"

As usual, Thea responded with silence. She turned on her Tivoli radio and raised the volume till it was deafening. She didn't want to hear Thea's silence. Not now.

Monday morning, the alarm woke Angela, and she didn't ignore it this time. She couldn't avoid work forever. She had bills to pay, and things would be tight now that she had missed a week of work. She got dressed, walked out the door, and hopped in Felicity for the drive to work.

Shelly called her as she was on her way.

"Hey, Shelly," Angela said after she pressed the speaker button.

"Hey, Angela. I'm assuming you're coming in since I didn't hear from you over the weekend."

"Yep, I'm on my way."

"I'm glad you're feeling well enough to work. I've missed you."

"Thanks, Shell. I've missed you, too."

"See you in a bit."

"Okay. Bye."

"Bye."

When Angela reached the front door of Phoenix Coffee, she hesitated. *What if I see him here?*

But she had to work—she wasn't rolling in cash. Even if she got another job, she needed to keep making money in the meantime. *You have to be here,* she told herself.

Shelly came and unlocked the door for her.

"Did you forget your key?"

"No. Just enjoying the autumn air." Angela forced a smile.

"You still feeling sick?" Shelly gave her a questioning look.

"A little. But I'm not contagious, don't worry."

Angela brushed past her and went to put on her apron.

Work passed uneventfully. That afternoon at class, her voice caught in her throat. She didn't answer any questions. Dr. Jones asked her during the break if she was feeling okay.

"I'm a little under the weather," she said.

"I hope you feel better," Dr. Jones said with concern.

"Thanks."

Tuesday passed in much the same way. There were moments at work when things got so busy that Angela didn't have time to think about Joseph. She began to crave those moments. Class wasn't nearly as distracting, and Professor McNear asked how she was doing. *Apparently I talk too much*, she thought as she considered the effect her silence was having on her professors. Ron asked how she was doing, too, but she brushed him off, saying she couldn't talk about it yet. He looked alarmed, but he respected her need for distance.

On Wednesday morning, Angela woke before the alarm. Her sleep had been broken as usual, but she was eager to get to work to get her mind off Joseph. The morning was busy before nine, and then it slowed down. Angela began to feel restless. When she left work, she had the rest of the afternoon and evening to herself. She didn't know how to spend them. She tried reading ahead for next week's classes, but she couldn't concentrate. She had no interest in taking up her contest proposal again. Cooking, which she normally loved, didn't appeal to her at all. Lacking other options, she took herself for a bike ride. She didn't know where she was headed when she set out, but she ended up at University Circle. Once there, she got on Euclid and rode east.

She pedaled for miles and miles. Cleveland turned to East Cleveland; East Cleveland turned to Euclid; Euclid turned to Wickliffe. As the sun sank on the horizon behind her, she suddenly realized where she was going: Borromeo Seminary.

Chapter 16

Angela's feet brushed the sidewalk as she rolled to a stop. Bare trees covered the front lawn of the brick seminary. No one was outside. Angela wondered if the bishop would be there now. What if Joseph was there? Panic crept into her belly, and she wheeled her bike around. *What am I doing here?*

She began to pedal back. She was thirsty, and her muscles were sore. She should have brought a water bottle, but she hadn't thought of it on the way out.

Angela was exhausted and parched by the time she reached her house again. She couldn't leave her bike out unattended out front, so she trudged toward the garage behind the house and opened it, rolling the bike in. Mama Sharon called to her from her back stoop.

"Good evening, Angela!" she called with a wave.

"Good evening, Mama Sharon," she said through labored breath.

"Out for a bike ride?"

"Yep. A long one."

"Where'd you go?"

"Wickliffe."

"On your *bike*?"

Angela walked in the direction of Mama Sharon after she closed the garage door. There was no fence between their yards. Janette's kids often played games using both yards. Angela liked seeing them enjoy themselves.

"I needed to get some energy out," she said.

"You look like you got out all of it," Mama Sharon said, eyeing her critically.

"I suppose I did."

"Would you like some tea? I just put the water kettle on."

"I'd love some."

"Come on in."

Mama Sharon led Angela through the back door through the dining room and into a large, homey kitchen. The walls were pale lavender, the curtains on the windows were white with lace trim, and the counters were white Formica. Off-white tiles covered the floor, and a picture of the Saharan desert at sunrise hung on the wall opposite the windows. Mama Sharon had told her once that it was an African portrait of Easter.

"How was Thanksgiving?" Mama Sharon said, after pouring hot water over a teabag in a mug for her.

Angela didn't know what to say. She didn't want to lie, but she didn't want to tell the whole truth, either.

"It didn't go very well," she said finally.

"Oh, sugar, that's too bad. Was something wrong with the turkey?"

"No. My company turned out to be a turkey."

Mama Sharon looked at Angela with surprise. "I've never heard you talk about anyone quite like that before. What happened?"

Angela shook her head. "I'd rather not talk about

it. It's over and done with."

Mama Sharon picked up her mug of tea and took a sip. "Well, if that's how you feel about it, I won't press you. I'm sorry it didn't go better."

"Me, too." Angela took a long swallow of the hot tea. It scalded the roof of her mouth, but she was too thirsty to care.

"Would you like some more?" Mama Sharon glanced at Angela's two-thirds-empty cup.

"Yes. Thank you, Mama Sharon." Mama Sharon poured more water over the teabag, and Angela let the steaming cup of tea steep.

"Do you have any plans for Christmas?" Mama Sharon asked.

"At this point I think I'll be staying home. I haven't really thought that far ahead yet. What are you guys up to?"

"We'll go to church Christmas Eve, open presents in the morning, and have Christmas dinner early in the afternoon—same as always. You're welcome to join in our festivities, Angela. You don't need to be alone."

"I'm not much of one for conventional church these days, Mama Sharon."

"That's right—you have told me that. Will you do your own service for Christmas?"

Angela blew on her cup. Her cheeks warmed, but not from the heat of the room.

"I'm not sure if I will. God and I haven't been getting along really well lately."

"I see." Mama Sharon took another sip of her tea but said nothing more.

Angela gulped down the rest of her second cup of tea. "Thank you for the tea, Mama Sharon. I should get back to the house. I have an early morning tomorrow, and I still have homework to finish up.

"All right, sugar. I'll let you out the front door." Mama Sharon set down her mug and led Angela back through the dining room and into the living room to the front door.

"Tell Janette and the kids I said hi."

"I'll do that. You have a good evening, now."

"You, too."

And with that, she walked down the steps of Mama Sharon's front porch and across the snow-covered yard to her house.

Angela opened her front door and went inside, shutting the door behind her. Then she leaned against the door, covered her face with her hands, and wept.

That night, after she dressed in her pajamas, she went downstairs to brush her teeth. Someone knocked on the front door. She spit and walked out to the living room, but panicked for a moment. *What if it's Joseph?*

Angela went to the picture window and peeked behind the curtain. It was Janette. *Whew.*

She opened the door and greeted Janette. Janette gave her a hug.

"May I come in? I'm sorry to bother you so late."

"No worries. Come on in." Angela moved toward the couch and Janette joined her.

"I wanted to let you know—that is, I was wondering... remember when we talked about the House of Blues?"

"Of course."

"Well, I got my first gig. It's in a week and a half."

"Congratulations, Janette! That's so exciting!"

"Yeah—I found a band that could back me up. They're really talented."

"A good fit for you, then."

Janette blushed at the compliment. "I was wondering if I could take you up on that offer to watch the kids so Mama can come out and hear me?"

"That's the weekend before Christmas, right? I think I can do that. Let me check my calendar." Angela took out her phone and scrolled through the month of December in her calendar app. "Yep, I'm free. I'd be delighted to watch the kids for you."

Janette grinned. "You just made my night. Thank you, Angela." She gave her a hug, then stood up. "It looks like you were just getting ready for bed, so I'll head back."

Angela looked down. "The pajamas gave it away, huh?"

Janette laughed and went to the door. Angela waved her goodbye and shut the door. She looked at the closed door to her prayer closet, and walked past it to the stairs. *Not tonight, Thea.*

Thursday morning, Angela was saying goodbye to a customer when Cassidy Henner walked in the door.

"Hello, Cassidy," she said as she approached the counter.

"Hi," she said, not making eye contact.

"What can I get for you?"

"A large latte with hazelnut."

"Branching out today, eh?"

"It seems like a good time to try something new." Cassidy looked up at Angela. There was fire in her eyes.

Angela took her payment, then started preparing her drink. When she was finished, she handed it across the counter to her. "Cassidy?"

"Yes?"

"Could I talk to you for a minute?"

Cassidy looked at her watch. "Sure, I've got a minute."

Angela called to the backroom. "Shelly, can you cover for me?"

"Sure." Shelly came out and greeted the next customer. Angela led Cassidy to a table in the corner.

"I wanted to let you know that Detective Winston talked to me about what happened to you."

Cassidy's lips grew tight with anger.

"What business was it of yours?"

"He came by to ask questions about what the staff might have noticed the day that it happened. Cassidy, I'm so sorry. I wouldn't bring it up, but I think…"

"What do you think?" she said coldly.

"I think I might know who your rapist is. Because he raped me, too." Angela's voice was at a whisper now. Cassidy's eyes widened.

"You were raped, too?"

Angela nodded, tears welling in her eyes. "By someone who was here the day of your attack."

Cassidy's eyes softened. "I'm so sorry. Can you tell me who it was?"

"His name is Joseph Warner."

Cassidy searched Angela's face. "I don't know anyone named Joseph Warner."

"Listen, I was wondering if you could tell me what happened to you that day—to see if there are any similarities with what happened to me."

Pain flashed across her face, and she looked at the table, speechless for a moment. "I was attacked in the parking garage across the street. One minute I was leaning into my car to put my coffee in a cup-holder, the next I was being held down by someone... someone strong. I couldn't see his face because I was facing away from him."

Angela nodded. She went on.

"When he was... when he was finished, he got up and ran off. I turned around, but all I could see was a shadow. He vanished somewhere in the garage, and I high-tailed it out of there."

Cassidy fell silent, rubbing the lid of her drink with her right thumb.

"What happened to you?" she asked.

"It was a little different," Angela said. "I invited him over for dinner. He drugged me, I passed out, and then I woke up sore."

"So you don't remember it?"

Angela shook her head.

"So the only similarity is that he didn't want to be seen either time."

Angela nodded. "Apparently."

"And it's possible that your attacker wasn't the same as mine."

"It's possible, but doesn't that seem like an extraordinary coincidence?"

Cassidy shrugged. "Coincidences happen."

"That's more or less what Detective Winston said. He said there wasn't enough to go on to make a case. It didn't help that my rape kit didn't turn up any DNA evidence other than my own."

"That's another thing we have in common. My attacker used a condom."

"He's covering his tracks."

Cassidy looked at her coffee cup for long moment, then looked up at Angela. "Why are you telling me about this?"

"I don't know. I thought… I thought it might help you to know that you're not the only one, and that your attacker has a name, and maybe eventually he'll be brought to justice."

"If he slips up the next time he attacks someone, you mean?"

Angela nodded. Cassidy was silent for a moment.

"If the guy who attacked you is the guy who attacked me, he's probably going to attack someone again. I *hate* the thought of that. But if he made a mistake and was caught as a result…."

"…maybe it would bring some closure," Angela said, finishing Cassidy's thought.

"Maybe, if he admitted what he had done."

He might never do that, Angela thought.

"I need to get to work," Cassidy said, checking her watch.

"I need to get back to work, too. Thank you for talking with me, Cassidy."

Cassidy pulled a card out of her purse. "Hey, if you ever want to talk again, about anything, here's my number."

Angela took the card. "Thank you, Cassidy."

Cassidy picked up her latte and nodded to Angela on the way out. Angela waved. She returned to the counter, where Shelly was all ears.

"What was that about?"

Angela sighed. "Cassidy and I have someone in common, it turns out."

"Is he cute?"

"Shelly," Angela snapped. Shelly backed off as if she'd been slapped. She had a questioning look in her eyes.

"Sorry, Ang. I know the matchmaking stuff gets old. I was just having fun."

Angela stared at her. "It's really not funny or cute," she said. She was angry, and she didn't have the energy to mask it.

"I'll stop then. I'm sorry, Ang."

Angela took a deep breath. "I'm sorry I snapped at you. I'm still not a hundred percent better after that illness."

Shelly patted her on the shoulder. "Water under the bridge. Let's get back to work, shall we?"

"I need to get out of my house and into the city again, Bill," Angela said on the phone that Thursday night. "I feel like my whole life has been infested. Everywhere I turn, a memory of him shows up, and I am goddamn sick of it."

The hum of Nighttown sounded over the line. "Why don't we do Little Italy?"

"Can't. I took a week off work and now I'm broke.

How about the art museum?" The Cleveland Museum of Art had a fantastic collection — and best of all, it was free.

"Saturday?"

"Sure. How about I meet you there at ten?"

Bill agreed and wished her a good night. She hung up the phone. The phone rang as she set it aside.

Ron.

Angela hesitated. She had avoided talking to him in class and hadn't called him once since Thanksgiving. He probably wondered if she was dumping him. *Not that he's mine to dump — we went to church and had brunch once. That's hardly a sustained relationship.*

Angela picked up the phone.

"Hello, Ron."

"Angela, hi. I wondered if you were going to pick up."

Angela bit her lip. She realized she had missed the sound of his voice.

"I just got off the phone with another friend of mine. You caught me at a good time."

"Great. Is everything okay? You've seemed rather distant in class the last couple of weeks."

"I haven't been feeling all that well." *If I can fib with Shelly, I can fib with Ron.*

"Yeah, you've been looking pretty pale. Is there anything I can do?"

Just keep talking to me.

She was silent for a long moment. Then she answered him softly. "Ron, I'm so sorry I've been so distant. I want you to know that it has nothing to do with you. Something… happened."

"Do you want to tell me about it?" His voice was gentle and soothing.

"I can't. I don't have it in me. Not yet."

"Okay, then. Well, hey, I was wondering if you might be interested in joining me for church and brunch again this weekend — but this time, brunch'll be at my place."

Angela laid her head on one hand, supported by her elbow. "I really enjoyed myself the first time around, Ron, but I don't think I'm up for any more church right now. God and I aren't on very good speaking terms lately."

"How about brunch then?"

"Could I take a rain check?" *I'd tell you why, but I can't tell you what happened, can't face the possibility of becoming a sopping mess in front of you. I'm sorry.*

"Um, sure. Some other time then."

"Thanks."

The line fell silent, as if he were waiting for her to say more. She didn't.

"Okay, I'll talk to you later then, Angela."

"Okay. Good night, Ron."

"Good night."

Damn.

She thought about calling him back, but decided against it.

She really wished it didn't have to be this way. She wished she could get back to the way life was before she even knew Joseph Warner existed. His existence loomed over her like a storm cloud, threatening to drench her at any moment. She thought again of

Thanksgiving night, of what he must have done to leave her feeling sore. Fury pounded in her ears. She could scream, but it wouldn't drown out the sound of him.

Angela pinched herself hard, willing herself to forget the dawning realization of what had happened to her that night. The sharp pain in her arm distracted her momentarily, relieving her.

I need to find myself again.

Angela crossed her arms and sat back in her chair. She hadn't eaten since lunchtime. She had no appetite to speak of these days—everything she ate, she forced herself to eat. Maybe she should eat again. She hadn't stepped on the scale recently, but her sagging clothing told her she was losing weight.

Angela went downstairs and took out a handful of saltine crackers. She ate them mechanically, chewing and swallowing each one as if it were an item she were ticking off her to-do list. She drank some ginger ale straight from the bottle, replaced the cap, and returned the bottle to the fridge. As she exited the dining room to the hallway, she ignored the quiet urge to sit and pray; she stomped up the stairs instead. Her feet ached when she reached the top, and her heart thumped. She went to bed without brushing her teeth and laid there for a long time, staring up at the ghostly memories that haunted her.

Saturday morning was cold and white, with thick lake effect snow coming down in waves from the clouds above. Angela drove Felicity to the art museum and met Bill in the lobby.

Recently renovated and expanded, the Cleveland Museum of Art was grand in both structure and content. There were certain rooms Angela made a point to visit each time: the room with the marble statuette of the Good Shepherd, dating back to the third century; the room with medieval illuminated manuscripts, including several books of hours; the Armor Court, which featured medieval armor and weaponry; and the numerous rooms featuring medieval and Renaissance-era European paintings.

Bill followed Angela as she took the lead, weaving through each room and its familiar offerings, stopping to gaze at pieces that caught her eye. When they reached the European paintings, Angela paused at Zurbarán's *Christ and the Virgin in the House at Nazareth*. She was drawn to the innocence of Jesus' youthful face as he looked down at a crown of thorns in his lap. Mary's face was pained as she looked past Jesus to the source of light that shone on him. The painting was a portrayal of Mary's sense of powerlessness at the foreknowledge of what was to come. *Is this how you felt about me, Thea? Did you see all this coming and weep for me?*

Angela pondered Mary's face thoughtfully, imagining Thea as powerless, rather than powerful. Then Angela considered free will, and the ability of people to choose their fate, as well as to influence the fates of others. *We are all connected, aren't we, Thea?*

What kind of man would choose to overpower a woman? One who felt powerless himself? One who had learned that he was the center of the universe and had never been challenged to think otherwise?

Angela turned her attention to the young Jesus and imagined him as Joseph. *Do you weep for him, Thea? Do you weep for what this son of yours has become?*

The kind of man who would attack a woman – drug her, rape her – is the kind of man who's no man at all. He's a nobody trying to be a somebody, and he's failing.

He's a future priest who has no holiness apart from the masks he wears from day to day. He's chasing a dream that doesn't and won't ever belong to him. And he'll never be happy, will he, Thea?

Angela looked over at Bill and he smiled at her with curiosity.

I have a life. I am whole, even with these wounds. I don't need to manipulate someone or rip someone else's life apart to be fulfilled. I am fulfilled from within myself.

I lead a life of integrity, and, in the grand scheme of things, I am happy.

I've got it better than he ever will, don't I, Thea?

She felt a pang of pity for him. His was a sorry life indeed.

She turned to Bill and held out her arms. He leaned over and gave her a hug. She squeezed him tight for a minute, and when she backed away her eyes were glistening.

"What was that for?" Bill said with a smile.

"I'm grateful for all the people I love. I am a lucky, lucky lady."

"And we're lucky to have you, my dear." He chucked her on the chin and her long peal of laughter echoed throughout the vast room.

Chapter 17

"You ready?" Bill asked. Angela nodded with a smile, and he opened the door to his apartment.

Inside, a seven-foot Christmas tree towered over the room with a glittering, lit star on top. Garlands of silver tinsel spiraled down the tree, and bright, metallic balls in jewel tones bedecked the tree branches. The scent of cinnamon and nutmeg hung in the air. Angela stood at the threshold, drinking it all in.

"I know it's still Advent, but I love this," she murmured.

"You always do," he said knowingly.

Angela walked in and sat on the couch, which had been moved to the middle of the room to make way for the tree. Bill turned on the radio, which was tuned to a station playing Christmas music. Normally Angela protested Christmas music before Christmas Eve, but this time she held silence. She thought back to last Christmas, which she'd spent at home for the first time. The liturgy had been wonderful and the food had been good, even if her table set for one was a little lonely.

"I was going to tell you that I'm planning to go to midnight Mass at the Community of St. Mary Magdalene," Bill said, sitting down beside her. "Do you want to come?"

"Is this the community that was booted out of the building on Superior?"

"One and the same."

"I haven't been up to praying since… well, since Thanksgiving. But I admit that I'm curious about this community. I've never heard of another church that got exiled from its denomination and still continued to meet. They sound like a hardy group. Maybe their hardiness will rub off on me. But is their liturgy any good?"

"I visited them before they were kicked out and I've visited them in their new space as well, and Ang, it's about the best Christian liturgy you're going to find in Cleveland."

"You're just buttering me up so I'll go, is that right?"

"Nope. This community is the real deal."

Angela gave Bill a long look. "Okay, fine."

Bill grinned. "You won't regret it."

"I'll be the judge of that."

Bill got up and walked to the kitchen. Angela heard the clink of glasses and looked over. He was pouring egg nog for both of them. Angela had a soft spot for egg nog. She accepted her glass gladly. Bill held up his glass, she held up hers, and they recited their usual toast.

"You seemed to enjoy the museum," Bill said, after taking a sip.

"I did." Angela sipped her egg nog and fell silent.

"You want to put some words around that?"

Angela closed her eyes and thought for a moment. Then she opened her eyes again. "You know, I haven't felt like myself for weeks. You and I both know why. And it isn't that I haven't wanted to feel like myself. Normally I like waking up in the morning. I like going to work. I like school. I like praying. I like sitting alone and pondering the universe. But lately all I've wanted to do is escape from myself. It's like I don't feel at home with me anymore.

"But at the museum, I felt grounded. I didn't want to be anywhere else. I wanted to be right where I was, doing exactly what I was doing. And it was such a fucking relief."

Bill regarded her seriously. "You're going to get through this, you know that?"

"Yesterday? I probably would have said no. But today? Yeah, I think so. I think so."

"So the moral of the story is that you're called to live at the museum."

Angela laughed. "Maybe. Or maybe I'm called to make my home wherever beauty and wonder may be found. And I don't have to go to a museum for that, you know?"

"That's right—you don't have to go any farther than my apartment!"

Angela nudged him with her palm. "No—I don't need to go any farther than my own house. I think I've been living in it wrong."

"Uh-oh. Do I smell the scent of paint fumes and wood stain coming on?"

"No, the walls and the floors are fine. But I think the furniture might need some rearranging."

"Really? What are you going to change?"

"I don't know yet. I just know that some

transformation is needed."

"Ooh, an intuition. I like it." Bill raised his glass again, and Angela clinked it with hers.

Angela's final week of classes was full as she scurried to finish up a term paper and two final projects. During the break in her Thursday night class, she talked with Ron and promised that she'd call him over the weekend to catch up. He seemed happy about that. She left class Thursday night pleased, but tired. When she got home, she poured herself a glass of chianti and warmed up chicken fajitas she had made the day before. She ate slowly, savoring the spices that crossed her palate. When she was done eating, she put her plate in the dishwasher and carried her glass upstairs to her room, still avoiding the prayer room.

At her desk, she clicked open her contest proposal and read through it. She hadn't looked it at in three weeks, so reading it was a bit like reading someone else's work. So far, she was impressed. She made changes as she read, adjusting the wording here and there and moving sentences. It was more or less finished—she just needed to add in the estimated costs associated with it. She could do that later, however. Angela wondered again about the secret hiding place that Adeline and Jeremiah had shared at the factory. There must have been something she missed when she was at the factory last time. What if Ebenezer Jones had found out where she went with Jeremiah and murdered her there? Or what if Jeremiah was a liar and baited her there to attack her? *Just like Joseph....*

Angela shivered.

Saturday afternoon arrived before she knew it, and soon she was bundling up to head over to Mama Sharon's house to watch the kids while Mama Sharon went to Janette's performance at the House of Blues. DeShawn and Jamal screamed when she knocked on the door. When Mama Sharon opened the door, the boys were nowhere to be seen.

"I think they want you to play hide and seek," Mama Sharon said.

"No DeShawn here!" a muffled voice said.

"Oh, no DeShawn here? Hmm, I wonder where he could be." Angela's vocal search of the first floor commenced as she peeked in various corners and nooks for signs of the hidden boys. Desiree came out and folded her arms, shaking her head and giggling. Angela spied a large lump behind one of the curtains in the living room.

"I wonder if he's over… HERE!" She snatched up the curtain, exposing the crouched figures of DeShawn and Jamal. They screamed again and ran into the dining room. Angela laughed as they went.

"Angela," Mama Sharon said, "dinner's on the stove, so just dish it up whenever you're ready. The boys can go to bed at eight thirty; Desiree can stay up till nine. You'll just need to help the boys get a bath before bed. Let me think. Am I forgetting anything?"

"Are you leaving behind booster seats?"

"Oh, right—just one, for Jamal. Let me go get that." Mama Sharon headed out through the back door to her garage. Meanwhile, Angela set off to look for the boys again. She heard the quick steps of Desiree running up the stairs.

Angela had just found the boys again (this time, in the kitchen pantry) when Mama Sharon returned with Jamal's booster seat.

"Oh, and you have a spare key to the house already, am I right, sugar?"

"Yes, ma'am."

"Good. I think I'll head out then."

"Have a good time."

"Thank you, sugar."

Mama Sharon walked out the back door and lumbered down the steps. Angela went to the kitchen to dish up some dinner for the three kids.

"Dinner's ready!" she called. Footsteps sounded throughout the house, and three youngsters appeared before her, pulling out chairs from the dining room table. Angela set plates before them. Jamal started to eat, but DeShawn hissed at him. "We have to pray first, Jamal!" Angela set her plate on the table and fetched glasses of milk for the three kids. Finally, with a glass of ice water in hand for herself, Angela sat down. Three faces stared at her expectantly.

"Oh, am I supposed to lead the prayer?"

They nodded in unison.

"Okay, but I pray a little differently than your granny and mommy do, just so you know."

Angela held out her hands. Desiree took her left hand and Jamal took her right. DeShawn reached across the table to hold Desiree's hand so they formed a complete circle.

"Let us pray," she said. "Mother God, we bless

you, our wonderful creator, and we bless the food before us, the fruit of your creation. May this food nourish our bodies, and may we remember with open hearts our neighbors who go without enough to eat tonight. Amen."

"Amen," the other three voices said.

"Did you say 'Mother God'?" DeShawn asked.

"I sure did."

"But God is our father, not our mother."

"Actually, the Bible says that God is like a mother eagle, carrying her eaglets on her wings. Did you know that?"

"It says that?"

"Sure does."

"Which book?" Desiree asked.

"I believe it's in the book of Deuteronomy. I'll look it up for you if you're interested."

"That would be cool," she said. "Maybe you can show us in our family Bible after dinner."

Angela smiled. "Sure thing."

They dug in to their turkey tetrazzini. It was delicious. Noodles, turkey, celery, carrot, cream of mushroom soup, and bread crumbs made for a tongue-tantalizing, belly-warming meal.

"Did Mama Sharon use leftovers from Thanksgiving for this?" Angela asked.

"Yep. She still has a bunch of turkey in the freezer," Desiree said.

"I'll bet."

Angela asked each of the kids how things were going with school. Desiree talked about her recent role in a school play. Then Jamal talked about how much he loved playing with the kids at daycare. DeShawn said he didn't like his teacher at school.

"Why don't you like your teacher, DeShawn?"

"She's mean. She's always telling me what to do."

"Teachers can be like that. I'm sorry you don't like her. You know, I had a teacher in second grade that I didn't like."

"You did?" DeShawn perked up.

"Yep, I did. And you know what I did?"

"What?"

"I drew pictures of her wearing funny clothes to make myself feel better."

DeShawn giggled. "That sounds silly, Angie."

"It was pretty silly, but it worked."

Their plates were empty now, and Angela began stacking them together to take to the kitchen.

"Angela, did you say that verse was in Deuteronomy?" Desiree yelled from the living room. Angela poked her head out from the kitchen.

"Yes, Deuteronomy. Let me check my phone and find out the chapter and verse."

Angela clicked into her phone's web browser and googled "mother eagle bible."

"Okay, it's Deuteronomy thirty-two, ten through twelve."

Desiree flipped to the thirty-second chapter of Deuteronomy and scrolled through with her finger till she found the tenth verse. She read the verses aloud. "He found him in a desert land, and in the waste howling wilderness; he led him about, he instructed him, he kept him as the apple of his eye. As an eagle stirreth up her nest, fluttereth over her young, spreadeth abroad her wings, taketh them, beareth them on her wings. So the Lord alone did lead him, and there was no strange god with him."

"But this says God is a he," DeShawn said.

"Yes, that's the convention for pronouns, but God is like a mother eagle, so God could be a she. Does that make sense?"

"How could God be a he and a she at the same time?" Deshawn asked.

"Well, tradition tells us that God is transcendent, which means God is beyond the images we have of God. When we say God is a he, we're assigning a particular kind of image to God, but God is greater than that image. God is more than merely a man, just as God is more than merely a woman. But we use concrete images like this to describe God anyway, because those images help us understand and appreciate God better."

"So we can say God is a she and it's not completely right, but it's not completely wrong, either?" Desiree asked.

"Just like we can say God is a he and it's not completely right or wrong. You've got it."

"What would Granny say about this?" DeShawn asked.

"Well, I don't know — you'll have to ask her."

"Okay. Can we play hide and go seek?"

Angela grinned and covered her eyes with her hands. "One, two, three…"

Mama Sharon got home just after ten. Angela was on the couch reading the latest copy of *Essence* when she heard the back door open. She got up and walked softly into the dining room.

"How'd it go, Mama Sharon?"

Mama Sharon shook off her coat. "My baby girl looked and sounded fantastic up there—and that's not just her mother speaking. Everyone around me was amazed by her."

"She sang for me on Halloween. Her voice is stunning."

"It is. She's got talent. I don't know if she's gonna make it big, but with a voice like hers, she could."

Angela gave Mama Sharon a hug. "I'm so glad you got to see her up there."

"Thank you for making it possible, Angela!"

"You are very welcome. Anytime I'm free, I'm happy to watch the kids again so you can go see her perform."

"And we need to get you to one of her shows. I have the feeling that tonight's performance was the first of many."

"Do you know when her next one is?"

"I don't know. Tonight was her first big gig, but I have the feeling they're going to invite her back. She has some other places in the works, too. I'll have her call you with the details."

"Sounds great. Oh, and Mama Sharon? I wanted to let you know that the kids and I had an interesting discussion about images of God tonight. We talked about the passage in Deuteronomy where God is compared to a mother eagle, and we talked about using different pronouns for God depending on the image we're using to imagine God. Is that all right? I mean, do you think Janette would mind?"

"That's right—you've told me before that you pray to God in feminine pronouns. That's all right, sugar. God is always going to be more than we can imagine, not less."

"Okay. I realized afterward that I probably should have asked you or Janette first. It came up because I prayed to Mother God during grace before dinner. Do you think Janette will be okay with it?"

"You might want to have a conversation with her about it yourself. She'll be here tomorrow afternoon if you want to call or come over."

"All right. I'll do that. Have a good night, Mama Sharon."

"Good night, sugar."

Angela called Janette the next day.

"Hello?"

"Janette, it's Angela, next door."

"Hi, Angela. Thank you again for watching the kids so Mama could come out and hear me sing last night."

"It was my pleasure. Listen, I wanted to talk with you about something that came up last night."

"Was everything all right? Mama didn't mention anything happening."

"The kids were all fine. I just wanted to let you know that we got into a discussion about images of God. When I said grace before dinner I prayed to Mother God. I realized afterward that I should have asked you about it first."

Janette was quiet for a moment. "You prayed to

'Mother God'?"

"Yes. It just came out when I was saying grace, and then the kids asked me about it. I showed the kids the passage in Deuteronomy where God is likened to a mother eagle. I realized after the fact that my ideas about God might not be welcome by you or Mama Sharon. Mama Sharon didn't seem to mind, but I wanted to check in with you."

Silence fell on the other end of the line.

"We pray to God the father. Like the Bible says."

"I'm sorry if I overstepped my bounds. I'm so used to praying to God in feminine terms that it just came out. I'm happy to stick with masculine pronouns and images in the future if you prefer."

"God is a he, not a she." Janette's voice was edged with anger. Angela thought this might not be the time to bring up all the instances in the Bible in which God was imagined as feminine.

"Angela, I thought you were a Christian."

"An unconventional one, but yes, I consider myself a Christian."

"But Christians believe in God the father—and Jesus the son."

Angela took a deep breath. "I believe a little differently than you do. But that doesn't mean I should have imposed my beliefs on your kids."

"No, you shouldn't have." Her voice was short.

"I'm sorry, Janette. I'll pray your way with them in the future."

"Maybe we should just keep our distance from one another for a while, Angela."

Stunned, Angela's mouth dropped open.

"I'm sorry, Janette."

"Thank you. Goodbye, Angela."

Angela heard a click. The call was over. She stared at her phone. Her cheeks flushed red with embarrassment and shame.

Several minutes passed. Eventually, Angela got up from the couch and walked to her prayer closet. She opened the door slowly; the scents of candle wax and incense greeted her. She breathed it in longingly.

Then, her cheeks burning, she shut the door to the prayer closet and ran up the stairs.

Chapter 18

The next day passed quietly. After work, Angela attempted to relax in her library with a book, but her mind drifted to Janette and her children. *Stupid, stupid, stupid Angela.* She had walked into Janette's house and shared her thealogy with Janette's kids without even thinking of how Janette might react. How could she have been so foolish?

Other people don't believe the way you do, Angela, she thought to herself. Old feelings of self-doubt and inadequacy washed over her. Her mother's voice sounded in her head, chastising her for her flawed faith. As hard as it was to talk to Thea after Thanksgiving, it was even more difficult now. She had screwed up, imposing her religious views on someone else's children. What kind of person did that? A selfish person. Or maybe a creepy person. The valley of difference between her and mainstream Christianity yawned wide before her. She was sorry, and she wanted to make it right, but now Janette didn't want her around her family.

Great, she thought. *Some neighbor I am.*

She made a half-hearted attempt to finalize her contest proposal Monday night, but her eyes wouldn't digest the words and images in front of her. She gave up and went to bed.

Tuesday morning at work went quickly, and in the

afternoon she went grocery shopping for Christmas. After work Wednesday, she wished Shelly a merry Christmas and headed to a tree lot to purchase her Christmas tree. She headed home with a spruce tree strapped to the top of her car with rope. When she got home, she dragged the tree out of the car and set it up in a tree stand in her living room by the picture window. She went down to the basement and found her box of Christmas decorations. It included decorations she had made when she was a child, and others that she had collected in the meantime. There were also strings of colored lights, ropes of tinsel, and a white star perched on a cone to hold it in place. She took her time adding the decorations, enjoying the annual ritual of dressing the tree. Once the tree was decorated and watered, she went to the kitchen, pulled a chilled cheesy potato casserole out of the refrigerator, and popped it in the oven. She was going over to Bill's parents' house for Christmas Eve dinner, followed by midnight Mass at the Community of St. Mary Magdalene. Before that, there was one last thing she wanted to do. Her contest proposal was as ready as it was going to be, and she wanted to send it off.

She headed upstairs and reviewed her proposal, checking it three times for errors. It now included details about the two women who had died in connection with the factory as well as narratives from the folks she had interviewed in the neighborhood. Her proposal told a story about real people, and it made a case for becoming a neighborhood center once again. She typed up the e-mail to the contest committee, and checked it for errors. She also checked to make sure her contest proposal was attached.

Then she clicked send.

A thrill ran up her spine as she read the message confirming that her e-mail was sent. It was out of her hands now.

When the casserole was ready, she put on her coat, gloves, and hat, and carried the casserole dish out to Felicity. Snow was falling softly around her. It was a winter wonderland—had been since Halloween, really, but this was Cleveland, after all.

Angela drove to Bill's place and picked him up, moving the casserole to the backseat to make room for him. He had a veggie tray in his hands, and he slid it onto the backseat next to the casserole.

"Thanks for picking me up. You remember the way?"

"I think so. And you're welcome. Thanks for inviting me."

Angela had visited Bill's parents' house a couple of times before. They lived in a 1950s house in University Heights. The bottom half of the house was lined with stone, and the upper half was lined with white siding. One car was parked in front of the house when they arrived, and Angela pulled in behind it.

"I have a surprise for you," Bill said.

"Ooh, a Christmas surprise. What is it?"

"Come on inside and I'll show you."

Bill headed up the front walk and opened the door for Angela. She brushed past him and spotted Bill's parents on the couch.

"Hello, Angela!" Bill's mother said. She got up and crossed the living room to give Angela a hug. Angela held the casserole in her left arm and leaned forward to return the hug. Bill's mother took the casserole from her and took it to the dining room, where the table was set with a table cloth, fine china, and real silverware. Angela walked over to where Bill's father was now standing and shook his hand with a firm grip.

"Ang," Bill said, "you remember Tony, yes?"

Angela turned around to see the black-haired, brown-eyed server from Mama Santa's.

"I don't think we were ever on a first name basis. It's nice to see you again, Tony."

"Nice to see you again, Angela," he said. "Bill's been telling me a lot about you."

Angela looked at Bill, who grinned sheepishly. "Surprise!" he said under his breath.

Angela was indeed surprised. Bill's parents were Catholic and stood on the traditional side of things. When Bill had come out after college, they hadn't reacted very well. Were they turning a new leaf?

The front door opened then, and a young woman with bobbed dark brown hair and soft brown eyes entered, carrying a pie plate in one arm. "Hi, Mom and Dad. Hi, Bill. Hi, Angela." She saw Tony, walked right up to him, held out her right hand, and said, "Hi, I'm Kate."

Kate was Bill's sister and only sibling. She was five years younger than Bill and worked at a law firm downtown. She wasn't shy.

Tony smiled at her and shook her hand. "I'm Tony."

"Nice to meet you, Tony."

Bill set the veggie tray and dip on the coffee table

and removed the plastic wrap. "Everyone dig in," he said.

Bill's parents, seated again on the floral-patterned love seat, leaned forward to pick out some veggies. Angela sat down on the matching couch across from the love seat. Bill sat next to her, and Tony offered Kate the third seat. She waved him off.

"I'll get a chair from the dining room. You sit." She took the pie into the dining room and fetched a chair from the table. Tony shrugged with a smile and sat. Bill beamed at him.

"How are you doing lately, Angela?" Bill's mother asked.

Angela picked up a carrot, ran it through the container of dip, and sat back on the couch. "Things are going well in general. I just finished up my third semester in my urban development program at CSU, and I'm pleased to report that I just submitted my proposal for an urban development contest that's happening in Cleveland." She took a bite of the carrot.

"Congratulations," Bill's father said. "What did you have to do for your contest proposal?"

Angela swallowed the bit of carrot she was chewing and began to describe the elements of her proposal. She left out the bits about the women who had died—those would have been a little too gory for Christmas Eve dinner.

"So you're redesigning a site in a neighborhood in Cleveland?" Bill's mother asked.

"Yes." Angela took another bite.

"What site have you chosen?"

"Bill helped me pick it out, actually. It's an old

textile factory on the corner of 61st and Euclid on the East Side."

"I didn't really help her pick it out, actually," Bill said. "I was just along for the ride."

"Yes, but you gave me a taste of the city's history, *and* you directed me to the Western Reserve Historical Society's research library, where I dug up all kinds of things about the history of the site I picked."

"Okay, maybe I helped a little," he conceded with a grin.

"Well, that's great news, Angela. Good for you," Bill's mother said.

"Thank you."

"What about you, Tony? How are you doing?"

Angela leaned forward so she could see Tony. She was curious about this man, and wondered about how serious he and Bill had become. She hadn't realized things were going so well. *I've been pretty caught up in my own shit,* she thought with dismay.

"Things are going fine for me. I started working at Mama Santa's a couple of months ago, which is where Bill and I met. In my off time, I freelance at the *Plain Dealer.* I'm an arts and music writer."

Ah-ha. No wonder.

"Really," Bill's mother asked. "What's your last name, dear?"

"Pacelli."

"Tony Pacelli? I think I've seen your work in the paper. Did you write one recently about children's programming the orchestra is doing?"

"I did. The orchestra has some excellent outreach programs for schools in the inner city."

"Well, a writer! That's splendid," Bill's mother said.

Tony smiled at her. He and Bill exchanged pleased looks. Angela thought of Janette and wondered if Tony might be a good contact for her. Would she be open to an introduction made by Angela? *Doesn't hurt to ask. Worst she can do is say no.*

"How about you, Kate? How's life as a lawyer treating you?" Bill's father asked.

Kate began discussing some of her recent cases in an animated fashion. Bill leaned over to Angela and said in a low voice, "What do you think?"

"Of you two? You're dashing together."

Bill nodded, smiling.

"I didn't realize things were quite so serious. I guess I've been a little preoccupied."

"With good reason. Anyway, I was excited to surprise you."

Bill looked back at Kate, and Angela rubbed Bill's shoulder encouragingly.

A few minutes later, a timer sounded in the kitchen. Bill's mother stood up and the room fell silent. "The ham is ready. Why don't we all take our seats at the dining room table?"

The conversation resumed as everyone took their seats around the table. Bill's mother and father sat on the ends of the table. Angela sat next to Tony, while Bill sat next to Kate.

Angela leaned over to Tony and said, "You know, there's a new act in Cleveland that you might want to look into. Janette Suggs. She's an extraordinary singer."

"Really? I've never heard of her, which means she probably hasn't been featured in the paper yet. Do you have her contact information?"

"All I have is her personal phone number. Let me text her and see if it's okay if I give it to you."

Angela took her phone out of her pocket and thumped out a quick text: "Janette, I just met an arts and music reporter from the *Plain Dealer*. He's interested in talking to you. May I give him your phone number?"

Angela put her phone in her pocket as Bill's father set the ham on the table. Angela's phone buzzed in her pocket, and she sneaked a peek. "Yes" was the reply.

She leaned over again and whispered, "She said I could give it to you. Remind me before we leave." Bill eyed her questioningly from across the table, but she just smiled.

The dinner spread consisted of honey-infused ham, Angela's cheesy potato casserole, candied yams, green beans, and dinner rolls. Bill's father said a table blessing, and everyone dug in. The conversation was jovial and varied, ranging from the latest Browns game, to the anticipation of Christmas gifts in the morning, to the weather.

After dinner, Angela helped Bill's mother clear the dishes and distribute dessert plates. "Keep your forks, everyone—Kate brought pie," Bill's mother said.

Kate stood up to cut the pie with a knife her mother handed her. "It's apple pie—I baked it just before I left home. Hope everyone likes it!"

Murmurs of approval rose around the table.

"Shall we take our dessert into the living room?"

Bill's mother asked. People stood with their pie plates and moved toward the living room.

"Mrs. Kinsman, would you like me to start the coffee?" Angela asked.

"Oh, yes, thank you, dear. That's right—you're the coffee expert."

"That's what they tell me." Angela grinned.

Kate joined Angela in the kitchen. "So Angela, what do you think of Tony?" she said, her voice hushed.

Angela looked over at her best friend's sister in surprise. Kate was a woman of many opinions; she had rarely asked for Angela's opinion on anything.

"He seems nice. Smart. And Bill seems happy," she said non-committally.

"It's so weird seeing Bill bring his boyfriend to Christmas dinner. I think Mom and Dad are still getting used to the idea of Bill being gay," she whispered.

"It's pretty bold on his part."

"Yeah. It's like something I would do." Kate shook her head, and Angela chuckled. Angela thought she detected some admiration on Bill's sister's part, which was unusual for her. Kate was the trailblazer in the family, and here was Bill, making his own path. Angela wondered, not for the first time, what it would have been like to have siblings.

Angela pulled coffee cups and saucers out of the cupboard and began pouring coffee. Kate, still lingering, took the first two coffee cups out to the living room and came back for two more. Angela took the last two out and handed one to Kate. They both sat down and set their coffee on the coffee table in exchange for their slices of pie.

"So what can you tell me about Janette Suggs?" Tony asked Angela after several bites of pie.

"She's a Cleveland native with a background in gospel music. I've never been to one of her shows, but she gave me a private performance of 'Amazing Grace' that sent chills down my spine."

"How do you know her?"

"She's my next-door neighbor."

"And you don't know if she has a website or anything?"

"If she does, she hasn't introduced me to it."

"Where has she performed?"

"She just had her very first gig at House of Blues."

"Wow. She must be talented to have landed a spot at House of Blues."

"She is. I speak as someone who can sing reasonably well—Janette can *sing*."

"Well, thanks for the lead, Angela. I'm working on getting my hours at Mama Santa's changed so I can go to more weekend performances. And see Bill more." Tony glanced Bill's way, and Bill met his gaze with a smile.

Angela set down her pie plate and picked up her coffee cup, taking a sip. Bill looked happy, and Tony seemed good for him. *Could this be the beginning of love for them?* Angela thought back to when she had a crush on Bill, and her mind wandered to other men she had dated. She had had many crushes, but she had never loved anyone. *Maybe that's because you back away from guys anytime they get close.*

Angela thought of Ron and sighed. She owed him more of an explanation than she had given him, but she didn't want to tell him what had happened on Thanksgiving. She thought of pulling out her phone to text him, but she didn't want to seem anti-social—she was the dinner guest of the Kinsmans, after all. She'd text Ron when she got to the car.

"Anyone want to play cards?" Bill's father asked. He pulled a deck out of the drawer in the coffee table.

"How about euchre?" Kate said.

"I'll play," Angela said.

"Either of you young men want to play?" Bill's mother asked.

Bill waved his hand. "You play, Mom. You love euchre."

His mother shrugged and picked up a chair from the dining room. Bill's father did the same. Angela and Kate were already seated together on the couch; Bill and Tony took the loveseat. Angela glanced over and smiled. This was the perfect way to end the evening—but as it happened, the evening was only just getting started.

At ten o'clock, after Angela and Bill's mother won twice as a team against Kate and Bill's father, Tony got up to say good night.

"Thanks for the lovely evening, Mr. and Mrs. Kinsman," he said.

"Thanks for joining us, Tony," Bill's mother said. Angela caught Bill's eye and grinned; he grinned back.

"It was nice meeting you by name, Tony," Angela said, giving him a hug.

"Likewise, Angela. Good to meet you, Kate," he said, turning to hug Bill's sister.

"Just a minute—I want you to take some leftovers, please," Bill's mother said as she hurried to the kitchen to prepare a plate for him.

"Oh, okay," he said, turning toward to the kitchen. Bill's mother returned a minute later with a plate heaped with ham, yams, and cheesy potatoes. Tony accepted the plate with a smile and met Bill's gaze as he turned toward the front door.

"I'll be right back," Bill said, and he opened the door for Tony. They walked out together, and Angela resisted the temptation to peek through the curtains and watch. Bill was back in a couple of minutes, and Kate moved to the door.

"Are you leaving, too, Kate?" her father asked.

"Yep. I don't want to be out too late on these roads. Have a good night, Mom and Dad. See you in the morning." Kate gave each of them a kiss on the cheek, then hugged Bill and Angela. She waved as she walked out the front door.

"That just leaves us," Bill said to Angela. "Midnight Mass isn't actually at midnight—it ends at midnight and starts at eleven. We can head over any time." Angela smiled. She was eager to experience the liturgy of the Community of St. Mary Magdalene.

"We'll get out of here so you can get to bed," Angela said to Bill's parents.

"You two have a good time," Bill's mother said. "Bill, we'll see you in the morning, yes?"

"Sure will."

Another flurry of hugs ensued, and then Angela

and Bill were heading down the front walk to Felicity. Angela pulled out her phone and texted Ron. "Merry Christmas, Ron. I'd love to see you soon. I've missed you," she typed.

It wasn't enough, but it would have to do for now.

Soon Angela and Bill were on Cedar Road driving toward Cleveland.

The Community of St. Mary Magdalene met in a converted factory building. The entrance was a single glass door in the back of the building off the parking lot. The parking lot was already half full, even though it was only 10:20 when they arrived.

As they entered, they found themselves in a long, wide hallway, with a statue of a woman just past the door: Mary Magdalene, presumably. They walked down the brick-lined hallway to another door, which opened onto a large room. Chairs were arranged on two sides of the space to face each other, and a low, velvet-covered bench stood in the center of the first row of one of the sides. A square altar table stood on the far end of the space, and a shallow stone baptismal font stood on the opposite side near the entrance. A wooden ambo, where the readings were proclaimed, was placed near the baptismal font. Iron candleholders were fixed to the walls at ten-foot intervals, and the candles they held were the pale yellow of real beeswax. Exquisite arrangements of red and white orchids stood near the ambo, the font, and the table, and a wide Advent wreath lay elevated just next to the table, all of its candles lit. A wooden triptych stood behind the ambo; it stood open to reveal Mary lying next to her swaddled child. A piano stood in a far corner of the space, and the sounds of a four-part choir warming up somewhere in the building drifted into the room.

Angela and Bill stood still, drinking in the sights, smells, and sounds of the sacred space. A greeter welcomed them, offering them worship booklets, which they took before heading toward seats near the table. People milled around the room, chatting and laughing. This community was new to Angela, but it exuded warmth and hospitality.

They found seats and sat down. Angela remained quiet, listening to the sounds of the far-off choir and the people who mingled about the room. It reminded her of her old church, her church as it was before she fell away from it. The community was knit closely together, and she felt at home. It had been a long time since she'd felt that way in a church.

Several people came up to Bill to say hello and to introduce themselves to Angela. The choir entered the room and took seats around the piano. At just past 10:30, the oboeist intoned "O Holy Night," and the choir and piano joined in with the first verse. The sound of voices swelled, and Angela noticed that the velvet stool was now occupied by a sharp-looking man with graying hair wearing white satin vestments. Without realizing it, she began to sing along. She surprised herself with the strength of her own voice. She hadn't sung loud and clear in community in years. Not since she'd left her church. Her voice had been subdued in the years since then. *I sang with Joseph at Thanksgiving, though.* The memory pierced her, and her voice fell silent. Bill looked over at her quizzically as he sang.

The lyrics to each carol were printed in the worship booklet, and Angela read along, allowing herself to be swept up in the sound of the voices around her. At eleven, the carols ended, and a bell choir began to play. The piano played under them, tapping out the notes to "Hark the Herald Angels Sing." The pastor stood, and everyone else followed his lead. The whole church, standing, sung together. Angela joined in, quietly at first, and then with her full voice. *He's not going to ruin this for me.*

The pastor began by making the sign of the cross while saying, "May the grace and peace of Jesus Christ, the love of God, and the fellowship of the Holy Spirit be with you all."

Many voices responded at once: "And also with you."

Then the pastor began the collect prayer without using a binder or book of any kind. Angela could and sometimes did improvise prayers, but she rarely memorized them. *That guy's good.*

After the collect prayer, an older white woman with curly salt-and-pepper hair wearing slacks and an oversized white dress shirt went up to the ambo to proclaim the first readings. She read slowly, thoughtfully, just the way Angela did at home, her voice lilting in an English accent. Then the choir began the psalm, intoning the refrain before singing it together with the congregation. They sang the verses in two- and three-part harmony. The whole congregation sang the refrain in full voice. Then a middle-aged black man with glasses, khakis, and a checked blue and white shirt crossed the room to proclaim the second reading. His cadence was similar to the first woman's, slow and articulate. After the second reading, the choir and congregation stood to sing an alleluia, and the pastor and two acolytes walked to the center of the space where one member of the congregation was holding a jewel-encrusted gospel book. The pastor read the gospel reading without a microphone, flanked by the candle-bearing acolytes. His voice was dramatic and strong, but not overly so. When the reading was over, the gospel-bearer returned to her seat, the acolytes returned their candles, and the pastor walked to the ambo. He waited a few moments, then began his homily.

He talked about Christmas as the foretelling of Easter: that this coming of light in the midst of winter darkness was a precursor of Easter light rising after Jesus' death. He talked about Advent bringing about the hope of a new thing, and declared that a new thing was happening this very night, in the midst of this congregation.

"And maybe," he said, "tonight we will encounter new light being born from deep within our own darkness."

As the pastor bowed toward the table and returned to his seat, Angela's thoughts turned to her rape. Tears filled her eyes. Could something new be born from this horror?

Angela hadn't heard from Joseph since Thanksgiving night. He knew that she knew — the police had questioned him about it. What must he be thinking?

I could call him. I have his number. I could ask him why he did it.

He wouldn't answer, though.

So was this it? No explanation, no conversation, no accountability? He just raped her and got away with it?

She wanted answers. Then again, the thought of talking to her rapist made her stomach turn. Angela put her head in her hands. She didn't know what she wanted, after all.

The voice of a man reading intercessory prayers jarred her from her thoughts. "For all who dwell in darkness, that they may find the light they seek, we pray." The choir and congregation sang, "O God, hear us, hear our prayer."

The pain and disorientation of Thanksgiving night gripped her. She searched her memories yet again for clues about who he really was. Nothing stood out. She hadn't seen who he really was because he hadn't wanted her to see it, just like she couldn't remember her rape because he hadn't wanted her to remember it. He was careful, so careful, to preserve a wholly appealing image of himself, to lure her into trusting him. *But why? Why become a priest if you're willing to plan and carry out the rape of women?*

Angela wondered if there were more than two women who'd been violated by him. Or was she alone—was Cassidy's rapist someone else entirely?

Bill tapped Angela on the leg. The congregation was standing and beginning to gather around the table.

Bill stood. "Peace be with you," he said to her, giving her a hug.

"Peace be with you, Bill," she said. She didn't feel peaceful. She felt like a storm swirling into a hurricane.

She began walking behind Bill toward the table, greeting those she passed with the sign of peace. She wondered if Joseph was celebrating midnight Mass at one of the Roman Catholic churches in the diocese tonight. *Maybe he just raped another unsuspecting woman.*

If he was a serial rapist, and if he did rape another woman, she hoped with all her might that he would be caught and revealed for who he really was.

But what if it was all a dream? What if he didn't rape me or anyone?

Her inability to remember what had happened that night chilled her. She *could* be wrong about all of this.

But if she was wrong, why hadn't he called her once since Thanksgiving?

Maybe he's waiting for you to call him. Maybe he's wondering why you accused him of rape to the police.

But if he were innocent, wouldn't he want to clear his name?

Not if he thought you didn't trust him and didn't want to speak to him. Again, maybe he's been waiting for you to make the first move.

The pastor began to chant the Eucharistic prayer as Angela argued with herself. Again, Angela noticed he wasn't using a book or binder. *He's got the whole Eucharistic prayer memorized?*

Clearly she needed to work on her presiding skills. Angela watched and listened as the pastor chanted back and forth with the congregation. She didn't know the chant they were using, but it was melodic and haunting. After several minutes, the pastor held up the bread and a gleaming silver carafe of wine and chanted, "Through him, with him, in him, in the unity of the Holy Spirit, all glory and power are yours, O God, forever and ever." The chant ended with the pastor and the congregation singing amen back and forth three times, each amen louder than the last. It reminded her of the great amen in her Eucharistic prayer. Apart from the masculine pronouns, the liturgy here was remarkably similar to the liturgy she did at home—and the liturgy she had grown up with. Angela imagined herself standing in the pastor's place, robed in white and leading the prayers. *That could be me.* Her call to ministry, the one that had driven her out of her church, filled her with longing. She thought of her liturgy at home, hidden in her prayer closet. What if she were to open it up to others?

That thought struck her and lingered a while. Communion lines formed as Eucharistic ministers took position in the center of the space where the gospel had been proclaimed. She was near the front of the line; as she stepped forward to receive the bread, the pastor looked her in the eyes, held up the bread, and said, "Body of Christ."

"Amen," she said, and took the morsel of bread. She put it in her mouth—it was soft and slightly sweet. It tasted good, just like the bread at her old church. She took the wine next. It was also sweet, and reminded her of strawberries in summer.

She returned to her seat, with Bill following close behind her. As the choir sang, Angela's vocation to ministry shimmered before her, and she closed her eyes. *What's next, Thea?*

"So what'd you think?" Bill said as he buckled his seatbelt.

"I thought Catholics were wafer people."

Bill looked at her and laughed. "They bake honest to goodness bread here. Maybe that's part of their rebellion from the larger practices of the Roman Catholic Church."

"If they're rebelling by using bread that actually looks and tastes like bread, then I'd say they're doing rebellion right."

"So you liked it?"

Angela gripped the wheel and held her breath for a moment. "I thought it was wonderful. Masculine, but wonderful. All my senses were engaged. It reminded me of why I want to be a minister."

"Was that present tense I heard? Do you still want to be a minister?"

"Well, I am a minister. Sort of. I just don't have a congregation."

"But you want one?"

Angela pushed the accelerator and pulled out. "I don't know. Community... it's been a long time since I've prayed in community and felt welcome, much less felt like I belonged. Not that I thought I belonged here, exactly, but I was able to remember here what belonging felt like. And the truth is, I miss having community."

"Maybe it's time you did something about that, then."

Angela glanced at Bill. She didn't know what to say to that.

Chapter 19

Christmas morning, Angela awoke early. For the first time in weeks, she got ready to lead liturgy, but this time she improvised, bringing her ritual items out of the closet and into the living room. She hauled her television out of the living room and into the spare bedroom, where she set it on top of the dresser. Back in the living room, she draped a fine white cloth across the television stand in folds, and then placed candles on top of the cloth along with her singing bell, her stoneware chalice and paten, and her thurible for incense. Her prayer book lay in her lap. Here on her couch she could imagine others sitting and participating with her—she had no idea who might join her for her unconventional liturgy, but now there was room for them. *Why didn't I think of this before?*

She knew why. Ever since she had moved here, she had hidden her unusual faith, not wanting to lay it open to scorn by others. She wasn't even sure she should call her faith Christian anymore—maybe "Thean" was a better word for it. It wasn't mainstream, whatever it was.

But it's authentic to me. And to Grandma Caroline.

Maybe she could invite Grandma Caroline to join her some Sunday. She was the one who had created Angela's prayer book; she was the one who had taught her to pray to Thea.

But could she lead prayer in the presence of the one who had taught her how to pray?

She made a mental note to call Grandma Caroline and finished her liturgy with renewed focus. It seemed fitting that she had brought her liturgy out of her dark closet and into her light-filled living room on the feast of the dawning of new light.

Once she had blown out the candles, she went to the phone and dialed her grandmother's cell phone. She picked up after the second ring.

"Hello, Angela. Merry Christmas."

"Merry Christmas, Grandma Caroline. Are you getting ready to head over to my parents' house?"

"I sure am. Are you?"

"No, Grandma. Not this Christmas."

"I didn't think so, but it doesn't hurt to ask."

"Actually, I called because I have a question for you."

"What question is that, dear?"

"I've been thinking about my call to ministry, and I think… I think it's time I led liturgy in the presence of others. I wondered if you would like to come over some Sunday or holiday."

"Can you hear me beaming over the phone? Because I am. I would love to, sweetheart."

Angela let out a sigh of relief. She hadn't realized she had been holding her breath. "Thank you, Grandma. Can we talk later and set up a time?"

"Of course we can. I look forward to it."

Angela beamed. "I love you, Grandma Caroline."

"I love you, my sweet Angela. Merry Christmas."

"Merry Christmas."

Angela hung up the phone and turned to face the front window of her kitchen. Her smile grew, and she clapped her hands together in excitement.

Her thoughts drifted to her parents, and she realized she should call them, too. She picked up the phone with decidedly less enthusiasm than she'd had a moment ago. She dialed their home phone number. Her father picked up after the third ring.

"Hello?"

"Hi, Daddy. Merry Christmas."

"Angela! Merry Christmas!" His voice sounded warm and happy. Guilt stung Angela's conscience as she thought about her decision not to visit them, but she pushed it back into the recesses of her mind.

"Did you enjoy liturgy this morning?"

"We did. It was beautiful. Poinsettias everywhere, as usual."

Angela remembered the flood of poinsettias that appeared at Christmas each year. It was a sight to behold.

"How's Mom doing?"

"She's doing fine. Would you like to talk to her?"

"Oh, um… sure."

"Here she is."

Angela heard a scraping noise as her father passed the phone to her mother, and then she heard her mother's voice. "Hello, Angela."

"Merry Christmas, Mom."

"Merry Christmas."

Silence broke into the conversation like a thief and left her breathless. She searched in vain for something to say.

"How's the weather up there?" her mother asked.

"Snowy and white. Picture perfect. How's the weather where you are?"

"There's a little bit of snow here." Silence again, and again Angela tried to think of something to say. Her mother saved her from the effort.

"Here's your father again."

That went well.

Her father's voice came on the phone again. "I don't suppose there's any chance we'll see you today, is there?" His voice was full of hope.

"Not today, Dad. But I was thinking, maybe we could get together for lunch again soon? You and me and Mom?"

"We'd like that very much, sweetheart."

"How about this Saturday at eleven? You want to meet at Aladdin's again?"

"That sounds just fine. We'll see you then, Ang."

"Okay, Daddy. Merry Christmas."

"Merry Christmas."

Angela hung up the phone. She could do this — she could have a relationship with her parents. She just needed to do it on her terms for now. *Or maybe forever.*

Angela returned to the living room where the last traces of incense lifted into the living room. She breathed it deeply.

"Thea, I've missed you," she whispered.

And that old blanket of silence wrapped around her, enfolding her in welcome.

The next two days passed uneventfully, and soon she was on her way back to Aladdin's for lunch with her parents. She was determined to make the most of it; she also intended to bring up the question of the house again.

She arrived in the parking lot of Aladdin's just before eleven. She walked in through the back door and down the hallway, then looked around for her parents. She spotted them at a table in front. They didn't see her yet. She called out to them as she walked toward the table.

"Good morning, Mom and Daddy!"

They looked up. Her father smiled. Her mother attempted to smile, but it came out looking more like pinched lips.

"Good morning, darling daughter," her father said. Angela sat down. A glass of water was already waiting for her, and she sipped it from the straw.

A server with long black hair and olive skin came by with a pad of paper. "What can I get for you today?" she asked.

"I'll have the V8 soup with chicken," Angela said.

"I'll have the spinach salad," her mother added.

"And I'll have the chicken shawarma," her father said. They handed their menus to the server and she hurried to the kitchen to deliver the order.

"So, I was wondering if you two had given any more thought to the idea of putting the house in my name." *Might as well get to the point.*

Angela's parents looked at each other. Her father opened his mouth to say something, but her mother beat him to it.

"I don't think it's a good idea, Angela. With your dad's health up in the air, signing the house over to you represents a lot of extra hassle for us that we don't need right now."

"So you're opposed because it's too much hassle?"

"Yes. We need to focus on your father's health. The house can wait."

Disappointment and frustration settled on Angela like a thick fog.

"How are things with your health, Daddy?"

"Well, the doctors are still keeping a close eye on me," he said. "I still don't feel like myself. I'm tired a lot."

In the weeks since Thanksgiving, Angela had hardly talked to her parents. She was alarmed that her father was still feeling unwell.

"I would have thought you'd feel much better by now," she said.

"Me, too. I go in for more tests in a couple of weeks."

"What are they going to test?"

"They want to make sure the cancer hasn't come back," he said.

Angela stared blankly at her father. "So there's a possibility that it might come back, even though they removed it?"

"Yes, there's a possibility."

Angela shook her head. She didn't know what to say.

"As you can see, we have more pressing things to think about than the title of your house," her mother said.

"Of course. We can talk about it later, when Daddy's in the clear." Angela folded her hands tightly in her lap.

The conversation hit a lull for a long minute.

"How was Christmas?" Angela asked at last.

The conversation turned to church liturgy and Christmas dinner. The food arrived at their table before long, and the conversation meandered along well-trodden paths for the rest of lunch. After they ordered dessert, Angela mentioned what she had found in Adeline Parker's journals and described her most recent visit to the factory.

"So you think that there's a trapdoor to a lower level somewhere on the first floor?" her father said.

"There must be," she answered. "She was hidden somewhere. They never found her after she screamed. And now I wonder if that hidden room isn't her final resting place. I'm thinking of taking what I've found to the police to see if they can reopen the case."

"Wow," her mother said. She looked impressed. Angela smiled a small smile.

As they got up to leave, Angela gave her father a long, tight hug. "Let me know how the testing goes, Daddy."

"I'll let you know, sweetheart. I've got you and lots of other people praying for me, so I know I'm in good hands."

Angela smiled at him and turned to her mother. She gave her a loose, awkward hug. Her mother patted her on the back a couple of times.

"Bye, Mom."

"Bye, Angela."

They went in opposite directions as they left the table—her parents went out the front door, and

Angela went out the back. As she walked toward Felicity, Angela worried about her father. She had been so wrapped up in what had happened on Thanksgiving that she hadn't given her father's health much thought. His mortality weighed on her now like an enormous stone, crushing her till she could hardly breathe. *I need to call him more. I need to see him more.*

She got in her car, took a deep breath, and turned the key.

"Hey, lady." Ron held out his hand, standing at Angela's front door. She stepped out carefully without taking it.

"Was it something I did?" he asked, frowning with raised eyebrows.

"No, it wasn't you, Ron. Let's just drive. I'll explain when we get there."

Ron opened the passenger door of his truck for Angela and she slid inside. Ron shut the door and got in on the driver's side. The truck rumbled to a start, and Ron turned the heater up full blast.

"Where are we going, by the way?" she asked.

Ron glanced at her with a small smile. "You'll see."

Fifteen minutes later, they pulled up next to Stonetown, a Southern Fusion restaurant near the corner of Prospect and East Sixth Street. Angela could see a fireplace inside. She looked at Ron appreciatively.

"Am I right? You've never been here before?" he asked.

"Nope, never been here before."

Ron jumped out quickly and opened the door for her. "Right this way, my dear."

They entered the restaurant and were quickly seated. Ron ordered a glass of sweet tea and a plate of chicken and waffles. Angela ordered the same.

"So, tell me what's been going on. I've been worried about you."

Angela stared at her fingernails. They were unpainted but well-kept.

"I was raped, Ron."

"Excuse me?"

She looked up at him and locked his gaze. "I was raped."

Ron sat stock-still, searching her eyes with his.

She continued. "It happened on Thanksgiving. I had someone over for dinner, but it was someone I shouldn't have trusted."

Ron said nothing for a while. She lowered her gaze again.

"Angela, I'm so sorry."

He tipped her chin up with his finger. When she looked up at him, she saw tears in his eyes.

"Who was it?"

"I'd rather not say. I just want to put it behind me, frankly. But I needed you to know." Angela took a deep breath. "It wasn't fair of me to leave you in the dark, especially when things were going so well between us."

"They were. And I think they are. Angela, thank you for trusting me with this. It can't have been easy for you to tell me this."

Angela blinked away tears. "No. No, it wasn't."

"Listen—I don't need anything from you. All I want for you is to feel safe. I'm going to let you make the first move from now on, okay? I want you to have all the control. I care about you, Angela."

Angela looked up at him. He had his arms folded in front of him. She reached out and touched his forearm. "Thank you, Ron. This is exactly what I need right now." She withdrew her hand and put her hands in her lap. She looked around. The heat from the fireplace warmed her back.

"This seems like a cozy place," she offered.

"It is. I've been coming here since they opened."

Angela searched for something to say. Adeline Parker came to mind.

"Hey, you want to hear a strange story?"

"Sure," he said, as their sweet teas arrived.

After sharing the story about Adeline Parker, things felt easy between the two of them again. They talked about school and about Cleveland history and culture, and before either of them knew it, they were on their way back to Angela's house. Angela gave Ron a kiss on the cheek when he dropped her off at home and said she'd call him soon.

Time settled into a slow, easy pace for the next couple of weeks. Angela called her parents every few days to see how her father was doing. The answer remained the same: he was tired, but otherwise felt good. The new semester began early in January, and with it, Angela's internship at the HUD field office in Cleveland. She was just finishing her first afternoon shift at HUD when a phone call from her parents came in. She let it go to voicemail, not wanting to seem unprofessional on her first day.

When she reached Felicity, she dialed her voicemail.

Her mother's voice came over the line.

"Angela, we got results back from the doctor. Please call." Her voice was as tight as a suspension cable. Angela dialed their home phone number immediately.

"Hello, Angela," her mother answered.

"Hi, Mom. What did they say?" she asked breathlessly.

"The cancer has returned. It's spread."

Angela swallowed hard and blinked back tears.

"They're giving your father the option of aggressive radiation therapy, but it may not help."

Her mother's voice broke. Angela felt as if she'd been punched in the stomach; she'd lost her wind.

"May I talk to Daddy, please?" she asked a few moments later.

Her father came on. "Hi, sweetheart." His voice sounded strange, hoarse, like he'd been in a screaming match.

"What are you going to do, Daddy?"

"I don't know."

Angela was silent. She could hardly breathe. "What happens if you do the radiation therapy?"

"If I do the radiation therapy, I'll be in a lot of pain, and I'll be weak. They estimate that I might live up to a year."

Her tears fell fast and hot.

"And if you don't do it?"

"I have a couple of months at best."

"No," she said slowly.

Her father didn't answer.

"No, Daddy."

"I'm afraid so, sweetheart."

"No," she whispered.

Angela felt dizzy. She leaned forward, resting her forehead on the steering wheel.

"I'm not sure what I'm going to do yet. Your mother and I need to pray about it."

"Is there anything I can do, Daddy?"

"You can pray for wisdom for me and your mom."

Angela took a ragged breath in. "Okay. Does Grandma Caroline know?"

"We're going to call her now."

"Can I call you tomorrow?"

"Yes, of course you can. You can call anytime you want, Ang."

"Okay. I'll talk to you soon, Daddy."

"Bye, Angela."

"Bye."

Angela sat still for a long time. Her tears stopped, and she felt like a dried-up well, vast and empty.

She started her car and headed home.

Angela drifted in and out of sleep that night. She thought about calling her parents before work, but she didn't want to wake her father. She imagined that he hadn't slept much better than she had. She went to work in a daze. Shelly asked her what was wrong when she arrived at work.

"Family stuff," she answered simply.

At her break time, she called her parents. Her father picked up the phone.

"Hello, Ang."

"Hi, Dad. Have you made a decision?"

"Not yet."

"When do you think you're going to decide? It should be as soon as possible, right?"

"Yes, sooner would be better. I think I'll give it till tomorrow morning."

Angela got off the phone and clutched her stomach.

Thea, help him, please help him.

The next morning, on her way to work, her parents called. She pulled into a parking lot and answered the phone.

"Honey, it's me."

"Hi, Daddy." She waited. She knew he knew she was waiting for his decision.

When he spoke, he sounded exhausted. "I've decided not to do the radiation therapy."

"But… why not?"

"I want to enjoy what life I have left as fully as I can. I'd rather have a few good weeks left than twelve unbearable months."

Tears welled up in Angela's eyes and began to streak down her face.

"Daddy, I love you."

"I love you, too, sweetheart."

"Can I come see you soon?"

"Of course you can. Anytime."

Half a minute later, Angela ended the call. She

leaned on the horn for a good five seconds, letting it bellow on her behalf. Cars on Chester Avenue honked back at her.

When Angela got to work, Shelly started at the sight of her.

"Angela, what is it?"

"My dad has cancer." Angela wiped her eyes with the back of her hand. "The doctors say he's got two months to live."

Shelly hurried over to her and wrapped her in a warm hug.

"I'm so sorry, honey."

Angela began to shake, soaking Shelly's shoulder with tears. Shelly rubbed her back.

"Take the day off," she said. "I can handle things here."

"No, Shelly, I need a distraction. Please?"

Shelly furrowed her eyebrows, as if she were assessing her.

"Okay, if it makes you feel better."

"Going home would make me feel worse." Angela sniffed and went to the sink to get a paper towel to blow her nose. She washed her hands, tied her apron behind her back, and began arranging carrot cake muffins in the pastry case, occasionally pressing the back of her arm against her eyes to dry them. Shelly got back to grinding coffee beans, and they worked together in silence until the first customer came in.

"Allison, good morning," Angela said, clearing her throat.

"Good morning, Angela! I'll have my usual," Allison chattered, pulling out her wallet from her purse as she spoke. She looked up and her smile turned to a quizzical frown, but Angela had already moved to the espresso maker to start her drink.

As customers stopped in throughout the morning, Angela concentrated on them, sweeping thoughts of her father to the edges of her consciousness like dust bunnies. She focused on the predictable tasks of customer service. Then it was noon: time to head to her internship.

It was only her second day on the job, and with the news of her father weighing on her, she was already dreading going back. Yesterday her supervisor, a lanky, blond-haired white man named Tom Fogel, gave Angela a detailed introduction to her job, which involved filing and responding to e-mail queries. Today she'd be on her own. At least at the coffee shop she could distract herself with real live people—at her internship, however, paper-pushing wasn't likely to take her focus off her father. And it didn't. She spent two hours at the filing cabinets and two hours at the computer, and all the while she thought of her father.

Two months.

And chances were, he only had a few good weeks left before he would need a constant regimen of pain medication. He would probably have to go to hospice.

When five o'clock rolled around, Angela straightened up the area around her work computer and got up. She said goodbye to Tom, who then asked her how her day was. She forced a smile and said everything was fine. He said he was glad, and then began a long speech about the work he had been doing that day. When he finally said goodbye, Angela sighed inwardly and walked with measured steps out the door. When she got to the parking garage, she broke into a jog. She caught a glimpse of her reflection in the driver's side front window, and in it she recognized features of her father's face. She got in the car quickly and drove off.

The first week of her internship ended on Friday evening. Angela decided to drive down to Cuyahoga Falls to see her father. The traffic on I-77 was jammed, and Angela began to wonder if Saturday might not have been a better idea. Nevertheless, she kept creeping south, and an hour and a half later, she arrived at her parents' house.

Angela rang the doorbell when she reached the front door. She had a key, but not having been back for over a year, she didn't feel comfortable using it. A minute later, her mother opened the door.

"Angela!" Her mother's mouth fell open.

"Angela?" her father's voice said from a distant room. He came to the door and stepped out into the chilly night to give her a hug.

"Hi, Daddy." Her face was moist from crying. Her father wiped her cheeks with his hand.

"Come on inside, sweetheart." Her mother stepped back to let them through and Angela stepped into the familiar warmth of her childhood home. The front door opened to a living room on the left with the kitchen at the rear of the house and a dining room to the right. Stairs to the second floor divided the living room from the dining room. A large crucifix hung over the living room couch. The house smelled of apples and cinnamon. *Home.*

"This is an unexpected surprise," her mother said.

"And a delightful one," her father added.

Angela removed her pea coat and sat down on the green and gold paisley couch. "It's been too long since I last visited here. I wanted to see you."

"Would you like some tea?" her mother asked.

"Yes. Thank you, Mom." Her mother walked to the kitchen and her father sat down on the couch next to her.

"Thank you for coming, sweetheart. This really is a wonderful surprise."

"Daddy—are you sure about not receiving radiation therapy?"

Her father's face went from smiling to serious. "Yes, Angela."

"Does that mean you're going to have to go to hospice?"

"It's very likely, yes."

Angela turned from her father to look at her hands. They were cold and the skin was dry from the winter air.

"You seem so calm," she said, tears forming in her eyes.

"I trust that God is leading me forward. How could I be anything but calm?"

"I wouldn't be calm if I were you. I'd be angry."

"'The Lord is my shepherd; I shall not want,'" he said.

Angela looked at her father and beheld his unwavering faith. Her grief spilled over, and she hugged her father tight.

"Here, Angela," her mother said. She held out a mug of steaming tea. Angela withdrew from her father and took it. She took a sip and held the mug between her hands, warming them up.

"I understand that you've made your decision, Daddy," she said, turning toward him again. "Is there anything I can do to help?"

Her father gave her a long look, then looked at his wife. "My life is in God's hands, Angela. There's nothing you can do to change that, nor would I want you to if there were.

"That being said, if you wanted to keep visiting your dear old dad, I certainly wouldn't object."

Tears fell freely from Angela's eyes. "Okay, Daddy."

"You know what we haven't done in a long time?" her father said.

"What?" Angela said.

"Played Monopoly. How would you like to play Monopoly?"

A small smile crept onto Angela's lips. "We haven't played Monopoly in years. Can I be the top hat?"

"If I can be the car."

Angela and her father looked at her mother. Angela's mother rolled her eyes and said, "All right, I'll be the shoe."

The three of them spent two and a half hours playing Monopoly. Angela's mother won the game after both Angela and her father landed on her hotel-laden Boardwalk.

"All right, that's enough of that," she said as she

began to put her winnings back in the bank.

"Mom and Dad, is it all right if I stay overnight tonight?" Angela asked.

Again, her mother's mouth fell open. So did her father's.

Her father recovered first. "You sure can, sweetheart. I think you'll find your room the same as when you left it."

Angela put her mug in the sink, gave both of her parents a hug, and headed up to her old bedroom. It had been years since she'd last stepped foot in here. A large framed poster of "Footprints" hung on one wall, faded with age. She crossed the room to her old closet and opened it. Clothing she had worn in high school and hadn't taken with her to Cleveland hung there. She checked the dresser for pajamas and didn't find any, but there were some old t-shirts tucked away, along with a pair of Mickey Mouse flannel pants. She undressed, put on her old clothes, and climbed into bed. Her bedspread was made of cotton, shaded a soft periwinkle blue. Periwinkle had been her favorite color in high school—her senior prom dress had been periwinkle. She'd gone to prom with Todd Mattingly, who had asked her to prom one day, completely unexpectedly. He told her at prom that he really liked her and had for a long while, but she knew he wasn't religious, and she didn't need any more complications in her religious life. Looking back on it, maybe someone who wasn't religious was just what she needed at the time. Her parents would never have approved, though, and she still wanted her parents' approval, even though she knew deep down that she wasn't likely to get it. Angela thought of Adeline Parker — had her father approved of her relationship with Jeremiah? Had he even known about the two of them?

Angela shook her head. Hers had been a strange rebellion. She departed from her childhood faith, not because she wanted to rebel, but because she couldn't reconcile her calling with the teachings of her church. If it had only been as simple as following her parents' wishes, she would have been glad to do so. But it wasn't that simple. She had to follow the calling of her heart first.

And now, almost ten years later, she was distant from her parents physically and emotionally, and her father was dying. Angela huddled under the covers for warmth and comfort. Her pillow grew wet. Her father would never see her return to the Missouri Synod. She had known for a long time that that would be the case, but she didn't think it would become final so quickly. She had hoped that, in time, her parents would come around and understand why she'd had to leave. And now her father was going to be gone before any real reconciliation was possible.

She cried softly into her pillowcase. Minutes turned into hours, and at long last she drifted into a dreamless sleep.

A knock on her door woke her. She rubbed her eyes.

"Yes?" she called.

"Angela, I made breakfast for you. Coffee, too," her mother said from the other side of the door.

"Thank you, Mom. I'll be right there."

Angela rolled out of bed. She changed out of her pajamas into a purple t-shirt and dark blue jeans—they still fit. Her curvy body was still curvy in all the same places. She ran her fingers through her hair and opened the door to head down the stairs. Smells of cinnamon rolls, bacon, and coffee wafted up from the kitchen, and Angela's mouth watered.

Angela's mother was standing at the sink washing dishes when Angela entered the kitchen. Angela walked to her mother and planted a light kiss on her cheek. Angela's mother looked up with astonishment, but Angela just smiled and poured herself a cup of coffee. Angela's father was at the dining room table reading the newspaper. The table was already set with plates and utensils. Angela took her coffee in, gave him a kiss on the cheek, and sat down. He smiled at her.

"Well, good morning to you, too. Gosh, it's been a long time since we sat around the breakfast table together, isn't it?"

Angela's mother set the rolls and bacon on the table and sat down, nodding. "A long time," she said.

"Angela, would you like to say grace?" her father said. This time it was Angela's turn to be surprised.

"Sure, Daddy." She grasped her parents' hands, closed her eyes, and said, "Let us pray."

She thought for a moment, then spoke again. "Loving God, the eyes of all wait upon you, and you give them their food in due season. Bless this food and the hands that prepared it, and make us mindful of those who go without enough food this day. Amen."

She opened her eyes, and her father looked at her

with warmth and appreciation. Her mother picked up the tray of cinnamon rolls and put one on her plate, then offered them to her husband. He took one and handed the tray to Angela. She took two.

"I'm glad to see you brought your appetite," her mother said.

"It's funny you mention that, because I haven't had much of an appetite lately." Angela took a bite out of one of her rolls. It tasted delicious. She took a long sip of coffee, then took another bite of her cinnamon roll.

Breakfast passed quietly, and when it was over, her mother headed upstairs, and Angela put her coat on.

"Are you leaving already?" her father asked.

"No, not yet. I'm just going for a walk."

"Mind if I join you?"

Angela paused, surprised at the request. "Of course you can, Daddy." She pulled on her gloves and hat as he bundled up in his own jacket, hat, and gloves.

Her father called up the stairs to let his wife know that he and Angela were both going for a walk, and then they headed out the front door. They walked along the sidewalk in silence, with snow crunching beneath their feet.

"Daddy?" Angela said at last.

"Yes, sweetheart?"

"Will you ever be able to forgive me for leaving the church?"

Her father looked at her and stopped walking.

"Angela, there's nothing to forgive."

"But you know by now that I'm never coming back."

Her father faced forward and began to walk again. "I know."

They walked in silence again for a while. Then Angela's father broke the silence.

"Angela, I want you to know that I respect the path you've taken. It's not my path, but you were never destined for my path. You were destined for the path God laid out for you. You've been faithful to that path, and I couldn't be more proud of you."

Angela looked at her father. This time she was the one who stopped walking.

"Really?"

"Really. Now, that doesn't mean your mother's ready to accept you — I'd be lying if I said she was. But I've been praying for you every day since you left home, and God has answered my prayers by assuring me that you're doing exactly what you're supposed to be doing."

"God spoke to you?"

Her father was quiet for a moment, then continued walking. "I had a dream a while back. It was right around Thanksgiving, actually. In it, an angel dressed in white came to me and said, "The message is this: your daughter's faith is strong and true. Be still, and know that I am God."

Angela absorbed these words. "Do you think the angel was real?"

"I've never had a dream quite like it," he said. "I've never been visited by an angel of God, but I'm inclined to believe that this was one. The message was clear. Your faith, even though it is quite different from mine, is valid. If anything, the message was about God: God is bigger and more encompassing than any single faith can imagine."

"You believe that?"

"I do now."

They continued walking without speaking. They had turned a corner a short while ago, and then another. Now they were walking back in the direction from which they'd come on a parallel road.

"Daddy, I don't know what to say except 'thank you.'"

"You don't have to thank me, sweetheart. Thank our marvelous creator, who speaks in many mysterious ways."

Chapter 20

Angela visited her parents the following weekend. They played more Monopoly and talked about the way things used to be. Angela's mother warmed up to her, and Angela welcomed the new attention. Her father, meanwhile, became more and more tired and wan. He was diminishing before her eyes.

As the contest banquet approached, Angela thought more and more of Adeline. Finally, she called up Detective Winston and told him what she had discovered at the Historical Society. "I visited the building with a commercial real estate agent and looked for the hidden room, but I couldn't find it. I thought maybe someone at the station could re-open the cold case and take a look," she said. Detective Winston said he'd pass the information along to one of the detectives who handled cold cases. Angela crossed her fingers.

Saturday, January 27, was the day the winner of the urban development contest would be announced, so Angela visited her parents early in the day and drove back in the early afternoon. When she got home, she put on a black dress and black flats and pulled her long hair back in a roll. Bill rang the doorbell when she was finishing her makeup, and she walked down the hall to let him in.

"Hello, gorgeous," he said.

"I'm so nervous I could puke," she said, closing the door behind him.

"That's attractive."

"I thought you'd think so."

A few minutes later, they climbed into Felicity and drove to the Cleveland Public Auditorium on Lakeside Avenue. Inside, several dozen round tables were set up with white and gold tablecloths, and people were milling around, enjoying drinks and *hor d'oeuvres*.

"Do you have your acceptance speech ready?" Bill asked, taking a sip of champagne.

"Yes. I don't know how I'm going to deliver it if I win, though. I'll be a basketcase. And look at all these hoity toity people." Angela gestured around the room at the well-dressed people who were walking in, claiming tables, and ordering drinks.

"Honey, you're one of them. Look at you."

Angela looked down at the snug dress she wore and blushed. "I guess I can be hoity toity for a night. But man, this is a lot fancier than I thought it would be."

Just then, Angela caught sight of Ron. He was there with his parents. She set down her champagne glass and hurried over to him.

"Hi, Ron. Hello, Mr. and Mrs. Walker."

"Hello, Angela," Ron's mother said. Ron's father nodded, and Ron took Angela's hands.

"Hello, lady. How are you holding up?"

Angela squeezed his hands. "Better, thanks in part to you."

Ron squeezed her hands lightly. "How about if we

go out sometime soon, just to talk?"

Angela smiled at him. "I've been visiting my parents on the weekends, but if you're free on a weeknight, you're on."

Ron returned her smile, flashing his bright white teeth. "Do you have a place to sit yet?"

"My friend Bill and I just set our things down over there. Would you all like to join us?"

Ron turned to his parents. "Would you like to join Angela and her friend at their table?"

"Sounds fine to me, son," his father said. Ron's mother took her husband's arm and the four of them walked over to where Bill was standing.

"Ron, Mr. and Mrs. Walker, this is my good friend, Bill. Bill, this is Ron and his parents, Mr. and Mrs. Walker. Ron is one of my classmates."

"I've heard so much about you," he said, shaking Ron's hand. He shook the hands of Mr. and Mrs. Walker next, and then returned to his seat.

"Would you like to get something to eat, dear?" Mrs. Walker asked her husband. He nodded and led the way toward the food tables. Angela sat down, and Ron and Bill sat on either side of her.

"So Bill, how do you know Angela?" Ron asked.

"We go way back. We met at Case when we were undergraduates. We've been good friends ever since."

"I see."

"And you two met at Cleveland State?" Bill asked.

"Yes. Last semester was my first semester in the program, and Angela was in two of my classes."

"And you entered this contest as well, yes?"

"Oh, yes. I couldn't let an opportunity like this

pass me by."

"What site did you pick?"

"I picked an abandoned ELCA church on the East Side."

The two of them continued to talk across the table, and Angela took a look around. There were hundreds of people milling around the auditorium now. The room was lit with blue spotlights, so everyone was cast in a bluish glow. Someone was wearing a long gold chain across his chest. Was that…?

Angela recognized the chain of the pectoral cross that Roman Catholic bishops wear. That was the bishop of Cleveland. Beside him stood Joseph, dressed in his black cassock. He hadn't seen her yet. She turned around quickly and tried to focus on what Ron and Bill were saying. Ron was describing his project to Bill. Mr. and Mrs. Walker rejoined the table a few moments later, and Angela forced a smile at them. To her relief, the emcee and several others entered the stage, and a hush fell over the room.

"Good evening, ladies and gentlemen. Welcome to the First Bi-Annual Amateur Urban Development Contest of Cleveland. My name is Sandra Wellington. I'm a professor of urban development at Cleveland State University, and I'm your emcee for the evening. I invite you to enjoy some *h'ordeuvres* and drinks. We'll get started in about half an hour." Angela recognized her; she had taken an introductory course with her during her first semester at Cleveland State.

"Would you like to join me?" Ron asked, looking at both Angela and Bill. They nodded and stood up to walk over to the tables where appetizers and cocktails were being served. They returned to their table about fifteen minutes later, armed with food and drinks. Angela and Ron discussed their projects as they took turns looking excitedly at the stage, waiting for the emcee to return. At last, she did.

"Ladies and gentlemen, I invite you to take your seats. I'd like to introduce you to the three judges of this contest. First, allow me to introduce Mr. Terry Keating, of Keating Architects, who created and funded this contest." Applause and catcalls rose in the auditorium. Terry Keating, a thin man in his sixties with white hair and pale skin, stood and took a slight bow.

"Second, I'd like to introduce Ms. Eleanor Headley, director of urban development at the Columbus field office of the U.S. Department of Housing and Urban Development." More applause followed as Ms. Headley stood. She had gray hair tied back into a ponytail at the nape of her pale neck, and she wore a green skirt and matching blazer.

"Finally, I'd like to introduce to you a familiar face, former Cleveland Mayor Michael R. White." Loud applause followed the introduction of former Mayor White, Cleveland's second black mayor, who stood at the sound of his name and waved to the assembly.

"The winner of the contest will be announced by Mr. Keating. But first, we'll hear a few words about his vision for this contest. Mr. Keating." Ms. Wellington sat down in her chair, and Mr. Keating stood, carrying with him a sheaf of papers. He cleared his throat and began.

"Thank you, Sandra, for introducing all of us tonight. Welcome to all of you. When I first imagined this contest coming to fruition, I had no idea that the response would be so tremendous. Tonight's gathering represents one hundred fifty-two contest entries from individuals across the Cleveland metropolitan region. For all your hard work, I'd like you all to give yourselves a hand."

More applause and catcalls erupted. Ron leaned over to Angela and whispered in her ear, "Good luck." She turned, smiled, and whispered, "You, too." When the crowd quieted, Mr. Keating continued.

"My hope for this contest was to bring new, fresh vision to the city of Cleveland. Cleveland has a vibrant history, and I wanted to honor that history with an urban development contest that put Cleveland's history and future side by side in harmony.

"The contest proposals we received were of a very high quality, and as you can imagine, it was difficult to choose one winner from among them. But choose we did, and I'm pleased to share that choice with you this evening. Ladies and gentlemen, please give a warm round of applause for the winner of the First Bi-Annual Amateur Urban Development Contest of Cleveland: Mr. Joseph Warner!"

Angela froze. She felt Bill's eyes on her. It wasn't long before the folds of Joseph's black cassock were brushing past her. He ascended the stairs to the stage and shook the hands of the emcee and the judges, one by one, till he had returned to the microphone. Mr. Keating patted him on the back, handed him a brass-plated wooden plaque, and returned to his seat. The emcee returned to the mic and faced the audience.

"Mr. Warner is a student at Borromeo Seminary, the Roman Catholic seminary of the Diocese of Cleveland. Mr. Warner chose the site of the former Church of St. Mary Magdalene at Superior Avenue and 40th Street on the East Side of Cleveland. His vision for this site is to create a shelter, resource center, and playground for women and children in need. The proposed renovation will include twenty beds and a bathroom with eight showers and eight toilets. The resource center will include a library for women and children; it will also include private offices for volunteer professionals such as lawyers, doctors, mental health counselors, career counselors, public housing advocates, and educational tutors to meet with the women and their children to offer their assistance. There will also be a kitchen where women can participate in communal cooking, and an interfaith chapel where women and their children can go to pray and meditate in whatever faith tradition calls to them.

"This renovation, as Mr. Warner writes in his proposal, 'empowers socially disadvantaged members of our city to rise up and assume a new identity of strength, competence, and joy.'" It is the hope of the judges that this empowerment will unite the disadvantaged and the advantaged members of our city for the common good. The judges are proud to award Mr. Joseph Warner as the winner of the First Bi-Annual Amateur Urban Development Contest of Cleveland."

All around her, members of the audience clapped

for Joseph. She looked up at him in disbelief. He caught her eye, held it for a moment, then looked on as if he hadn't seen her, smiling all the while.

"Are you okay?" Bill whispered, leaning over.

Angela shook her head.

Ron leaned over and murmured, "Well, we didn't win, but it sounds like a wonderful project." Angela gave a slight nod without looking at Ron. He was right—it sounded like the proposal of a warm, decent human being. *But he isn't. He spends his spare time raping women.*

As the clapping subsided, Joseph took the microphone. "I'd like to thank the judges for their selection, and also my bishop and brother seminarians for their support. I'd especially like to thank Professor Seamus McNear, professor of urban development at Cleveland State University, for encouraging me in my reimagining of this beautiful city of ours. I'm grateful for the opportunity to have that reimagining come to life. Last but not least, I thank God for daily inspiration in all I do. Thank you."

Joseph walked right past her on his way back to his seat. She flinched as his cassock brushed her dress. Chatter resumed around the room. Angela looked behind her and saw the bishop give Joseph put his hands on Joseph's shoulders. He was smiling at him.

Angela thought she might throw up. She said a quick goodbye to Ron and his parents and began to walk out. Bill hurried to keep up. Ron jogged after her and touched her on the shoulder.

"Hey. You're really unhappy with the results, aren't you? It's just a contest, Angela."

"You don't understand, Ron. I know the man who won. He's a piece of shit."

Ron looked at her quizzically. "You know him?"

"He's the one," she confirmed.

Understanding dawned on his face, and he turned toward the table where Joseph stood, talking with his bishop. Fury etched his face. He turned back to her. "I'm sorry, Angela. Is there anything I can do?"

Angela's eyes were swimming in tears. "You can make sure never to befriend that man."

Ron touched her shoulder. She shrank back. "I won't." He looked into her eyes with sympathy. "Is it okay if I call you tomorrow?"

Angela took a deep, ragged breath. "Yes. I'd like that."

"Are you okay to go home?"

"Yes, yes, I'm fine. The cold air is helping."

"Okay. If you're sure. Take care, Angela," he said. He gave her one last long look, and walked back to where his parents were standing, talking.

Angela turned and walked out the door. Bill kept pace with her without saying a word. When they got into the car, Angela gripped the steering wheel without turning on the car.

"Do you want to talk about it?" Bill asked quietly.

"I want that bastard out of my life. I cannot believe he won—with a proposal that supports disadvantaged women. What kind of twisted asshole is he?"

"A very twisted asshole," Bill said.

Angela turned the key in the ignition. "You know, this world is really fucked up sometimes."

"It is," he agreed. Angela turned left on East 6th Street, then left on St. Clair Avenue instead of going up to Superior. She didn't want to drive by the cathedral.

Angela dropped Bill off in the parking lot next to his apartment building.

"You want to come up? Have a drink? I have some Montepulciano Stella, 2007."

Angela hesitated. That was one of her favorite wines. "You still have some?"

"I have one bottle left."

"I don't want to ruin a good bottle of wine with my sour mood."

"But it'll taste so good!"

Angela rolled her eyes. "It's a good thing I'm not an alcoholic. You're such an enabler."

Bill smiled. "If you become an alcoholic, I'll never open my liquor cabinet to you again. But meanwhile…"

Angela grinned. "Fine. Enable me."

She nursed a single glass of wine over the first two hours of her visit while nibbling on Irish Dubliner cheese and rice crackers. She had forgotten to get something to eat at the contest gathering, so she ate over half of the block of cheese. Bill turned on *Gaslight*, one of their favorite black and white movies.

"You know," Angela said as the movie ended, "I can relate to Paula. She thinks her husband is one person, but he's really a manipulative bastard trying to make her think that *she's* got issues. She has no issue at all. It's all him."

She looked over at Bill. The wine bottle was

empty, and he was asleep.

"Oh, dear Bill." She got up, covered him with a blanket, and headed out of his apartment, shutting the door softly behind her.

The liturgical season of Lent came just days after the contest gathering, and Angela found herself reflecting on the sin of the world and her role in it. She also found herself reflecting on Joseph's role in the sin of the world, and wondered if she could ever forgive him. Continuing to be angry at him would only hurt her—it would do nothing to him. *But he deserves to be punished—he should be put in jail.* Angela thought about calling Detective Winston, but she refrained. If there was anything new to report, he'd call her.

She met up with Ron for dinner in Little Italy the following Wednesday, and at her request, they didn't talk about the contest at all. Angela was relieved—she didn't want to think about it anymore. Not until the next round of the contest came up again, anyway.

Angela pondered her relationship with her parents. She visited each weekend, and each weekend, her father looked more pale and less substantial, as if he were turning into a ghost. Her resolution for Lent was to work on repairing her relationship with her parents, especially her mother.

February came and went. Her father deteriorated so much that, at the end of February, his wife decided to place him in hospice. Angela helped her mother pack up some of his things—clothes, books, his Bible, a gold-plated cross—and went with both of them to drop him off at the hospice center.

Lifebreath was a hospice located in Fairlawn, a town just north of Akron. Angela's mother took Route 8 to I-77 and navigated toward a busy shopping area on Market Avenue. Lifebreath was on the southwest side of the road. The paperwork had been submitted in advance, so when they arrived, a nurse guided them to the room where Angela's father would be staying. The room had one wall of windows that looked out onto a parking lot. Angela was dismayed at the view, and turned toward her mother.

"Are you sure he has to be in hospice?"

"I can't give him the care he needs. He's in pain, Angela."

They spoke in quiet tones as Angela's father sat down in a green gliding rocker. Angela looked at him. His skin sank and drooped around his face and arms. His once stout frame was now thin and bony.

"Susan," he said in a raspy voice, "may I have my Bible?"

Angela's mother hurried across the room to give him his Bible. He turned the pages until he reached the gospel according to Mark. "'When Jesus heard it, he saith unto them, they that are whole have no need of the physician, but they that are sick.'"

Angela knelt down next to her father and hugged him. He hugged her back with effort. "My girl," he whispered. When she looked up, her father's shirt was wet from where her face had been.

"Angela, may I have some time alone with your father?" The look in her mother's eyes was one of pleading. Angela nodded and stepped out of the room, shutting the door gently behind her. She paced slowly up and down the warmly lit hall, with her arms folded against her chest.

A quarter of an hour passed, and her mother opened the door, inviting her back in. "I want you to have some time with your father. I'll be down in the lobby. Why don't you meet me down there when you're through?"

"Okay, Mom," she said. Her mother left, and then it was just Angela and her father.

"Angela, sweetheart, come here," he said.

Angela returned to her kneeling position next to him.

"Sweetheart, I want you to know two things. First, that I love you."

"I love you, too, Daddy."

"And second, that everything is going to be okay. It really will be. I will always be with you, even if I'm not here in my body."

Angela leaned her head against her father's legs and cried silently. There had been too many tears these last few months, and there would be even more before they finally subsided. *Thea, take care of my father. Be his shepherdess in the valley of death.*

Angela's father tousled her hair. They sat together that way for a long while. Then her father spoke.

"Angela, I think I need to sleep now."

Angela stood and helped her father to his feet. "I'll help you get into bed," she said, and she walked him to his bed and turned down his sheets for him. He climbed in slowly and got under the covers. When he was settled, Angela planted a kiss on his forehead.

"I love you, Daddy."

"I love you, sweetheart."

She flipped the light switch and left the room quietly. She met her mother in the lobby. Her mother's eyes were rimmed with red. Angela moved toward her. "Daddy's sleeping," she said. Her mother opened her arms for a hug, and Angela stepped into her embrace. They held each other tightly. After a couple of minutes, her mother took a step back.

"Let's go," she said to Angela.

They drove back to Angela's parents' house in silence.

On Thursday, March 5, when Angela got home from her internship, her mother called.

"Angela, it's me," she said when Angela picked up. Her voice was hoarse.

"Honey, he's gone. He passed away in my arms."

Angela didn't answer. She felt like a kite that had just lost its wind. She sank to the floor with the phone in her hand.

"I can come down," she whispered.

"Yes. Please come down. I'll be at home."

Angela drove down to Cuyahoga Falls and let herself in the front door with her key. It was just past seven, and there was a single light on upstairs. Her mother met her at the top of the stairs, illuminated from behind. She was still dressed. She looked disheveled. Angela gave her a long hug. When the hug was over, she said in a choked voice, "What do we do now?"

"I've already dealt with the hospice. Tomorrow we'll go to the funeral home and make plans. The funeral will probably be Sunday or Monday. Then there'll be the will to sort out with our lawyer."

"The will? Didn't he leave everything to you?"

"He left his part of your house to you. We changed our will a few weeks ago."

"Oh," she said. Tears threatened again.

"Angela, I've thought about it, and I want you to have my part of the house, too. There's no reason not to give it to you."

Angela was still. The house she wanted so much was finally hers—it had only cost her her father's life.

"If I could choose between the house and having Daddy back, I'd have Daddy back in a heartbeat."

"I know you would."

They stood there in the hallway, silence shrouding them.

"Angela, I want you to know that I love you as much as your father did. And I don't ever want to lose you."

Angela's mother held her arms open again, and Angela rushed into them.

The funeral took place the following Sunday afternoon. Angela drove up to her house to gather something suitable to wear, then drove back down to Cuyahoga Falls with Bill, who was dressed in a black suit and a dark blue tie. He took the day off from work to go to the funeral. They drove to Angela's mother's house. Once her mother was in her car, they drove in a caravan to Angela's former church. They arrived at two o'clock with an hour to spare before the funeral was scheduled to begin.

Angela walked into her old church with Bill by her

side and drank in the scent of incense. It smelled like years of prayer. Her father's casket stood near the entrance to the church.

"Come help me," her mother said to her. They walked toward the casket. Her mother took a white folded cloth from the altar and handed a corner to Angela. They unfolded it and draped it over the casket. Angela smoothed it with her hands. Tears fell freely. She'd avoided wearing makeup for just this reason.

Congregants began to arrive and take their places among the pews. The pastor, Reverend George Weber, walked out fully vested and greeted Angela and her mother.

Angela, her mother, Bill, and Grandma Caroline sat down in the front pew, and the funeral began. The church choir sang "Amazing Grace" as the casket was rolled to the front of the nave, and Angela listened, remembering. After a homily about death and resurrection, the pastor received the thurible filled with incense and walked around the casket, swinging the thurible back and forth as he went. That was what stood out the most for Angela: the sound of the thurible chain swinging, and the scent of sweet frankincense filling the nave with its spice.

After communion, Bill and Angela stood with four men and took places around the casket. They lifted it in one swift movement, and as the choir sang, they processed to the front doors and placed the casket in the hearse. Those who had attended the funeral snapped magnetic funeral flags on top of their cars and followed the hearse in a long procession to

Oakwood Cemetery in Cuyahoga Falls.

During the interment, Pastor Weber invited Angela and her mother to cast dirt over the casket. "The Lord is my shepherd; I shall not want," Pastor Weber said. He recited the rest of psalm twenty-three. When he concluded, silence fell, and those in attendance lingered a few last moments before walking to their cars. Angela, her mother, and Bill were the last to leave.

Bill gave Angela a hug, and she squeezed him back. Angela gave Grandma Caroline a hug, and Grandma Caroline kissed her forehead. Then Angela gave her mother a hug, and they stood there for a long time. "I love you, Mom" Angela whispered.

"I love you, too, Angela."

"I suppose we ought to get back to the church hall, eh?"

"Yes, I suppose we should."

Bill and Angela got in Felicity, Angela's mother got in her car, and Grandma Caroline clambered into hers. As they drove off, Angela looked in her rearview mirror at her father's grave. She wept.

Chapter 21

A few days later, Angela was praying evening prayer in her living room when her phone buzzed on the dining room table. Just in case it was her mother, she jumped up to get it. It wasn't her mother; it was Detective Winston.

"Detective Winston?"

"Hello, Angela. Did I catch you at a good time?"

"I was just finishing up with something, but we can talk."

"You may want to sit down."

Angela returned to the living room couch and sat.

"We've caught him."

"You've… caught him?"

"We caught Joseph Warner. He raped another woman, but this time the condom broke. We got a warrant for his DNA, and it came back as a match. He's under arrest."

"You arrested him?"

"Yes. Aren't you glad?"

"I'm… stunned."

"Stunned in a good way, I hope."

"Yes. Stunned in a good way. I was beginning to give up hope that he'd be caught."

"It'll be all over the papers tomorrow. We're charging him with three rapes, including yours and Cassidy Henner's. Unless, of course, you want to drop your charge against him."

"No… I don't want to drop the charge. I'm just amazed that he got caught. He seems like the type of person who could get away with anything forever."

"Some guys get away with it forever, but we caught this one. Hopefully you'll rest a little easier tonight knowing he's behind bars. The judge set his bail at one million, and so far no one's stepped up to pay it, so it looks like he's going to stay put."

"Thank you for letting me know, Detective."

"One more thing, Angela. I spoke with the cold case detective, the one I passed the information about Adeline Parker to. She and her partner reopened the case and got a search warrant for the factory. Last week they found a trapdoor to the basement. There was a female skeleton there. They also found Jeremiah's name written in blood on the floor next to the skeleton, right next to a heap of old-fashioned women's clothing. It must have been the last thing Adeline wrote before she died. They think Jeremiah raped her, stabbed her, and left her to die."

Angela took a sharp breath in.

"Thank you for bringing your research to our attention. Thanks to you, we can close this case. I doubt we could have done it without you."

The phone call ended, and Angela sat back on the couch with her hands on her face, absorbing everything Detective Winston had just told her.

Thank you, Thea.

The trial wasn't scheduled to take place for another two months. Angela was due to testify, and she was nervous—she'd have to face him again.

As the date approached, she steered clear of the media, who wanted to interview her every chance they got. In other parts of her life, however, things were going well: she grew to love her internship, and she applied for several positions, including a position that had opened up at the site of her internship. Things at Phoenix were as busy as ever. Angela spent Saturdays with Bill or Ron, depending on the weekend, and she spent every Sunday afternoon with her mother. Sometimes Grandma Caroline came over, too, and the three generations of women talked, ate, laughed, and even prayed together.

Angela's mother and grandmother were equally surprised and dismayed when they found Angela's name in the news as one of Joseph Warner's alleged rape victims. Angela told them she still wasn't really ready to talk about it. They let it go at that, but Angela suspected they talked about it with each other and worried on her behalf.

With an introduction by Detective Winston, Angela met Joseph's third rape victim, Rachel Thompson. She invited Rachel and Cassidy to her home for dinner early in March. Both women were impressed by her table blessing and asked about her prayer life. Encouraged, she invited them over for the Easter Vigil at her house, promising that it would be a ritual of female empowerment. Her grandmother came, too. So did Janette, who had secured a number of gigs since being featured in the paper by Tony. She came around to the idea that there were many ways to imagine God, and when Angela invited her to sing the

Exsultet for the Easter Vigil in Angela's Theanized form, she agreed, to Angela's surprise and delight.

Angela's Easter Vigil was an experience for the senses. The scents of beeswax, incense, and fresh flowers from her garden filled the room; candlelight scattered the darkness; and a clay bowl splashed with baptismal water. The return of alleluias after their Lenten absence was as sweet as the bread and wine. Angela led it all, vested in a baptismal alb and white stole that she had purchased for the occasion. It was her first communal liturgy, and she fell into the role of priestess as if she'd been playing it her whole life.

Easter Sunday, Angela drove to Cuyahoga Falls before dawn and picked up her mother for the Easter sunrise service at Emmanuel. They sang alleluias together to the sound of a trumpet, and Angela smiled tearfully at the reconciliation she and her mother had planted together.

Joseph's plea of not guilty to all three counts of rape during his arraignment made national headlines, so the lead-up to Joseph's trial received a lot of attention on the local and national level. When the bishop of Cleveland was questioned about the matter, he declined to comment.

The trial began Monday, May 4. Angela was to serve as a witness. Her lawyer, who was serving on the prosecution team and who was just a touch older than Angela, reminded her to stay calm as she answered the questions from Joseph's lawyer, because his lawyer would try to make her look like an overly-emotional, raving, unreliable witness.

After the judge, a stout man named Clarence

Winn, entered the courtroom and took his seat, the prosecution and defense presented their opening statements. The prosecution laid out the facts of the case and called Joseph Warner a serial rapist; the defense, on the other hand, portrayed Joseph as an innocent victim.

Cassidy was called to the stand first. The lead prosecutor, a tall, athletic-looking white woman named Joanna Winkle with dark hair held back in a French twist, asked her to describe in her own words what had happened on November 3, 2014.

"I went to work downtown. It was a Monday morning. When it came time for my lunch break at 10:45, I drove out to Phoenix Coffee, where I'm a regular customer. As I put my coffee cup in my car around 11:15, I was attacked from behind. I was pushed down into the seat and pinned, and then I was raped by my attacker. When he was finished, he ran off. I looked at him, but all I could see was a shadow, and then he disappeared. I drove out of the parking garage immediately. I went to the emergency room the next day to have a rape kit done."

The prosecutor thanked her and said there were no further questions. When the defense cross-examined her, however, the gap in her testimony became apparent.

"Ms. Henner, do you know who attacked you on November 3, 2014?"

"No, I don't."

"So you have no proof whatsoever that Joseph Warner attacked you?"

"No."

"Did you know Joseph Warner before the day of your attack?"

"No."

"Did your rape kit give any trace of your attacker?"

"No."

"So there's really no reason to believe Joseph Warner did this. No further questions, Your Honor."

Cassidy shook her head at the prosecutor as she exited the stand. The prosecutor stood stock-still.

Angela was next.

"Ms. Bridges, please describe what happened on November 27, 2014."

"November 27, 2014 was Thanksgiving. I was celebrating Thanksgiving in my home for the first time ever. I got all the food ready, got the table prayer ready, and then waited for the arrival of my guest, Joseph Warner. I had invited him to Thanksgiving when he told me on the phone that his parents had passed away.

"When he arrived, we sat down and I poured two glasses of wine. I had forgotten the water carafe, however, so I returned to the kitchen to pour water into the carafe. When I returned, I sat down and we prayed our table blessing. About fifteen minutes later, I felt dizzy. About five minutes after that, I had to lay down. Joseph helped me to the couch, and I blacked out before I got there.

"When I woke up, I was in bed, wearing all my clothes from the evening, and I was sore. I went to the bathroom and realized I was bleeding. That's when I realized I had been raped. I drove myself to the emergency room at the Cleveland Clinic and they performed a rape kit. Then I called Detective Winston, who had questioned me about the day of Cassidy Henner's rape because I worked at Phoenix Coffee, and I told him I'd been raped. He invited me in for questioning. I went home a couple of hours later."

"Thank you, Ms. Bridges."

The defense came up next.

"Ms. Bridges, did your rape kit turn up any evidence against your alleged attacker?"

"No.

"And you have no memory of being raped?"

"No."

"So it's possible you weren't raped."

"I was bleeding."

"Isn't it possible that you could have been menstruating?"

"Yes, but I wasn't due for my period for two weeks."

"Isn't it possible that, say, a spike in hormones would have brought on your period early?"

"Yes, but..."

"Ms. Bridges, did you find Mr. Warner to be attractive?"

"Objectively speaking, he's an attractive person."

"So you were attracted to him?"

"No."

"But you invited him to spend Thanksgiving with you?"

"Yes, but..."

"Don't you think it's odd that you, a single, unmarried woman, would be inviting a Roman

Catholic seminarian to a dinner in her home, particularly on a holiday?"

"No."

"Doesn't an invitation to a holiday dinner indicate feelings of intimacy with the person invited?"

"Well, yes…"

"So you felt you had an intimate connection with him?"

"Yes, I had a connection with him…"

"Isn't it true that you had romantic feelings for him?"

"No."

"And isn't it the case that when your feelings weren't returned by Mr. Warner, you retaliated by accusing him of rape?"

"No!"

"No further questions, Your Honor."

The next witness from the prosecution was Rachel Thompson. She was a slim woman with blond, well-styled hair and gray eyes. She took the stand, and the prosecution began.

"Ms. Thompson, please tell the court what happened on March 4, 2015."

"I went to work downtown as usual. At lunchtime I stopped at the Clevelander Bar and Grill. When I left, I returned to my car in the parking lot on the next block, near Progressive Field. When I was putting my drink in the cupholder, I was attacked, pushed down into the seat, and raped. I didn't see who my attacker was."

"I immediately went to the Cleveland Clinic emergency department and requested a rape kit. I called the police from the hospital, and I was put in touch with Detective Winston of the Cleveland Police Department, who invited me in for questioning. I went home a couple of hours later."

"Thank you, Ms. Thompson."

The defense was brief. "Ms. Thompson, did you see who your attacker was?"

"No, I didn't."

"You didn't see your attacker. No further questions, Your Honor."

The prosecutor called up a member of the Cleveland Police Department's forensics team, Don Wilson.

"Mr. Wilson, would you please state your position with the Cleveland Police Department?"

"I'm a forensics analyst."

"And how long have you held this position?"

"Twelve years."

"About how many court cases have you been called to testify for?"

"Over two thousand."

"So it's fair to say that you're experienced in your field—even an expert."

"Yes, it's fair to say that."

"Mr. Wilson, when you found DNA evidence in Ms. Thompson's rape kit, did you find a DNA match?"

"I did."

"And whose DNA did it match?"

"Joseph Warner's."

"Thank you, Mr. Wilson."

The defense waived the opportunity to question

Mr. Wilson, and he stepped down.

"The prosecution has no further witnesses, Your Honor."

"The defense would like to call Mr. Joseph Warner to the stand, Your Honor."

A hush fell over the court as Joseph Warner, wearing orange prison garb, went to the stand.

"Mr. Warner, can you describe, in your own words, where you were on the morning of November 3, 2014?"

"Yes. On the morning of November third, I had a meeting scheduled at eleven thirty with my bishop at St. John's Cathedral. I drove downtown from the seminary and stopped at Phoenix Coffee on my way to pick up coffee. After I ordered coffee for me and the bishop, I headed to the cathedral and had my meeting with him."

"Did you stop anywhere else on your way?"

"No. I went straight from the seminary to the coffee shop, and straight from the coffee shop to the cathedral."

"Did you rape Cassidy Henner?"

"No, I did not."

"Would you please describe for us where you were and what you were doing on November 27, 2014?"

"Yes. I was having Thanksgiving dinner with Angela Bridges, with the permission of my rector. Angela became faint during dinner, so I helped her to the couch. She fainted, so I carried her upstairs to her bedroom and put her in bed. Then I put the Thanksgiving food in the refrigerator and returned to the seminary."

"Did you ever have any sexual contact of any kind with Angela Bridges?"

"No."

"Please describe what happened on March 4, 2015."

"I had a meeting downtown with my bishop. I drove from the seminary to the cathedral directly and had my meeting. When the meeting was over, I returned to the seminary."

"Did you rape Rachel Thompson?"

"No."

"No further questions, Your Honor."

The prosecutor stood.

"Mr. Warner, there is DNA evidence linking you to the rape of Rachel Thompson. Do you deny this?"

"It's not mine."

"Our forensics analyst says otherwise. You seem to have trouble remembering that you raped Rachel Thompson. Is it also possible that you forgot you raped Angela Bridges and Cassidy Henner?"

"No!"

"The prosecution has no further questions, Your Honor."

"Would the defense like to call any other witnesses?" Judge Winn asked.

"Yes, Your Honor. We would like to call The Most Reverend Paul Obermann to the stand."

Angela turned as a man clad in black approached the stand. He wore the gold chain of a pectoral cross across his chest. Angela recognized him as the man who had accompanied Joseph to the contest gathering.

"Bishop Obermann, would you please describe your relationship with Joseph Warner?"

"He is one of the students at my seminary. He and I have gotten to know one another through frequent meetings at the cathedral chancery over these last few months."

"What kind of man would you say Joseph is?"

"He's a man of impeccable character. I chose him especially for a pastoral position at the cathedral because I thought so well of him."

"Do you believe any of the allegations against Mr. Warner are true?"

"No, not at all."

"Thank you, Bishop Obermann."

The prosecution declined to question the bishop, so he sat down. The next witness was the rector of the seminary. He answered much the way the bishop had. Then the defense asked a new question.

"Tell us what you knew about Mr. Warner's visit to Ms. Bridges' house on Thanksgiving."

"Joseph asked me for permission to go to dinner at the house of a friend of his."

"What did he say about the friend?"

"He said her name was Angela Bridges, and she lived in Cleveland."

"Did you have any concerns about Mr. Warner's visit to Ms. Bridges?"

"None at all. Joseph is one of our finest young men at the seminary. I had no doubts about his character whatsoever."

"Do you have any doubts about his character

now?"

"No, I do not."

"Thank you. Your witness." The defense nodded to the prosecution. The prosecutor stood.

"You admit that you allowed Mr. Warner to go to Thanksgiving dinner at Ms. Bridges' house. Is that correct?"

"Yes."

"And it never once occurred to you that sending a young man to a young woman's house alone might be a bad idea, particularly a young man for whom celibacy is required?"

"No."

"It never occurred to you that Mr. Warner's character might be called into question because of the way he singled out Ms. Bridges?"

"No."

"One might wonder about your ability to judge character, given the evidence mounted against Mr. Warner today. No further questions."

The defense had no further witnesses. Judge Winn called for a one-hour recess, which would be followed by closing statements.

An hour later, the court reconvened, and the closing statements began. Angela listened to the prosecutor review the evidence, in particular the DNA evidence that linked Joseph to Rachel Thompson's rape. The prosecutor painted a portrait of Joseph as a slick, selfish, power-hungry man who would do anything to make himself look good, and would likewise do anything that made him feel powerful, including raping three women. "If Mr. Warner is not found guilty," the prosecutor said to the jury, "who will be next on Mr. Warner's list of conquests?"

The closing statement of the defense, however, described Joseph as an upstanding young man with the highest moral values and integrity. His lawyer portrayed him as a victim of opportunistic, misguided young women who sought to place blame where no blame belonged.

When the closing statements were finished, the judge called for a recess until tomorrow morning.

Angela barely slept that night, wondering what would come of it all.

The next day, red-eyed and exhausted, she returned to court just before eight o'clock. The room was packed. Angela took a seat next to Cassidy and Rachel at the prosecutor's table.

Judge Winn entered the courtroom, sat down, and called the room to order. He asked the jury if it had come to a verdict. A representative of the jury stood and said, "We have."

"How do you find the defendant?"

"We find Joseph Warner guilty of two counts of forcible rape against Cassidy Henner and Rachel Thompson and not guilty of one count of forcible rape against Angela Bridges."

Angela exchanged looks with Cassidy and Rachel. Rachel and Cassidy were both smiling through their tears. Angela felt horrified.

"Let the defendant come forward for sentencing," Judge Winn said.

"It is the judgment of this court: for the crime of the forcible rapes of Cassidy Henner and Rachel

Thompson, I sentence the defendant to sixteen years in prison. The defendant is given fifty-nine days' credit for time served." Judge Winn adjourned the hearing, and Joseph was placed in handcuffs and escorted out of the courtroom.

Chapter 22

Reporters pushed for room as Angela, Cassidy, and Rachel exited the courthouse.

"How do you feel about the ruling in this case?" one blond-haired, perfectly primped woman asked. Angela kept her head down and continued walking. Cassidy and Rachel stopped to talk to the reporters.

Angela called Bill when she got home that night.

"Hello?"

"Hi, Bill."

"Hi, Ang. How'd it go?"

"The jury acquitted him of one charge of rape: mine. I guess there wasn't enough evidence that I was actually raped."

"Honey, I'm sorry."

"Hey, he's behind bars for the next sixteen years, and he'll be a registered sex offender for the rest of his life. That's something."

She spoke with her mother and grandmother, too. They each sounded angry about the ruling. She told them they didn't need to be angry on her behalf—she had spent enough anger as it was, and she wanted to let it go.

On the news that evening, Angela listened to the comments made by Rachel and Cassidy.

"I'm happy to see my rapist behind bars," Rachel said.

"And how do you feel about the ruling, Ms. Henner?"

"I'm glad that he's serving time, even if it isn't nearly the amount of time he deserves."

The reporters tried to get a statement from the bishop, but he declined to comment. The diocese issued a statement later talking generally about the importance of integrity and virtue among seminarians, who represented the diocese's future priestly leadership.

Guess that means he's not going to be a Roman Catholic priest.

Angela thought about Joseph as she laid in bed that night. What could have possessed him to ruin his future so spectacularly? What was he trying to prove, and to whom? Did he really believe he was invincible? For that matter, what possessed any man—or woman—to commit rape?

Angela didn't understand it. She wanted to—she wanted to know what could possess someone to be a monster to someone else. Was it just the draw of power? Did he have an unquenchable thirst for it?

When Angela thought about it, she realized she had never had much power, and maybe lack of access to it was enough to keep her from wanting much of it. But if she had always been in control, would she do anything for more power? Maybe his parents' death left him feeling powerless, so he asserted his power in desperate ways.

Angela thought of her father's death. She'd had some time to prepare for it, so it hadn't swallowed her whole when it happened, but it still devastated her.

Yes, but you gained a renewed relationship with your mother from it. Joseph lost both his parents — the only family he had.

The faces of those Angela loved appeared in her mind's eye, and she found herself grateful for her circle of support, and once again, she felt pity for Joseph. He would have to rebuild his life from scratch with support from no one — no one but strangers.

That night, Angela wept for him, and eventually fell into a dreamless sleep.

The next day, Angela headed to work early in the morning. Customers who had seen her on the news mentioned the case and rallied behind her, saying they were glad her rapist was behind bars, even though the jury didn't convict him for her rape. She thanked them and tried to focus on making coffee. When she got to her internship that afternoon, she was relieved not to have to talk to many people.

When she got home, she turned on the six o'clock news. The three faces of the contest judges appeared on screen, and Angela's eyes widened. She turned up the volume. It looked like they were having a press conference.

"The judges of the First Bi-Annual Amateur Urban Development Contest of Cleveland have decided, in light of yesterday's court decision in the case against Joseph Warner, to award a new contest winner. Our new winner is Ms. Beth Weaver. Coincidentally, Ms. Weaver also chose the former site of the Church of St. Mary Magdalene, so that site will still be revitalized, albeit according to Ms. Weaver's vision. We congratulate Ms. Weaver for her excellence and look forward to seeing her proposal come to fruition."

Beth Weaver? Jessica Lyle will have a fit.

Angela grinned and hummed a little ditty to herself.

Graduation took place that Saturday at two in the afternoon. Angela's mother and grandmother were there, as were Bill and Ron. Angela heard them cheer as her name was called, and she crossed the stage to receive her diploma, her academic hood swinging behind her. After the ceremony, Angela wove her way through the crowds to meet them all. Ron handed her a bouquet of a dozen red roses; her mother, grandmother, and Bill all gave her cards.

"I'm not sure I'm going to be able to carry all this," she laughed.

"Well, here, let me hold those beautiful flowers, dear. It's been a while since I got a good whiff of red roses," Grandma Caroline said.

Angela handed the flowers to Grandma Caroline and stacked the cards on top of her degree.

"Where should we eat?" Angela asked.

"How about Aladdin's?" her mother said. Angela gave her mother a side hug and agreed.

Lunch was a rowdy affair filled with laughter and joking. After lunch was over, Ron pulled Angela aside.

"Hey, I wanted to let you know that I'm going to be doing my internship this summer in Columbus."

"At HUD?"

He nodded.

"I wondered if you might like to join me—get

away from Cleveland for a while."

Angela looked at Ron with wonder. "You want me to move in with you?"

He nodded again, holding her hands tightly and looking earnestly into her eyes.

"Ron, that's very sweet of you, and I do care for you, but I think I need to focus on getting back on my feet here in Cleveland. Besides, a local urban design and architecture firm offered me a job up here. I start full-time next week, and I want to make the most of it."

A twinge of regret flashed in his eyes. He took a deep breath and kissed her on the cheek. "Okay," he said.

She smiled at him. "What do you say we visit each other on the weekends?"

He smiled back. "I'd love that."

That evening at home, Angela settled onto her couch with a mug of tea. She had just lit several candles and rung her singing bowl. Now she lit some incense and allowed the scent to fill her nostrils.

"Thea, I'd like to talk to you tonight—just you and me," she said aloud. She closed her eyes and wrapped her hands around her steaming mug.

"It's been a long time since I read that scripture about Anna and turned away from the Missouri Synod, but the call has never faded. I think I know what you've been calling me to, Thea. I think you've been calling me to be a minister, a priestess, here in my home."

Angela paused. The silence around her urged her

on.

"Thea, I commit this space to the worship of you. I pray that I will be a good and faithful servant in your sight, and that I will teach and preach in ways that open hearts to your enveloping presence. I no longer walk in fear of my vocation; I embrace it with my whole heart. I have come to do your will, Thea, and I embrace it all.

"I've been thinking about the First Bi-Annual Amateur Urban Development Contest. I know now that I'll never be eligible to take part in it again, because the next time it comes around, I'll be a paid urban development professional, not an amateur. But Thea—the firm that hired me loved my proposal for the contest, and they want me to be involved in future urban renewal projects. I'll be helping renew neighborhoods for a living, starting right here in Cleveland."

Angela set her mug down on the coffee table, which was covered with a velvety cloth in muted shades of gold, purple, and blue.

"And Thea, thank you for putting this contest in my life. Thank you for giving me the opportunity to bring closure to Adeline Parker's case—and for helping me find closure with my own rape. I'm doing better now, Thea. So much better." She rested her hands on her knees, palms up and began to chant the fifty-first psalm: "Create in me a clean heart, O Thea, and renew a right spirit within me...."

Then she sang Bobby McFerrin's "Twenty-Third Psalm." As she sang about being led by her shepherd, she knew she was right where she belonged.

Afterword

and

Discussion Questions

Afterword

Six years after the initial release of *Memory Stands Still*, one of the many features of Cleveland I mention in the third chapter is now making national news. The Guardians of Traffic of Cleveland's Carnegie Bridge are the inspiration for the new name for Cleveland's professional baseball team, the Cleveland Guardians. This name change is not the first that this team has experienced, but it is the first in over a hundred years.[1] With this change, one division ceases and another is born. Those indigenous people and their allies who have protested the team name "Cleveland Indians" and its well-known icon, "Chief Wahoo," celebrate a firm step toward anti-racism. Meanwhile, others who are attached to "the way things have always been" protest that the name is part of the team's history, that it's not intended to be racist (and therefore isn't racist), and they wonder what difference a team name change will really make anyway.

Memory Stands Still is a novel about the development and persistence of memory. It is therefore also an argument in favor of the claim that

---

[1] For more on the history of the Cleveland's professional baseball team, including the history of the team's names, see https://case.edu/ech/articles/c/cleveland-indians.

the choices individuals and groups make around people, names, and places matter. The choice to make a change is only one part of memory-making—the discussions that precede and follow change represent a powerful, tense pull between differing ideas. In the tension between those ideas resides the possibility of new and potentially shared understanding on which collective memory may be built.

Changes like this, from the "Cleveland Indians" to the "Cleveland Guardians," are not neutral.[2] Memory itself is at stake, and not just the memory of those who live through the decision. In a hundred years, will Cleveland baseball fans still remember its history of having caricaturized a segment of people who did not consent to (and vehemently protested for years) that caricature? If they do remember, will they dismiss baseball fans of the previous two centuries as feeble-minded or unenlightened? Will they believe that they are immune to the kinds of thinking that they assume led their forebears astray? Will Cleveland baseball fans even remember that there was a team name change in 2021, or will this change be lost to the city's collective memory like previous team names for all except specialized historians?

My hope is that Clevelanders of the 22nd century and beyond will remember well this piece among the many pieces of Cleveland's history. All of it, the

---

[2] For an illuminating discussion of the non-neutrality of memory-making and memory-keeping in a city context, see *Ghosts of Berlin: Confronting German History in the Urban Landscape* by Peter Ladd (Chicago: University of Chicago Press, 2021).

beautiful and the ugly, the laudable and the despicable, the charming and the challenging, deserve to be remembered in one way or another. If the next generations of history-makers are not merely victors but those who have come together with wildly different views of things to spend time in intentional, shared listening, and if they hold that tension between their varied experiences as something worth remembering, then the intersection between past and future will be a place where memory stands still.

M. Kate Allen
December 13, 2021

Discussion Questions

1. Angela Bridges is committed to living in the city of Cleveland.

What difference does it make that she wants to live there? Would it make any difference if she were to leave? Why or why not?

2. The idea that buildings and memory are inextricably linked is a theme throughout this novel.

Think of a building you know of that exudes memory. How does it do this? Are any of your own memories woven into its history? Is it a place where memory is for the living, or for the dead, or for both? In what ways?

3. Angela has a challenging and unconventional relationship with her childhood faith.

In what ways do Angela's significant connections — with friends, co-workers, customers, neighbors, classmates, family members, and others — illuminate her relationship with her faith, and vice versa? How does this change throughout the story?

4. Belief and memory are argued to be tied together in one way or another in the context of place during heated debates held in one of Angela's graduate classes.

What beliefs does Angela espouse religiously, politically, creatively, interpersonally, and otherwise? How do these beliefs affect Angela's personal memory as well as her pursuit of memory in her urban development contest entry?

5. Buildings and places are described in great detail throughout this novel.

In what ways do the details about buildings and places impact the novel's plot? In what ways are buildings and places portrayed like characters in this story?

6. Angela has struggled to relate to her mother, and this is challenged further by what happens to her father during the course of the story.

What kinds of stories does Angela tell about her family? What kinds of stories do her family members tell about her? How does this storytelling shift throughout the novel?

7. Angela works at a locally owned coffee shop in downtown Cleveland, Phoenix Coffee.

How does Angela's place of work facilitate memory-making? How might the story have turned out differently if she had worked in a different profession to support herself through graduate program?

8. The story takes an unexpected turn at Thanksgiving.

In what ways, if any, does the unexpected turn of events impact and/or shed light on the story as a whole?

9. The opening quote in this book is from the Book of Revelation: "Then I saw a lamb, looking as if it had been slain, standing at the center of the throne…"

Discuss the connection between this quote and the title of this novel.

About the Author

After a childhood spent with her nose in a book, M. Kate Allen now spends her grownup life weaving magical tales of her own.

M. Kate Allen lives in Tempe, Arizona, with her daughters, both of whom are voracious readers, and her husband, who is a hoot.

9 781956 604009